Victim of Circumstance

W9-AJI-799

Other Gil Beckman Mysteries
by W. E. Davis

Suspended Animation

VICTIM OF CIRCUMSTANCE

A GIL BECKMAN MYSTERY

W.E. Davis

CROSSWAY BOOKS • WHEATON, ILLINOIS

A DIVISION OF GOOD NEWS PUBLISHERS

Victim of Circumstance

Copyright © 1995 by W.E. Davis

Published by Crossway Books
          a division of Good News Publishers
          1300 Crescent Street
          Wheaton, Illinois 60187

Cover illustration: Nicholas Jainschigg

Series design: William Paetzold

Art Direction/Design: Mark Schramm

First printing 1995

Printed in the United States of America

ISBN 0-89107-843-6

03		02		01		00		99		98		97		96		95
15	14	13	12	11	10	9	8	7	6	5	4	3	2	1

To my folks, Ed and Betty Davis.
Thanks for bringing me up in the fear
and admonition of the Lord and
for never ceasing to encourage me.

ONE

The warm, early morning sun reflected golden off the wet pavement. The air was crisp, the sky clear, and there was peace and quiet on this big city downtown street; no shrieking horns, no rumbling flathead V-8s, no shouts from the corner newsboys. That would all come later. Few people were out yet, and those who were seemed detached, disinterested, meandering slowly in small, huddled groups.

The Bijou Theater was open. It was always open. The hit movies of the early 30s played around the clock, catering to people of all habits and preferences. At this hour, mostly sleeping winos and deviates occupied its red velvet chairs, along with those who were still awake from the revelry of the night before and unable or unwilling to go home and face the music. From among the general populace, only the foolhardy or the dangerous went to the show this early.

This was when the mob went to the movies.

Not as a group, of course, but individual gangsters—hit men with their girlfriends, men with names like Light-Finger and Creepy, men who distrusted crowds because crowds could camouflage G-men. The F.B.I. The good guys.

The ticket seller sat in her booth out front, stiff, appearing wooden, her mouth frozen in between chews of her stick of Blackjack gum. She stared straight ahead, her tired, disinterested eyes unblinking. Ten, fifteen feet away a man in a checkered coat, white saddle shoes, and black fedora nestled back into a doorway, his fingers nervously drumming against the brick facade of the art deco building. He glanced at his watch, coughed into his hand, and looked furtively out to the street in both directions.

As I watched him from a second-story balcony across the thoroughfare, I noticed more men; nondescript, fedora-wearing men in gray suits and subdued ties, all falling into place in doorways up and down the street, or peering over newspapers while standing by the curb. Something was up.

I wasn't the only one to notice. Other people had begun to gather, curious at the suspicious men, yet, keeping a respectful distance. None of them challenged the men; they, in turn, pretended not to notice the growing crowd of onlookers.

A child broke free from her mother and bolted toward the ticket booth. Mr. Saddle Shoes saw her and stepped out of his hiding place to quickly intercept the girl, giving her back to her mother. The grateful woman said something to him by way of apology; he smiled, and she hurried back with her daughter to the vantage point the rest of their family still occupied. The ticket seller seemed not to notice, never flinching.

A few people began emerging from the theater, drawing the discreet attention of all the men of the stakeout. But they didn't leave their cover, letting the theater patrons stagger into the sunlight in all directions. Suddenly, all eyes locked onto the doors as the Bijou divulged its final patrons. The men in hats signaled each other with looks, waves, and whistles. Somewhere in the distance, a dog barked.

A man had emerged from the lobby, flanked by two women, one wearing a single red rose on her bodice. The man's coat was unbuttoned, his felt hat cocked lazily back, exposing his forehead. He wore a thin, nicely trimmed mustache and had a pleasant face that belied the evil behind his clear blue eyes.

The woman on his right arm, the one with the rose, suddenly stopped and fell back, as if to light a cigarette. Though her head was down as she opened her bag, her eyes were up, searching. When she and Saddle Shoes locked gazes, Rose nodded nervously then turned and retreated hastily up the sidewalk in the opposite direction.

In an instant, it was happening. Saddle Shoes stepped out of his doorway in front of the movie couple, at the same time pulling a revolver from the shoulder holster under his coat. He pointed it at the man's chest and shouted, loudly enough for the whole block to hear him.

"F.B.I.! John Dillinger, you're under arrest!"

Dillinger was surprised, but not unprepared. With his left hand he shoved aside the woman still with him, with his right he drew an automatic pistol from his waistband and commenced firing.

G-men emerged from everywhere, guns blazing, shouting, running toward the gangster. The air was filled with violence, angry words, the smell of gunpowder, and the pops of small arms fire.

Dillinger fell in a writhing heap on the sidewalk, still shooting and still taking slugs. As he died a slow death, having wounded two G-men, the rest moved in like vultures, their weapons trained on his head in case he made a last attempt. Yet even as he breathed his last, a car accelerated up the street toward them.

Staccato tommy-gun fire erupted from the auto, surprising the G-men, the spectators . . . everyone but me. I had seen this before.

About twenty-three times, I think, but I had lost count. Four times a day John Dillinger was gunned down in front of the theater, only to be avenged by his cronies in their Plymouth with their burp guns and double-breasted suits. Not historically accurate, to be sure, but loads of fun.

When the car had passed and disappeared, two or three of the untouchables who had been shot off the running board by G-men, Dillinger himself, and several other dead men casually picked themselves up and bowed to the scattered applause of the crowd. Little children cried as always, and I saw the mother of the errant girl kneel to console her. The gunfire was too much, echoing off the closely set buildings and frightening the little ones with its intensity and duration.

Although it only took about two minutes, it seemed like forever—except to the bored ticket seller, who never once moved during the whole episode. That she was a mannequin may have contributed to her dispassionate response.

The combatants disappeared backstage to change clothes and hurry to the Wild West Zone for the gunfight at the O.K. Corral, while the spectators, guests of the theme park, wandered off in all directions to see what other productions awaited them in the Flapper Zone and regions beyond.

I was on a break. Reassigned from Park Security to Design and Planning six months before to oversee the implementation of a major rebuild of much of the park, including several new rides, it had been awhile since I had been able to stroll casually through the park, taking in the sights and sounds and smells, the people, the disobedient children and fawning parents . . . .

The transition had been rather abrupt for me. I had been a security guard—security officer, I mean—working the graveyard shift, when I stumbled onto a murder victim inside a ride one night; my old cop-instinct took over and forced me to solve it.

I had spent almost sixteen years on the force, deciding to chuck it all when circumstances seemed to indicate I should. I'll not bore you with the details now. Suffice it to say, I left police work only to discover how much I missed it, especially homicide investigation.

But working here had its benefits. Good medical plan, profit-sharing, I could hang out with people less than half my age . . . . And now, elevated temporarily from security officer to production supervisor with a healthy pay raise, why, who could ask for more?

The whole sequence of events boggles my mind, really. The murdered kid had been knocked off for his ideas; ideas that could transform the park from an also-ran to a contender. Maybe not a Disneyworld attendance threat, but a major force nonetheless.

But with the kid dead, who would take his plan and run with it? My investigation had familiarized me with many of the details, so I was asked to get the project rolling. His girlfriend, a ride operator, was assigned to assist because she also had some knowledge of the plan.

Hey, if they want to take me off graveyard and pay me more, who am I to argue? Besides, I had learned through the affair to take things as they come, to sit back and let God do His work, to not thwart His plan before He could put it into action.

So here I was, Gil Beckman, former cop, security guard, dressing up and making nice with the big shots. What a hoot!

I retired from the balcony to make my way back to the ride that was being refurbished. The Time Machine, a dinosaur spectacular inexplicably located in the center of the Flapper Zone, was being expanded to allow for larger—and preferably scarier—dinos.

As I approached a glass door to go outside, I saw a familiar face coming in: Lt. Theo Brown, homicide detective and my former partner. He saw me at the same time and we both stopped, just short of the door, waiting for the other to pass through it first.

"Move it, buster," said a female voice behind me.

I turned to see a tall and elegant woman in casual clothes, her auburn, cascading hair framing a pretty face.

"Oh, pardon me," I said as I stepped aside. "Here, let me get that for you." I reached over to open the door but got a scolding in return.

"I can open my own door!"

Something told me, detective that I was, that this woman paid dues to the National Organization for Women. I ignored her and continued to hold it open, smiling at her excessively. I love a challenge.

"Pig," she muttered as she passed. I followed her outside.

"You're welcome . . . ," I replied as she blew by Theo and advanced out of earshot, ". . . you . . . you . . ." I faded out without finishing.

"Now now," Theo scolded. "You have a standard to uphold. Besides, I've never known you to be at a loss for words. What was that all about?"

"She was insulted that I held the door for her."

"So don't. Let them get it themselves; they're liberated."

I gave him my best raised eyebrows. "It's my right to be polite, and no bra-burning feminist is going to take it away from me!"

Theo laughed. "Gil, you beat all. I don't know how you do it."

"Do what?"

"Turn everything into a cause."

"What's right is right, Theo. The times may be a-changin', but God's laws aren't."

"You have to open doors for women? That's one of God's laws?"

"Verily I say unto thee," I replied in round, pious tones. "Hezekiah 3:12. Look it up."

Theo *hmmmed*, and I strolled up the street.

"Buy you a cup of coffee?" I asked when he caught up to me.

"Sure."

"So what are you doing here? We have another homicide I don't know about?"

"No, thank God."

Don't get the wrong idea. Theo wasn't a Christian. He was just uttering a cliché, a familiar phrase. He could just as easily have said, "Thank Zeus," or, "Thanks Higher Power," and it would have meant the same to him. Theo believed that something out there in the Great Beyond put us all here, but not necessarily the God of the Bible, the God of Abraham.

"I'll accept the concept of a singular God," he once told me during a lively coffee shop discussion precipitated by our arrest of a drunk in a brown robe who claimed to be the messiah. "I've seen the kind of decisions committees make. Only a single God would have been successful. But the idea of a *personal* God, who cares continually about each individual here . . . well, that's something I can't accept. I've seen too much of man's inhumanity to man to believe God cares. Maybe for some of us. Maybe even for you. But not for all of us."

I pointed out that I had seen as much inhumanity as he had and tried to explain all the major doctrines of Christianity to him that day, four or five years ago. He listened, even asked a few questions, but nothing came of it. He shrugged it off as something that was okay for me, but he would rely upon himself and get religion in his old age.

Then my wife Rachel died, and he carefully avoided the subject, thinking I was afraid that my God had failed me.

I snapped back to the present.

"So, if you're not here for a homicide," I asked, "what is it? You didn't come just to see little old me, now, did you?"

"Actually, I did. They told me you were over here."

"Snitches," I muttered. "So you found me, copper, now what?"

"I need you to do a favor for me."

"How much do you need?" I reached for my wallet.

"Knock it off, you know I don't need money. And if I did, you'd be the last person I'd come to.

"Prove it," I challenged. "Pay for the coffee."

"Cops never pay for coffee," he said, mocking the erroneous attitude held by most of the adult population. He accepted his cup from the vendor.

I passed a couple of dollars to the girl and got a dime back. I stared at it incredulously. "That's it?" I wheezed.

She nodded and smiled sweetly, but I know she enjoyed inflicting pain. You could see it in those green eyes of hers.

"Enjoy it," I muttered to Theo. "It's worth its weight in gold."

Theo dumped three packets of sugar into his steaming brew while I winced.

"So, what's the favor?" I prodded as we took a seat on a park bench near the square. We could talk openly here. In our suits, plus Theo with his overcoat and hat, we blended right in. Nobody paid us any attention except for one rather robust woman who snuggled between us for a second to have her picture taken by a guy in pink bermuda shorts and black socks. She thought we were part of the decor.

"I'm here officially," Theo said when the woman departed.

"Officiously?"

"You heard me. I'm looking into a disappearance."

"That's like grabbing a handful of air, isn't it?" I queried. "How can you look into something that's not there?"

"Knock it off, Gil, it's too early."

"I love you too. So what's up? You're still in homicide, aren't you?"

"Yeah." He took a chew of his coffee. "I'm doing someone a favor."

"And you're about to pass it on to me."

"Part of it. Michelle—uh, Miss Yokoyama asked me to check it. It's probably nothing."

"Go on."

"A ride maintenance employee hasn't shown up for work the past couple days. Up till now he's been highly reliable, only had a couple sick days, never late. Suddenly, *poof.* Gone. No trace."

"Why does Michelle care?"

Theo shrugged. "You know how it is. She doesn't care. It was handed down to her from her boss, who got it from someone else. Maybe he was a friend of one of the owners, I don't know."

"Whatever." I did indeed understand how it was. "Did you check his house? Family?"

"Lived alone. Manager of his apartment let us in, just in case he was sick or injured inside. Nothing was disturbed, everything looked normal."

"Clothes missing?"

"Didn't look like it. Closet and dresser were sparse but there were no empty hangers or drawers. Two empty suitcases were in the corner."

"So what do you need from me?"

"Check his employee file, see if there's anything in there you can find that might tell us where he's headed."

"You think he just up and took off?"

"It's possible. There's no obvious alternative explanation. His car is gone, no evidence of violence anywhere, no reason for someone to kidnap him that we can figure out. His apartment manager said she saw him leave for work two days ago, regular time. He never made it."

"What's regular time?"

"Three A.M.. She had the . . . she was a little, shall we say, irregular. Heard a noise and looked out, saw him driving off. He was alone."

"That all?"

"No. She said he seemed to be in a hurry."

"Maybe he was late."

"Hmm. Maybe."

This was a puzzler but didn't concern me too much. People sometimes do that. Up and leave one morning. Something snaps and off they go. Even people with families.

Theo handed me a slip of paper with the guy's name on it. Russell Albright. Didn't ring a bell. I figured I'd recognize him if I saw him, though. Having worked graveyard for two years, I had seen most of the ride maintenance guys when they came in at three-thirty in the morning to get the rides ready for the day. Unless, of course, he had been hired during the last six months.

"When did he get hired here? Do you know?" I asked.

"Not exactly," Theo admitted. "Miss Yokoyama said something about eight or nine years ago, she thought. She wasn't sure."

I nodded. "I'll find out. If he's been here that long, there's bound to be something in his file that—wait a minute. Why don't you check it yourself?"

"Like I said, I need a favor," Theo repeated. "I've been on duty since oh-dark-thirty, interviewing his fellow employees. I'm bushed, and I've got other stuff to do. Real police work. Look, if you're too busy—"

I held up my hand. "I'm not trying to get out of it. You know me, I just like all my ducks in a row. I need to know everything. I hate mysteries."

"I thought you already knew everything."

"Har har."

"Well, so you won't pout, let me tell you everything I know so far."

"Shoot."

"Nothing. Not a da—sorry. I mean, not a darn thing. Albright's driving record is clean, no criminal history, no contacts with the P.D."

"How long's he lived in that apartment?"

"Five years. Gave no previous address."

"What did his coworkers have to say?"

"Nothing. He was sociable, no girlfriend or family. Kept to himself but not so much they thought anything about it. He wasn't reclusive. In fact, he was very personable and dependable. That's what makes it so suspicious. They could rely on him. One guy said you could set your watch by him. He was just the opposite of you, Gil."

I ignored the slam. It was an easy shot, not worth enough points to require a response. "When do you need the file?"

"Whenever you can get it. This afternoon is fine. If there's nothing there, leave a message for me. Otherwise, I'll stop by in the morning for copies of whatever's relevant. We wouldn't be bothering without some evidence of foul play except it came from Miss Yokoyama."

"I'll bring the file to you," I volunteered. "Tomorrow's Saturday."

"Oh yeah. I forgot." He pushed himself up and tossed his styrofoam cup toward a trash can. He missed but made no effort to pick it up.

"Oh, and see if you can dig up a photo," he added, adjusting his fedora. "His DMV soundex won't be in for a few days. Probably won't be much good, anyway. He's had several extensions. Last DMV photo was taken six years ago."

"That's just as well," I agreed. "Those things never look like the person. We keep current photos of everyone on file for employee of the quarter announcements and stuff like that."

"Good enough." Theo stuck out his hand. "Wish you'd come back," he admitted.

"Over Capt. William 'Don't-Call-Me-Bill' Fitzgerald's dead body," I said. "Even if I wanted to, he'd never let me."

"I know," Theo conceded. "I was just wishing."

I grinned. "I've done a little of that myself."

TWO

Theo thanked me for the coffee and ambled off more or less in the direction of the security office where his unmarked, American-made sedan with the tiny hubcaps and tell-tale antennas was probably parked. I could check the dino ride later. I had other work to do and needed to check on the excavation for a brand-new ride before I could go to personnel to check Albright's file.

The new ride was going in where an old ride had been. It would be no loss. They had already torn down the Starcoaster, basically just a dolled-up Tilt-A-Whirl inside a building with no lights, just stars and planets projected on the domed ceiling and loud noises designed to destroy your equilibrium. It had gotten so decrepit over its life that it was due to be mothballed anyway, so when the plan was formulated for the park's makeover, this was one of the first checked off to go.

It would be superceded by another space ride—to maintain the continuity since this area was called the Future Zone—and would also be an indoor ride, but that's where the resemblance would end.

Everett Curran—the genius kid who had been murdered—had designed a moonscape, which guests would traverse in little moon cars like those used by the astronauts in the seventies. First, though, riders would sit in a landing module and slowly descend, feeling what the astronauts felt, and hearing what they heard. It was all simulated, of course, with special effects, moving chairs, and a sound track.

Once landed, folks would move into the moonmobiles, over which they had no actual control, and begin their excursion. At this point, all resemblance to the real moon ended. The guests would then be assaulted with space creatures, meteor showers, alien spacecraft, and all kinds of exciting emergencies. I don't want to spoil it for you, but suffice it to say, the experience promised to be exciting.

The really neat part is, although computer driven, it would all be random. The ride would never be the same twice. The mechanized creatures and computer generated components would all function independently of each other.

That was the plan, at least. Right now all we had was a big hole in the ground. The Starcoaster had been mounted on a thick concrete slab that had to be broken up, and now a deep basement was being dug by heavy machinery, since the new ride—Moonraiders—took place mostly underground.

Because of the high water table in the city, we had to build a pump system to keep the new ride dry. That had to be completed and operational before construction began and was actually the first thing done when the new plan was instituted. It had been operating for about three months now.

I watched the construction crew; tough, tanned men in hard hats wearing T-shirts and heavy boots and Levi's that had a tendency not to cover their backsides when they bent over. I marveled at how precisely they manipulated their bulldozers and graders, following the directions of the foreman and the markings of little stakes with colored cloth tied around them. I smiled to myself. I had a tough time cutting a block of cheese into equal slices.

And Rachel; she couldn't park a car to save her life. . . . My smile faded quickly. Why did everything remind me of her?

Everything in the pit appeared to be under control. I waved to the foreman who had just noticed me. He acknowledged my greeting and turned back to his duties, knowing I wasn't there to stick my nose in it. As I skirted the area to make my way to security, I noticed a familiar figure on the far side of the pit surveying the scene with his hands on his hips. His wide girth and gray hair identified him easily, and I wondered what monumental occasion caused him to venture out from his office and his $3,000 tufted burgundy, leather, heated, vibramassage easy chair.

Since coming to the theme park as president, Jerry Opperman had never been seen actually doing anything. The rumor was that he was a genius of ultimate proportions, one of those guys who is so far above everyone else that they operate on a different wavelength altogether. He's FM, everyone else is AM. That much was true, I knew from experience. What few conversations I had had with him were priceless, short exchanges that left me scratching my head. It was like he couldn't hear a word I was saying and was reading my lips only in a foreign language. Perhaps that was part of his genius; he was so advanced he knew the questions I *should* have been asking, and those were the ones he answered.

That he had been the one to promote Michelle Yokoyama from vice president of merchandising to senior vice president of operations—second only to himself—was a surprise, although everyone suspected it was a directive that came down from the owners' group. It was a good decision, one of the few made by the park in recent years.

Hiring me was the other one.

Opperman moved off now, flanking the pit, waving his arms and pointing and shouting. He was ignored by the construction workers. I pressed on and in a few moments was next to him. He hadn't seen me.

"May I help you, Mr. Opperman?" I asked.

His head turned abruptly toward me. "Huh?" His eyes met mine but didn't stay there, drifting off to some point beyond my left ear. "Jerry Opperman, president," he said. He extended his hand but withdrew it when I hesitated.

"What are you doing here? This is a restricted area," he informed me.

"Well, I work here," I said. "I'm in charge of this." I waved my left arm in an arc, taking in the whole construction area. His brow furrowed, and he leaned toward me.

"Gil Beckman," I said, anticipating him. "Michelle Yokoyama assigned me to oversee the construction of this and a few other things. You know, the Curran Plan."

"Why?" His face was completely blank.

"I'm the most familiar with it."

"Curran?"

"Yeah, you know. The kid who developed the plan then was murdered by John Hayes?"

He scowled. "Oh. The dead kid." He looked at the construction then back at me. "Well, you're doing a bang-up job, just bang-up. But tell me, do they have to dig right here? Why not over there a bit more?"

"They're following the plans, sir," I said. "It may not look like much, but it will come out all right in the end. Surely you know that from your experience. Your miniature golf courses didn't look like much when they started, but when they were finished, all the little windmills were in just the right places I'll bet."

He thought about it, then beamed. "So, you've seen them, then? Aren't they wonderful?" He took a second look at me. "Say, aren't you a security guard?"

"Security officer," I corrected. "But not for the last six months."

"Then it wasn't you."

"What wasn't me?"

"Who sat in my chair."

My face flushed suddenly. Actually I had sat in his chair. I had messed with the settings on his vibrathingy and the heat dojigger, and he'd gotten all upset. Only he didn't know it was me, and I didn't want to tell him. I couldn't lie either, so I did an end run around the issue.

"Are you talking about recently?"

"Last night."

"Oh." *Whew!* "No, it wasn't me." *This time at least,* I thought.

He turned away from me and said no more. I waited for a few seconds, and after I was sure he was done, I moved on. When I looked over my shoulder a minute later, he was gone.

It was a sparse day at the park so far—a yawner—and when I pushed through the rear door of the security office several of the guys were there, taking it easy. Danny Hill, a transfer from catering, ate his tuna fish sandwich out of a sack in the squad room adjacent to dispatch, apparently putting his intimate knowledge of the park's food preparation to good use. Todd Carter, the dayshift sergeant, sat at the console with Wendy. He was sweet on her—who wasn't?—but she only had eyes for a city fireman.

Formerly the graveyard dispatcher when I pounded the all-night pavement, Wendy was put on dayshift by Harry Clark, the security chief, in a last-ditch effort to keep her from hiring on at the P.D. They were close to offering her a position—so close that they had completed her background investigation—and Harry began trying to tempt her to stay, trying to avoid losing a good employee. Nice little raise, dayshift with weekends off, small stuff like that.

To no avail. Wendy was not going to trade her dream for a few baubles.

"Morning, Wendy," I greeted.

"Well, look who's slumming," Carter said. "Nice jacket."

"Sergeant Carter. How's Gomer Pyle?" I asked.

"Very funny, Gil. Not very original, though. You know, you can't be in here," Carter said. "No one allowed in the dispatch center."

"You're in there."

"I'm the supervisor."

"Thanks to me," I said. "I created an opening for you."

"What a pal."

"Besides, I'm not in dispatch. I'm outside dispatch. See?" I pointed to my feet at the edge of the doorway.

Our intelligent repartee was interrupted by a radio call, and Carter had to leave, taking Hill with him.

"Thanks," Wendy said. "He's a jerk."

"That's how he got promoted," I observed sarcastically, but meaning it.

"He was right, though, that is a nice jacket," she said.

"Thanks. Got it for five bucks at a yard sale."

"Stop it," she cautioned.

"I can't stop. I love yard sales."

"You know what I mean, Gil. You didn't get that at a yard sale. . . . Did you?"

I just smiled. "Any news from the P.D.?"

Her grin widened. "If I tell you, I'll have to kill you."

I laughed. My trademark line, and she beat me to it. She had been waiting two years to do that.

"Must be good stuff," I ventured.

She squirmed. "I start in three weeks!"

"Hey! Great!" I gave her a hug but broke it off quickly when I saw Harry Clark's door came open down the hall and Sally Foster, his secretary, emerge. "Have you told Harry yet?"

"No," she admitted. "Not until the last possible second."

"Probably just as well," I nodded. "I hate seeing grown men cry."

"Yeah. Oh, and thanks for the recommendation."

"Biggest pack of lies I ever put on paper . . . next to my last resume, of course."

Sally grinned when she saw me through the glass and headed for dispatch. She was moved from dayshift dispatcher to being Harry's secretary when Harry put Wendy on dayshift. He raised her pay a bit, too, even though secretary was in the same classification as dispatcher. It was Harry's way of compensating her. Sally didn't mind and wouldn't have complained if she did.

Sally was a really nice woman, a genuine peach, and also the only woman I had dated since Rachel. I enjoyed her company nearly as much as she enjoyed mine. But things weren't serious, as least as far as I was concerned.

Sally attended my church—or I hers, since she actually started there a couple years before I did—and some time after Rachel died, I noticed her. Then I quit the P.D. and went to work here at the park and discovered she worked in security. That's when I entertained the idea of getting to know her better. We were in different Sunday school classes, and ours is a large church, so we had never spoken much more than a greeting to each other there, at least until we dated that first time. But things hadn't changed much.

When I got to thinking about it, I wondered if Rachel had known her. Rachel went to all the women's things: Bible studies, retreats, quilting parties, barn raisings. Whatever they did when they got together. It was possible they were acquaintances.

"Uh oh," Sally said, apparently seeing the sheepish looks on our faces. "I interrupted something."

She looked a little hurt, but I couldn't figure out why until I realized I still had my arm on Wendy's shoulder.

"No, heh heh, not at all," I assured her, giving Wendy a pat then pulling my arm back.

"Well, if you were congratulating Wendy for getting hired by the police department, go ahead. I already know. Congratulations Wendy."

"Thanks," Wendy said. "How do you—? Does—?"

"Harry?" Sally laughed. "Not a chance. I called the records supervisor over there, Margaret, and asked her point blank. Hey, I've got to replace you, I need a head start. Don't worry, I won't say anything to Harry until you want me to. Or you can do it yourself."

"I think I should do it," Wendy said. "And thank you."

"Good girl. Now Gil, what may we do for you? You know, you look sharp in that suit." She leaned closer and picked something off of my shoulder. "These long blonde hairs don't do a thing for it, though."

I'd been caught, and I hadn't even done anything. Just then Sergeant Carter came back. Saved by the dullard.

"You still here?" he asked.

"No, I left just after you did."

"I see you're in dispatch."

"Keen observation, Sherlock. Ever think of becoming a detective?"

"If I did become a detective I wouldn't quit."

Sally, seeing my face flush and my eyes begin to widen, gave me a look Carter couldn't see—a look that said *control yourself*—then she made up some excuse to get Carter out of the office, some errand she had for him. When he left, I thanked her.

"I wasn't protecting you as much as I was him," she explained. "You could say a word to Michelle Yokoyama, and he'd be history. I don't think he realizes it."

"Neither did I," I admitted.

"That's just as well. Don't you even think about it."

"Furthest thing from my mind." I turned to Wendy. "Get Michelle on the phone for me, will you?"

"You know, Gil," Sally said. "You've got to stop being so sensitive about your quitting the police department. People are going to hit you with it every chance they get. They think it was a dumb move, and they love throwing it in your face."

"I wouldn't be so sensitive if people would stop flogging me with it. Do you think it was a dumb move?"

"How should I know, Gil? The Lord moves in mysterious ways, sometimes. Maybe He has something better lined up for you, something that you wouldn't be prepared for if you hadn't gone through that. Maybe it was a wrong decision, but God will work it out for good."

"Besides," Wendy added cheerfully, "it's too late now."

"That's the truth," I agreed. "What's Carter's problem, anyway? What did I ever do to him?"

"He was tight with Jaime," Wendy said.

Jaime Brito was the former sergeant I had fingered for the murder of Everett Curran. He did the actual deed, following the orders of Senior V.P. John Hayes. Jaime had friends, and even though they didn't approve of what he did, they still held it against me for exposing him. People are strange.

"Ah, don't fret about him, Gil," Sally said, waving Carter off. "The world's full of guys like him. We just have to do our best and let the chips fall where they may."

"And keep our noses to the grindstone," I added.

"Our shoulders to the wheel," Wendy said.

"Whatever will be, will be," said Sally.

Just as I was sure we were about to break into a rousing rendition of "Climb Every Mountain" in three-part harmony, the door opened and Harry rushed in, putting the kibosh on it. His face was red and beaded with sweat, and he was panting like a dog, his tongue dangling over his thin lower lip. Harry had been running! I checked my pockets for my CPR card to make sure it was still valid.

Sally glided swiftly to him and eased him into a chair. I drew a cup of water from the cooler. He drank it in a single gulp, wiped his sleeve across his mouth, and looked up at me, wide-eyed.

"I'm glad you're here," he said between breaths.

"You didn't have to run," I told him. "I'd've waited."

"What's the problem, Harry?" Sally asked.

Harry jerked his thumb over his shoulder and started to speak but didn't have enough air. We waited patiently. Finally, he heaved and spit it out all at once.

"Your new ride, Gil. They found. . . something."

"What? Who?" Harry was so excited, it was contagious.

"The backhoe operator. He scooped up a load of dirt and when he raised the bucket—"

"Gold? Oil? Jimmy Hoffa?"

"—something dropped back into the hole." He sucked in a breath. "It's a skull. A human skull."

THREE

I was stunned. I had only been kidding about Jimmy Hoffa.
"Cool!" I said, inciting looks of disdain from Sally and Wendy.
"As in interesting," I explained. "Hey, there could be a lot of possible explanations for this."

"Like what?" Wendy asked.

"Like. . . a lot," I said with a shrug. To Harry I said, "They're not messing with it, are they? I mean, you made them stop digging and back off, right?"

"Well, I didn't exactly say anything. . . ."

"Great." To Wendy I said, "Call the police, see if Lt. Theo Brown is there. He'll be interested in this."

"Shall I have the police respond, or stand by?"

"Tell them to come on in. Even if it's no big deal, they'll want to be in on it from the outset. Oh, and no radio traffic about it. We don't need a bunch of onlookers."

"What's so important about stopping the construction?" Sally asked.

"If it's a crime scene, we don't want it disturbed. It'll have to be processed properly for evidence. I need to get out there. Sally, would you call Trish? I think she's in Design and Planning right now. Have her meet me there with a camera and a notepad."

"Okay Gil."

"Thanks, Sal. You too, Wendy."

I patted Harry on the shoulder and trotted over to the pit. The construction crew was gathered around the foreman, and the heavy equipment had been shut down. I figured the foreman, Joe Daniels, had the prize, and everyone was gathering around him to gawk. I was right.

Hopping down into the pit, I shouted to Daniels, and the men parted to let me through, then closed back in behind me like the Red Sea on the Egyptians.

I was a little surprised by what I saw. The skull was dark brown and blotchy, the teeth stained. Conditioned like everyone else to television and the movies, it took me a second to remember that only bones bleached by the sun turn white. Buried bones will be the color of the earth they are in.

The skull appeared greasy, not at all clean, with dirt and what could only be soft tissue still attached in spots, tissue that was brown and leathery. Small patches of hair were stuck to the top and side of the skull. They were somewhat long and appeared to be brown, but that could be from dirt. I suspected Daniels had tried to brush it off at first, and I couldn't blame him, really. He wasn't a cop, wouldn't understand the importance of not disturbing it, and was undoubtedly intrigued and puzzled by their find.

I gingerly took it from him and asked for a paper bag or something to put it in. While I waited for someone to get it, I inspected the artifact.

It was small, with delicate teeth. The mandible—jawbone—was not attached. Probably still in the dirt. I turned it over.

"Adult female," I mumbled to no one in particular.

"Now, how in the world do you know that?" the foreman asked. "Looks like a kid to me. Look how small it is."

"Lots of ways to tell," I said. I showed him. "Permanent teeth, the skull sutures—these wiggly lines here—are completely joined. They're loose on a kid so he can grow. And see this?" I pointed to an area on the underneath of the skull in the center, about where the spine would attach.

"Yeah. So?"

"On a kid there's a separation there. It grows together around age twenty or so." There was more, but I thought I'd save it for Theo.

"Well, I'll be," said Daniels. "I suppose you'll have her name and phone number shortly." He grinned a construction worker's grin and lit a cigar with rough calloused hands.

"She's not your type," I suggested.

"If she's dead," shouted one of the workers, "she's his type."

When the laughter died down I asked, "Where'd you find it?"

He pointed to the deepest part of the pit, a hole three, four feet lower than the adjacent ground.

"When Tommy scooped that area and pulled the shovel out, the skull kinda fell out of the wall of dirt he left. See the hole it made?"

I could. It was either great news or terrible news. If the body—if indeed there was a whole body—extended away from the hole, it could still be intact. If not, the bones would be all mixed up in the pile of dirt Tommy was making.

"That last shovelful," I said, "where'd he dump it?"

"Nowheres. As soon as he saw the skull pop out—he didn't know it was a skull at first, you understand, but he knew it was something other than a rock—he stopped the backhoe. Dirt's all still in the scoop." He pointed and I saw Tommy standing proudly in front of his machine, his T-shirt too short to cover his expanded gut. I gave him a thumbs up. Construction guys like that.

"Good," I told Joe. "Leave it there. We're calling the police. They have to check this out. We can't disturb it for awhile."

"Police? You think this might be something. . . like a murder or something?"

"Could be." *I hope I hope I hope.* "If it is, you'll have to find something else to do for a day or two."

"No problem. It's your nickel." He wandered off and began directing his men to tasks outside the pit.

Trish Smith showed up about then and joined me in the pit. She was a blonde, a different blonde than Wendy, more honey-colored, and just shy of twenty. She had been the adoring almost-girlfriend of the bashful Everett Curran—the bashful, late Everett Curran. She had worked, as had Everett, as a ride operator, and when I got kicked upstairs I suggested I needed an assistant and thought she would be perfect. Besides myself, she was the only one who knew anything about his plan. Michelle agreed, and here we were.

I was happy to have her working with me. For one, she was young and gave the project a much needed insight: The folks from Design and Planning were okay, but some of them had been there a long time and were somewhat set in their ways. Like me, they hadn't changed with the times.

And it was especially good for Trish. It gave her something to keep her mentally stimulated—pressing buttons on rides all day long gave her too much time to think, to remember her dead boyfriend. She had enough time at home to do that. Here, she could actually contribute something of lasting value to the park as Everett's representative—plus, I needed a woman's point-of-view and input on some things. After all, at least half the park's customers were women.

"What's up, Gil?" she asked, handing me the camera and notepad I had requested.

I told her, showing her the skull now nestled comfortably in a brown paper sack.

"Yuck. Is it . . . ?

"Human? I'm afraid so."

"It smells." She wrinkled her nose.

"You would too if you'd been buried under the Starcoaster."

"Where'd it come from?"

"Down there. Tommy-Bob Belly dug it up." I jerked my thumb toward Tommy, still standing sentinel by his backhoe. He grinned again, knowing he was the subject of our conversation.

"Are you going to dig for the rest of it?" Trish asked, somewhat apprehensively.

"No." She looked relieved so I added, "The cops'll do that. There's most likely some evidence down there."

She considered the ramifications of that, and I saw the look on her face when it dawned on her that meant murder.

"This place gives me the creeps. What's this mean? To the park, I mean."

I shrugged. "Not much. A delay for a day or two. To the park, some free publicity."

"Good? Bad? What?"

"I don't know. It depends, really, but I don't think it'll be bad. There could be a lot of explanations for this, most of them interesting but not necessarily sinister. Now, if Lucy here had a bullet hole in the back of her head, that'd be different."

"Lucy?"

I scrunched my shoulders and grinned. "First thing that popped into my mind."

"Nonsense. You named her after the missing link, that Jinzan . . . thropus thing."

"Zinjanthropus."

"Yeah."

"Don't know what you're talking about."

"You've never heard of Dr. Leakey."

"Sounds like a plumber. 'Let Doc Leakey fix your drippy.'"

"You're mocking the theory of evolution, aren't you?"

"Of course. It's a hypothesis based on an assumption, with no basis in fact. It's not science. Science requires the study of what is in the present that can be tested. Evolution is a religion, based on faith in a theory for which there are no provable facts. Our Lucy has as much of a chance being the missing link as Leakey's Lucy."

"How long do you think she's been there?" Trish asked.

"At least as long as the Starcoaster. She was pretty deep. She might be ancient." I had a pretty good idea that wasn't the case. There was too much soft tissue still attached to her. But I didn't want Trish to freak too badly.

"Why does it smell?"

Because she was probably buried alive or immediately after death and has been rotting in dark moist earth, I thought. What I said was, "What did you expect?"

Trish screwed up her face. "I don't know. Clean and white, I guess." I didn't say anything, and she asked uneasily, "How do you think she got there?"

That answer was obvious too, even without the rest of the body: someone had put her there. "That's one of the questions the cops will have to answer," I said. "But I think we can rule out burrowing."

"Let them handle it," she said. "I'm going back to work. Have fun with your camera." She shuddered visibly and left.

"See you later," I called after her, and she waved.

No sooner had she gone than someone else appeared, like a vulture to a carcass. I saw him coming and groaned inwardly. I had hoped the cops would get here first.

"What's going on?" Jerry Opperman demanded. "You there, why has the work stopped?"

Surely Harry Clark had told him about the find. Why else would he have come out? I kept my back to him and turned my head slowly, my face expressionless. He stood on the rim, his hand characteristically on his hip, the other pointing a chubby finger at me. I hate finger-pointing.

This was twice in one day Opperman had emerged from his den and both times to torment me. What were the odds? I should have rushed right out and bought a lottery ticket. Either he had decided to become more directly involved in the operation of the park, or birds had eaten his trail of bread crumbs back to his office.

"Oh, good morning again, sir," I fawned disgustingly, pretending not to hear the question.

"Well?"

"No sir, it's not going to be a well," I said with all truthfulness and sincerity. "We're putting in a new ride."

Yeah, I know, I probably shouldn't be such a smart aleck. But sarcasm and irony are art forms, in my humble opinion, and should be practiced whenever possible. In this case, it was lost on him. He just assumed I was stupid.

"No, no, that's not what I mean. Why have the workers stopped?"

"Oh. Well, sir, to be honest, we, uh . . . they dug up something that more or less forced them to stop, at least until the police get here."

"The police? What do we need the police for? It's just an old Indian or something."

So he definitely had been told.

"I doubt that, sir," I said. "I believe it may be a murder victim."

31

His scowl faded into nothing. Blankness. Zero on the Richter scale. Then slowly his forehead creased as the realization set in. His mouth opened, but he said nothing and looked around furtively, as if searching for something to provoke a response. Finally the thought formed, and he glared back at me.

"So what? You've got the thing. Give it to the cops and let's get back to work."

"It's not that simple, Mr. Opperman. This could be a crime scene. There may be evidence here that—"

"Evidence of what?"

Opperman's mouth hadn't moved, and the voice came from behind me. I turned my head to see Lieutenant Brown standing on the rim, his hands pushed deeply into this overcoat, his eyes puffy. A blue suit was with him. I breathed a proverbial—and literal—sigh of relief.

"Come on down and check it out," I said, pointing to the paper bag. After telling the uniformed officer to wait there, Theo hiked down into the pit, inciting a protest from Opperman.

"This is outrageous! Who are you?"

Without flinching Theo yanked his shield out and displayed it, then flipped the black leather badge holder quickly shut and into his pocket in one motion.

"Lieutenant Brown," he said. "And you are . . . ?"

"President Opperman," I offered.

"Oh. Well, let me take a look, Mr. Opperman."

Without waiting for a reply from Opperman, I opened the bag and Theo peeked in.

"Where?" he asked simply.

I pointed to the hole where the skull had popped out. Theo assessed it quickly. "Is the rest of it in there?"

"Could be," I said. "Or in the bucket." I pointed to Tommy who went into his routine one more time.

"Looks suspicious," Theo concluded. "We'll have to search the area carefully, see if there's any more," he said to Opperman, leaving no room for argument.

"Come here," I said to Theo. I led him to the scene, and we scrutinized the hole. Dusting off the loose dirt around the indentation, I stuck my finger in, pointing out a piece of bone with an attached tooth. "Mandible."

"Looks that way," Theo agreed. "There might be more."

When we looked up, Opperman complained.

"Well, what about it? We need to get these men back to work." Without waiting for an answer, he turned to Joe Daniels, who was leaning against Tommy's backhoe. "You there," Opperman called, "get on that machine, get back to work."

"Negative!" Theo shouted. Like most cops, he didn't like his authority circumvented. Daniels looked at me, and I shook my head. The foreman shrugged and folded his arms.

"Mr. Opperman," Theo said, his jaw tight, "we have a possible homicide here. At the very least we have a questionable situation, but this area will remain as it is until I say otherwise."

"This is private property," Opperman asserted. "You need a warrant."

Theo turned to me. "What's his problem?"

"Too much TV as a child," I said. "Or maybe it's his diet. He probably eats bean starch sandwiches, or birthday cake pot roast. He's got a real . . . authority complex. He thinks he's president of the park."

"He is."

"Oh yeah. Never mind."

Theo gave me his I-don't-need-this look. "Yes, Mr. Opperman, I need a warrant. That is, unless I have the permission of the property owner. I can have my chief call the owners of the park and get it, explaining to them in the process that you refused to cooperate with a police investigation. Or I can call a judge from my cell phone—" he pulled his phone out of his pocket and held it up so Opperman could see it, "and he'll give me what I need. Both of those options will take considerably longer than you simply giving me your blessing. But either way, I don't have to take a step, and nothing in this pit is going to be disturbed."

Opperman was beaten and knew it. Maybe he was smarter than I gave him credit for. He grumbled for Theo to go ahead and do whatever he needed to but urged him to do it quickly. Then he stormed off, probably back to his office and his easy chair to plot revenge against the detective.

"He'll call the chief," I warned.

"Big deal," Theo said. He shouted to the uniform up on the edge to get the coroner rolling and a forensic team. The works. The uniform disappeared, and in a few seconds I could hear his unit radio crackling faintly.

"Now what?" I asked.

"We wait."

"Want to hear my theory?"

"Not particularly."

"Aw, c'mon," I pleaded.

"How can you have a theory already?"

"Well, I don't know who killed her or how—"

"Her?"

"Yeah. I looked at the skull before I bagged it."

Theo sighed. "Look, we've never had a buried victim before, at least not since I've worked homicide. And all the homicides you and I worked together, they were not only fully clothed but had their skin on too. Good grief, we only have one or two a year, and most of those are family deals or drive-by shootings. What makes you think you know so much about it? We'd only been in homicide for only two years before you quit."

"I've done some independent study, I guess you could say."

"You go to the movies a lot now that you've got all that free time?"

"Ouch." I feigned injury. "No. Actually I'm just interested in forensic anthropology. For a while there, I was entertaining the idea of getting my master's degree in it."

"Do tell. Well, in that case, Mr. Smarty Pants, you might as well go ahead. You won't give me a moment's peace until you do."

I grinned like a kid. "Adult female, at least twenty, buried near or at the time of death, burial perhaps the cause, modern—"

"Wait a minute. How do you know it isn't an Indian relic or something? Or a war memento from Vietnam? That's not unheard of, you know. A lot of vets brought them back."

I gently brought out the skull. "Indians—native Americans, that is, from the last century and before—have well-worn, almost flat teeth because of the grit in their diet." I turned the skull over.

The fillings in the bumpy molars were unmistakable. "I doubt that Doc Holliday did this dental work. A war prize is pretty much eliminated too," I ventured. "She looks Caucasian to me."

I went on to explain why I thought it was a female and that the presence of soft tissue virtually precluded an antiquity.

"That would make it fairly recent, wouldn't it?" Theo asked.

"That's the puzzler," I admitted. "She would have had to have been here before the ride—the one we just tore out—was completed. And yet she still has soft tissue. Plus this greasy stuff." It looked like a coating of brown soap. In fact, that's what it was called. The proper term was adipocere, and I told Theo so.

Theo looked at me wryly. "You read too many books. You have just enough knowledge to make you dangerous. Any other brilliant deductions?"

"No, but a suggestion. I think you should call Professor Ellison at the university."

"The anthropologist?"

I nodded. "The sheriff's department uses her on occasion, like when a hiker finds a body in the mountains or a dirt biker falls over a skull in the desert. Even if this turns out to be nothing, it'll be good training for her students. A nearly pristine site."

Theo thought about it. "Yeah, I hate to admit it but you're probably right." he said. "But it's not my call. The coroner decides what we do, you know that. He'll be here pretty quick. So will forensics."

Theo fell silent, gazing at the scene while working something out in his mind. He jotted down an occasional note. I got out the camera and took some photos and on my notepad, drew a few quick sketches. No reason, just habit. I liked doing it. Gave me something to look at later, to help me think.

We found out about the coroner all too soon. He arrived a few minutes later, before the crime scene investigators had had time to do more than set up their gear.

When I saw him coming, I groaned out loud. Theo gave me a skewed up look, "What's your problem, Gil?"

"Franklin Willis," I said quietly. "The coroner's answer to Barney Fife."

"Yeah, I guess he is pretty stupid."

"It's not that he's stupid, he just has no sense. He's the only deputy in the coroner's office that I ever had a problem with."

"Yeah, they're all pretty good guys. What'd Willis do to you?"

"Nothing to me. He did it to the widow. About three years ago, I backed up patrol on a medical aid. You were on vacation or something or I'd've told you about it. Anyway, the old guy was dead when we got there, natural causes. His wife—she was about 80—was pretty staggered. They'd been married for sixty years. His death wasn't really a surprise; he'd been sick with lung disease for several years. But they'd had dinner a half-hour before. Then, while she did the dishes, he walked into the bedroom and died.

"Needless to say, she was upset, but she had enough presence of mind to remember they'd already made funeral arrangements for themselves. She told ol' Franklin there—he was just a rookie then—that she wanted her husband's body taken directly to a certain mortuary. Willis got the old boy's doctor to agree to sign the death certificate so an autopsy wouldn't be necessary—although he was obviously peeved about the number of phone calls it took to get it—but he didn't think the transport company would take the body anywhere but to a contract facility.

"She insisted, though, and Willis finally caved in and called them. When he gets off the phone he turns to the old gal and says, 'This is your lucky day. They'll take him to your mortuary.'"

Theo was aghast but couldn't help snickering. "You're kidding."

"I was standing next to a paramedic. We both grabbed our lips and beat feet outside so we wouldn't bust up in front of everyone."

Theo was still shaking his head when Deputy Coroner Franklin Willis made it down to us.

"What'cha got?" he asked, sounding for all the world as if he had something else more important to do. He was chomping on a wad of bubble gum that I expected to find later on the bottom of my shoe.

"Human skeletal remains," Theo said. He let the coroner peek in the bag.

"That's just the head," Willis said.

"Duh," I said, rolling my eyes.

Theo threw me a glare, but I let it bounce off.

"Didn't you used to work in the park here?" I asked Willis. "In management?"

Willis looked at me, perplexed. "No, I don't believe so. Why?"

"No reason." I waved him off and turned away so I could grin at my little inside-joke.

"I recognize this is just the skull," Theo said, trying to ignore me. "The rest of her is in there." He pointed.

"Her?" Franklin Willis sounded insulted. We should have left that for him to figure out. Theo just gave him a dead stare, the kind I'm sure he used to give his kids.

"Well," Willis said slowly, apparently resigned to accepting our assessment without argument, "let's go get the rest of her."

"I really don't think we should," Theo said.

"Oh? And why not? That's our job, isn't it?"

"I think this should be done properly, by someone trained to excavate remains."

"How long has the . . . subject been there, do you suppose?" People were all subjects to King Franklin.

Theo glanced at me for an answer. I shrugged. "Decade, maybe more. She was under a ride."

Willis snorted. "Let's get someone over here with a shovel. We're gonna dig her out. We can study her later on a table." He moved toward the site.

"Not so fast, hot shot," I said, moving in front of him.

"Who is this?" Willis said, turning to Theo and poking a thumb in my direction. I shook my head at Theo who kept his mouth shut, forcing Willis to turn back and address me.

"Gil Beckman," I said. I didn't offer my hand. "Lieutenant Brown will back me up on this. We tried to be nice, but you won't take a hint." I redirected my gaze to Theo. "What's the deal? Why is everyone so hot to dig these bones up?"

Theo could only shrug.

"You look familiar," Willis said to me.

Theo said, "Used to work with me in homicide."

"That so? That explains the attitude." Willis stared at me for a second, then said my name several times slowly. He snapped his fingers. "Didn't your wife croak a couple years back? In a school or something?"

My chest tightened, as did my fist. I felt the heat rise up my neck, but I swallowed back my anger. I wasn't going to let this twerp get to me.

I moved closer to him and spoke softly, but firmly. "I don't know why you want to be such a jockey, but you're not going to storm in there and disturb a crime scene. I don't care if you are the reigning authority figure here, you're wrong. But if I let you go ahead, then prove you're wrong later, it'll be too late. I'm sorry to have to talk to you this way, I expected a coroner's deputy to have more sense. You don't disturb the crime scene."

"I'll have your job," Willis said, his voice shaking now.

"You can have it, Willis, but I doubt you could do it. You're not qualified."

"That's not what I meant."

"He's not a cop, Willis," Theo said. "Your threats don't hold water."

"You said he used to work with you in homicide."

"That's right. The operative word is *used to*. When he left homicide, he left the department altogether. He's an ex-cop. Works here at the park, in charge of the new construction. As completely devoid of tact as Mr. Beckman the civilian might be, he's right. This is going to be processed like an archaeological dig so we can collect all the evidence that's there. It's hard enough to catch crooks when they have a several-year head start that we shouldn't go around destroying the only evidence we have."

"I say what goes here."

"Talk all you want, but get your keister out of this pit. How many buried victims have you dealt with in your short career?"

"Well . . . none."

"Big surprise," I said.

"Shut up, Gil," Theo ordered. He turned back to Willis. "If we thought you'd listen to a reasonable argument, we'd've given you one. These things take time, they have to be done right. When the forensic anthropologist gets here, you can oversee the whole operation, do your job the way it's supposed to be done, even tell everyone it was all your idea, I don't care. Until then, hands off. Gil would be within his rights to bust you one after your crack about his wife, and I wouldn't see anything if he did. You wouldn't be able to do your job with a broken nose. Lucky for you Gil's a gentleman."

Willis seethed, but slowly backed off and climbed out of the pit.

"He'll call his supervisor," I said.

"So will I. It's been a long time coming."

"I hoped he would have improved with age," I said quietly. I gave Theo a puzzled look. "Break his nose?"

Theo just smiled. "Worked, didn't it?"

"Our bosses are gonna love us at the end of the day," I observed.

"I'm staying down here with you," Theo said. "They'll never find us."

FOUR

An hour or so later, the construction zone more resembled an archaeological site than the beginnings of a thrill ride. The forensic anthropologist, Judy Ellison, had arrived with her entourage, and within minutes they were as busy as one-armed paper hangers, each having his or her own little task and doing it with very little instruction. Professor Ellison, who had testified on untold homicide cases over the years, took the skull from me with a cheery thank you and an appreciative *ooohhh* when she looked in the bag, like a kid who had just gotten the present she'd been waiting a year for.

She was a short, unassuming woman, totally unlike what we've come to expect a lady anthropologist to look like from the nature shows on PBS (tall and thin, with longish hair in a pony-tail, wearing shorts and hiking boots). Ellison wore baggy Levi's and tennis shoes and a UCLA sweatshirt, and was, shall I say, a little plump.

Although a PhD, she wouldn't let anyone call her Doctor. Said it was too presumptuous. Then she'd laugh and say she preferred "Your Majesty." Her heart was as big as all outdoors, and she often caught one quite by surprise. Expecting her to talk like someone's mother, she would occasionally let slip a surprising—although always accurate—descriptive word, causing anyone near her who happened to be sitting in a chair to fall out of it.

Slowly, methodically, the group dug toward the remains, moving from the top down even though that was not the most direct route. Judy (as she liked to be called) explained to Theo,

Willis, and me that if they tried to pull the skeleton out from the side, the heavy dirt on top would collapse, destroying evidence and endangering her people. Also, it was important to see the whole skeleton *in situ* before moving it, because that would tell them much. There was also the possibility of evidence below the remains that would be destroyed from carelessness.

Willis accepted her explanation without comment and went back to his car to sulk. I buzzed around, taking photos of everyone and everything. One never got too many chances like this.

Two students were soon sifting through the dirt still in the backhoe and in the pile Tommy had left just before the grisly discovery but quickly learned there was nothing there. If there was anything else to be found, it was still in the ground.

I knew from experience that the head might be all we'd find. It was not uncommon for killers, especially serial murderers, to cut off their victims' heads and bury them someplace else. I didn't think that was the case here, though. They usually don't go to the trouble of putting them this deep . . . unless it had been convenient.

"Here you go, Gil!" Professor Ellison called. She held up the mandible as if it was priceless china. "What do you make of this?"

"Well," I said thoughtfully, closing one eye and tilting my head, "I could make a centerpiece for the dentists' convention."

Theo walked over. He suddenly seemed a little grumpy, although I didn't know why.

Professor Ellison laughed graciously. "No, Gil, I mean what can you tell me about this?"

Taking the jawbone, I studied it. I could imagine what it might have looked like when it was covered with flesh and full pink lips. I examined the teeth and wondered how the man who loved her felt when he looked at that mouth, those straight, white, near-perfect teeth, now stained and brown and fully exposed in a permanent sardonic grin. I suddenly felt a butterfly in my stomach, a brief stab of sorrow for her and the people who loved her that she left behind—and who probably had no idea about her fate. For all I knew, they were still holding onto hope that she would return.

My feelings turned angrily into outrage toward the monster

who buried her. There was no doubt in my mind, even though nothing had yet been dug up to verify that she'd been murdered, that Lucy's remains were not here by accident, or by her own choosing.

"She ate properly, for the most part," I ventured. "Only one filling. No apparent damage to the jaw. I take it it fits the skull."

Judy nodded and took the mandible from me, sticking it in place on the skull. Perfect fit. Pointing the skull at me, she worked the jaw and said, "Hi, big boy. What's your sign?"

I couldn't help but laugh. Here was this college professor, an intellectual academician, having fun with human remains. The incongruity alone was absurd.

"Nice teeth," Theo said, reminding us he was not only present, he was the investigator in charge. "No overbite."

"And high cheekbones," Professor Ellison said. "She was probably an attractive girl. At least she had no obvious structure problems. Jaw is in good proportion, eyes not too narrow or too wide set, head nicely shaped—"

"Stop it, Doc, I'm falling in love," I deadpanned. In a way, though, I was. Intrigued might be a better word. Sometimes I react to intrigue the way others react to love: pursuit. I had to go after it, find out what happened, who she was, who buried her, why. . . .

I shook it off. It wasn't my problem. This was one of those times when I didn't just miss being a cop in a mental sense, I really felt it, got a lump in my throat; the vacuous stomach, that sense of loss and longing not unlike sitting in an empty house after Rachel was gone and hearing that special song on the radio.

"What about the rest of her?" Theo inquired dispassionately. "Are there more bones?"

"That's going to take some time," Judy explained. She's deep, there's a lot of dirt on top of her. We aren't even sure there's anything else there yet. Won't know until we dig down to her."

Theo checked his watch. "Do you need me to stay, or can I check back with you later?"

"That's up to you, Lieutenant. It's liable to be pretty tedious for awhile. How about I give you a jingle when it gets interesting?"

"I'd appreciate it. Gil?" He stuck out his hand. "Thanks. Once again you've given me a shovelful of work to do. Literally."

I shook his hand. "Don't blame me. I didn't find this one."

"This is your hole. That makes it your responsibility."

"Just find the guy who put her there, and we'll both blame him."

Theo's sly grin faded. "Later, buddy. Good-bye Professor. I'll be waiting for your call. Try to make it as soon as possible, okay?"

"He's been up all night," I explained to Judy.

"Oh, you poor dear," she sympathized. "Why don't you go get some sleep in the meantime?"

"Crime doesn't sleep," Theo intoned in his best Joe Friday, "and neither do I."

"Oh?" I said. "Have you changed since we worked graveyard patrol together?"

He ignored the comment as he hiked out of the pit, then turned as he made the rim and said, "Don't forget that favor you're doing for me."

"Huh? What favor?" I asked, then remembered. "Oh, yeah. No problem, I'll do it right now." I waved and Theo disappeared. "I'd love to stay and watch," I told the professor, "but I'm afraid I've got work to do as well. As soon as you find something, have the security officer over there call me on the radio, okay?"

"Sure, Gil." As I turned to leave she continued. "Excuse me, Gil."

"Yes?"

"How come you left the police force? If you don't mind, that is. When I saw you here, I figured you and Lieutenant Brown were still working together. I didn't realize you were working for the park. I don't mean to pry."

"That's okay," I said with a sigh. "To be honest, I'm no longer sure why I left. I've heard so many theories, well . . . suffice it to say, I wish now I hadn't. If only so I wouldn't keep hearing how stupid it was. But, then again, things have happened that I'm glad I was a part of."

This was weird. I had worked with her a few times, taken a

class from her on forensic anthropology (which is why I knew what I knew about it), but didn't know she took any interest in me. Maybe she was just curious, although she wasn't the prying type. Usually I took offense at intrusionary questioning like this from all but my closest friends, and most of them didn't ask. They knew better. If I was forced to analyze myself, I'd have to admit my umbrage probably was born out of embarrassment over what was probably a bad decision on my part. No one likes to admit their shortcomings, except members of Something Anonymous groups.

Fortunately, I can take some comfort in the Bible. I've read Job, and Psalm 37, and the story of Joseph, who said to his brothers, "You meant it to me for evil, but God meant it to me for good." Whatever happens, if we're really His children, is for our good even when we make mistakes and use poor judgment.

Of course, that's not always easy to remember when you're in the middle of the swamp wrestling alligators. Thank the Lord His grace doesn't require our conscious awareness of it.

Professor Ellison moved close to me and put her hand on my arm. "Lieutenant Brown told me he wished you were still working with him, how you were a good cop." She paused, but I couldn't say anything. I lowered my head and she went on. "Theo told me your wife died just before you left. I hadn't known that. I'm sorry."

I accepted her condolence and wanted to say something, but her tenderness touched me, and I couldn't get the words out. I swallowed hard and strained to keep my composure.

Had Theo equated Rachel's death with my leaving the department? That's not why I left, but I didn't have time right now to go into it with Judy, nor did I have the desire.

She sensed my discomfort. "I'm meddling. I'm sorry, Gil." She patted my hand. "I'll call you later."

She immediately returned to her work, engaging one of her students in hushed conversation with much pointing and nodding. I watched them for a minute, my hands pushed deep into my pants pockets, thinking about what Professor Ellison had said and of Rachel.

But mostly of Rachel. With a pain forming behind my eyes,

I turned slowly and picked my way out of the pit, stopping to tell the security officer guarding the site—Danny "Tuna Fish" Hill from the squad room earlier—that Professor Ellison would be having him call me later.

I don't know what it was—perhaps the Lord, perhaps just my own subconscious thoughts—but, instead of heading directly to Personnel to look up Albright's file, I meandered toward one of the stage doors that led into the amusement park, past the place at the edge of the western ghost town that used to be the American West Museum.

The museum was too close to where the new space ride was going in (although the Wild West Zone and the Galaxy Zone were completely different areas and physically isolated as far as the guests were concerned, they backed up to each other). The new ride, being largely underground, needed a lot of space for the construction, so we dismantled the museum building and sold it, along with its contents, to some historical, western, tourist place out in Arizona somewhere.

Management intended to build another museum in its place, a bigger one, when the new ride was done. That was a good thing, really. The old museum was a non-authentic building— one of the structures they built to look old—and had been rather small. About all it had inside was an old safe with some phony gold and silver bars and coins behind a piece of plexiglas, along with a few saddles, old guns, photos, and strands of barbed wire.

I had heard a rumor that somewhere in the bowels of the park was a warehouse full of real antiques they had been saving for such a time as this, really valuable and genuine western memorabilia. I would love to see that kind of stuff, western fanatic that I am, but the location of the warehouse was unknown to us peons. Some folk guessed it wasn't even on the property, but there were so many old buildings here, built with no master plan, that this secret warehouse could easily be inside any one of several other structures, or occupying space in the center of a group of buildings, or even in some basement or attic, and no one would be the wiser.

The amusement park was crowded now, with waves of folks moving in all directions, intent on their quest for fun at any cost.

My mind was empty as I strolled, picking up scattered bits of conversation from passersby.

"Then we're going to the arcade to. . . ."

"I want a candied apple and a. . . ."

"Billy, get back here this instant or I'll. . . ."

". . . all the way from Utah for this bunch of. . . ."

"Do you want to eat now or later . . . ?"

"I don't have the money, I thought you had the money!"

I wondered how God was able to keep track of everyone and all their problems, their life histories and their goals and aspirations, not to mention the number of hairs on their heads. Boggles the mind.

A distressed shout broke through my thoughts.

"Amber!"

It was a male voice that repeated the cry almost immediately, then was joined by a female. A lost child. Not an uncommon occurrence here. Even the most attentive parents can lose sight of their kids very easily. I hoped they had a plan, telling their children in advance what to do if they got separated. I expected they would find her momentarily. Usually the kid was right there, out of sight behind some grown-up, gazing with eagerness into a store window, or racing to hug a costumed character.

I stood by for a moment waiting for the happy reunion, but the calling of her name continued, growing more frantic each time. Making my way to the distraught parents, I identified myself and asked if I could help. They told me where they last saw her, and I suggested they look for her together for a few minutes, then split up and meet in a prearranged place in fifteen minutes, then one of them go to the security office to wait while the other continued to search. I explained that park employees are trained what to do with lost children, but it was difficult to reunite little ones with their parents if Mom and Dad weren't able to be found.

I told them I'd notify security immediately and obtained a description of the girl. From a nearby call box, I phoned Wendy, and she alerted the roving guards. I was confident connections would be made momentarily; it was one of the things the park did right.

With nothing pressing to do at the moment, I decided to take a stroll around the park toward the main entrance. Maybe I'd see the girl. If nothing else, I was an extra pair of eyes.

You never notice things like this until you are looking for them, but it seemed half the little girls in the park fit Amber's description. Everywhere I looked there was a little brunette four-year-old wearing a white sweatshirt and blue pants.

But only one stood out, only one made me look long and hard. It wasn't anything about her that caught my eye, it was the person she was with that set off the alarms. None of the little girls were alone; they were with Mom and Dad or Grandma and Grandpa, and no one looked particular stressed. But this little girl was with a man about thirty-five, with a balding forehead and scraggly hair lightly touching his collar. He wore a heavier jacket than the day called for, not appropriate attire for someone who planned to spend a day at the amusement park with his little girl. He had plastic-rimmed glasses that sat crooked on his face and needed a shave. He stooped repeatedly as he walked, talking to the girl, as if to reassure her. He held her hand, and it seemed to me he was doing so a bit too tightly. She was going with him willingly but didn't appear too sure about it.

I knew his type. He had ex-con and pedophile written all over him. After fifteen years on the street and in the detective bureau I had become acquainted with many child molesters—of all types. In my book, he fit the profile. Call it sixth sense, a hunch, whatever you like, I knew this guy was up to no good.

And very rarely did guys like this let the child go. The opportunistic-type molesters usually tried to take advantage of family members or neighbors, rarely abducted kids, and hardly ever murdered. This guy, on the other hand, had paid his way into an amusement park—probably to take advantage of the multitudes, the noise, and the confusion to facilitate escape—and was rather bold in his abduction tactic. He had no intention of letting the girl go.

The child's safety was my primary concern. I couldn't shout at him without endangering the girl. Besides, what had he done yet that I could prove? It's one thing to know deep inside what someone is doing, or intending to do—it's quite another to prove it. He could say he found a lost girl and was taking her to security, and how could I demonstrate otherwise?

I wanted to get the girl back unscathed and emotionally intact as well, but I also wanted to nail this creep. To do both would require caution and restraint, and perfect timing. In the worst case scenario I might delay too long and lose him. I decided to hold back, keep my distance and follow them, and if it began to look bad, I'd just move in and take the girl, even if it meant losing my quarry before he did anything we could pin on him.

You might question the wisdom of this, but you need to see the big picture. In the first place, I wasn't absolutely certain this was Amber. She might have been this man's little girl. I didn't believe that for one second, mind you, but I wasn't absolutely positive. In addition, if it was Amber and I took her away from him too soon, before the creep committed a provable crime, he'd walk. Some other day, some other place, he'd find another little girl to steal. He needed to be put away.

Normally, a security officer could be found hanging around the main exit, either to watch people come and go, prevent gate crashers from sneaking in, or to have lengthy conversations with the new redhead working the reentry turnstile. I hoped today would be no different. If he was there, and the man with Amber walked past him, I'd have the evidence I needed: the pervert couldn't argue that he was turning the child over since he'd missed an opportunity to do so. But that wasn't going to happen, at least not here. The alarm about Amber had apparently drawn the security officer into the park to assist searching the area. He wasn't at his normal post when we approached, and the man passed with the girl out of the amusement park.

He didn't get his hand stamped for reentry, either, despite the early hour. He wasn't planning on coming back. My heart began to pound.

When I exited about twenty yards behind them, I told the redhead what I was doing and to call for a plain-clothes backup. I hoped she was as smart as she was cute and understood my brief directions.

Mr. Greaseball did what I expected: headed straight for the

parking lot, his pace quickening once he was out of the amusement area and the crowd had thinned. Whatever doubt I may have entertained before now slipped away unnoticed. This was Amber, and she was being kidnapped, most likely by a child molester. Even if he was the world's nicest guy—and all child molesters will tell you they love children—he had no business taking her away.

As I followed cautiously, I watched the little girl, wondering how our little one—Rachel's and mine—would've looked. She would have been about the same age. And how would I feel if I was her father, standing by helplessly while some pervert was dragging her off. . . . I didn't want to think about it.

Any time now I could move in, but I wanted help. I didn't want to risk getting into a hassle with him and have Amber run off unattended, or worse, get caught in the middle of it. Nor did I want to give him too much warning and turn it into a hostage situation. At times like this, I wished I could carry dart guns or phasers, something with which I could instantly immobilize him. I wouldn't have had a problem just shooting the creep, but I wasn't packing heat and there might be a law or two I'd violate in doing so. Darn the luck.

So I was left with my wits, not an entirely happy predicament. I thought a quick prayer, something like, *Lord, help me,* but no magnificent plan popped into my brain. I kept going, following as he weaved his way through the parked cars to his own. Occasionally he turned his head to cast furtive glances over his shoulder, but his movements were so exaggerated that I was able to anticipate them and fade behind a vehicle or a light pole, or pretend I was looking for my car.

A white vehicle caught the corner of my eye. I turned my head enough to see it was Harry Clark, looking for me. Redhead had done it. I thought about thanking her with dinner then remembered propriety and decided a simple word or two would be sufficient. I signaled Harry that our quarry was up ahead and for him to drive around the perimeter of the lot and box him in. He waved and took off.

As the cars thinned out, I began to look for Mr. Greaseball's ride. It was easy to find. A generic, white panel van, some ten years old and in dire need of a wash and wax. He'd carefully parked it where access to the side rollback door was not inhibited. It was one of those vehicles pedophiles could stuff their victim inside, drive to a secluded place, and torment that victim to their heart's content, then drive leisurely to the desert or forest and dump the body, with no one the wiser. They could also store their implements of debauchery, magazines, cameras, alcohol or drugs, and still avoid detection during a routine traffic stop because of the curtains behind the front seats.

I had to make my move soon, before he made it to the van. Once inside and mobile, the whole affair would get really complicated—and dangerous for Amber. And I didn't want her to get more frightened than she was already. She knew she was being taken by this man to his car, and, despite what he might have been telling her, she wasn't at all comfortable about it, but there was nothing she could do. I sped up, crouch-walking so I could hide easier, and got close enough to make a run for him when the opportunity presented itself.

He began to fish in his pocket for his keys. I tensed myself for the confrontation.

Then he came to an abrupt halt. He looked at the van, then scanned the lot. *What's going on?* I wondered, watching him from behind a Lexus. Then I realized what was troubling him as I saw him stop looking and turn to his left, heading off in another direction. I followed him with my eyes and saw another van just like his about a hundred yards away. He'd gotten the wrong van.

Uh uh, I thought. I sent Harry the wrong way. I was alone now, at least for awhile.

He arrived at his vehicle in a few moments and once again began to extract his keys. That was it. My window of opportunity. He had to let go of Amber long enough with his right hand to stick it in his pants pocket while reaching for her with his left hand. I shouted her name, and she turned.

"Run!" I cried. I broke into an open field sprint as Greaseball jerked his head around toward me. Amber obeyed and took off.

Before Greaseball could yank his hand out of his dirty khaki pants, I dove. The last time I had done that was in high school, during a junior varsity football game. I tackled the runner with such force that I knocked him out of bounds, cleared five guys off his bench, and woke up on the sidelines with blood streaming down my face. But I had prevented the touchdown and gained the respect of my teammates. We still lost 40 to zip, but that didn't matter. Something more important was gained: the attention of all the girls the next day when I showed up to school with a shiner and ten stitches above my eye.

This was different. No glory here, no impressing the girls. I smelled blood, and this creep was going to regret the day he came to my amusement park.

I struck him at full speed, knocking the wind out of him as we both crashed into the side of the van with a metallic crunch, the cracking of bone, and cries of pain. The rebound turned us as we fell, and he landed on top. I remember being aware of his stench, that oily odor of filth and alcohol, of unwashed clothes and stale breath. I wanted to take a shower.

Without any break in motion, however, I disregarded my disgust and drove my knee up into his groin as I pushed him off. He cried out and rolled off as I spun away and tried to regain my feet.

I will never cease to be amazed how agile some people are, even in their brokenness. Although he probably maintained an inadequate diet, drank, observed lousy health habits, and didn't exercise, Greaseball recovered his wind quickly and jumped up, despite nursing some bruised or broken ribs. But my anger (righteous indignation?) drove me, and I rose to meet the challenge. I couldn't look to see how Harry was faring, hoping he had corralled Amber and was calling for backup. My concentration was on this deviate and on securing him for the cops, hoping he forced me to hurt him in the process.

I heard a car accelerating up the row. It sounded like Harry's Chevy. I hoped he'd seen what was happening. The car slid to a gravelly stop and Harry called to me as he jumped out to go for Amber. I was too busy to acknowledge him.

The code of the Samurai says to strike, and strike again, and keep striking relentlessly until your opponent is beaten or concedes, and then show mercy. I planned to do just that, but deep down I hoped he would keep fighting, for awhile at least.

I have a holy hatred for people who victimize children.

I don't know if it was the menacing look in my eye or the half-dozen police cars screaming into the lot, but Greaseball abruptly gave up before he even started to fight, despite encouragement from me to take a chance. He turned and spread out against the side of his van, fingers splayed and legs spread wide, and stayed that way until the blue suits cuffed him and hustled him off, all the while crying about how I'd brutalized him and how he was just trying to help the little girl who'd come crying to him.

I gave my statement to an officer, a veteran who knew me, and soon a security officer arrived with Amber's parents, who bundled her off to their car clutching free passes Harry had given them, good for a return trip to the park another day.

Harry patted me on the back, started to say something, then changed his mind and got back into his car. He rolled the window down.

"Would you mind writing a quick report? I could have you give a statement to Todd, but I think it would be quicker just to write it yourself."

He left without waiting for an answer . . . and without offering me a ride.

I checked my watch as I left the security office. That little diversion had used up an hour, not that time was particularly precious today.

This was turning out to be quite a day. I needed a cup of coffee. In fact, lunch wouldn't be entirely out of the question, I realized as I smelled the pies cooking in the pastry kitchen of the Frontier Oven, the only good place to eat in the park. With no further encouragement necessary, I quickened my pace and beat a path to the employee entrance at the rear.

The swinging gate to the backside of the Oven was across an asphalt walkway from the trailers that housed the merchandisers. Michelle Yokoyama, before she was promoted to senior vice-president of operations, had been head of this division, and despite her new title and responsibilities, she still oversaw merchandising. With all that, plus the myriad of new products and stuff that would be arriving in conjunction with the new rides and attraction—and the new park mascot, the cartoon dinosaur—I didn't know how she could keep up with it.

Perhaps that was why she hadn't moved into her new office, opting instead to stay in her trailer. She was busy, and to take up John Hayes' old digs would put her too far away from the action.

Michelle was an unassuming, although elegant, woman, and I imagine she was more comfortable in her office of eight years. Not one to rock boats, she probably didn't wish to give the appearance she was tossing her weight around, or that the promotion had blown her head up like a Macy's parade balloon. Then again, maybe she was just waiting for new carpet and drapes to be installed. What did I know?

As I pushed on the gate, I cast an absent-minded glance over my shoulder at her trailer thinking I should talk to her after I ate about the goings-on in the pit, when I noticed the back of a familiar bald head in her window. Stopping, I strained to listen. The window was open a crack, and I could hear Opperman's whining simper as he spoke in harsh tones to the unseen Yokoyama, who was apparently seated behind her desk. The trailers were elevated as trailers usually are, and I couldn't see anything but the ceiling.

With a furtive scan around to make sure I wasn't seen, I let the gate go quietly shut, stuck my hands casually into my pants pockets, and moseyed over to the shadows under the window. If I had started whistling, I doubt I could have looked more conspicuous. Fortunately, most of the employees here were self-absorbed teenagers who wouldn't have given me a second glance or a second thought, their tiny brains filled with trivialities, like *Who's that cute new girl?*, *What movie should we go to tonight?*, and *How much gas can I get for seventy-five cents?*

I settled in under the window and leaned casually against the trailer.

". . . And I don't think we can afford these delays," Opperman was saying. "This is private property, not the Oldevil Gorge—"

"Olduvai," Michelle said pleasantly.

"Whatever. That place in Africa. We can't have an archaeo-logical exhibition—"

"Expedition," Michelle corrected, her voice calm and quiet.

"It's an exhibition!" Opperman shouted, unwilling to stand corrected a second time. "We're paying a whole construction crew to stand around and watch people with spoons and tooth-brushes dig their pit for them!"

"From what you've told me, Jerry," Michelle offered sweetly, "isn't this a police matter? I mean, we really don't have a choice, do we?"

"Well it seems we don't now, but before your man . . . what's-his-name got there, we could have scooped it all up and dumped it in a box and handed it to them with a thank-you note and an apple pie!" His voice rose into an angry, cracking crescendo, and I could imagine him spraying spit all over her desk. "I even called the coroner. . . ." He fell into a coughing spell.

Aha! I thought. Franklin Willis' motivation exposed.

"What man of mine are you talking about?" Michelle asked coyly.

Outside, under the window, I smiled proudly and poked myself in the chest with an extended thumb.

"Uh, Bill . . . Beckler, something like that. That guy who used to be a security guard."

Officer, I corrected in my thoughts.

"Gil Beckman," Michelle said.

"Whatever. Whose big idea was it to promote him, anyway?"

"Mine, and you approved it, Jerry." She paused, then added, "And it was a good decision."

Her voice was suddenly louder and clearer, and I looked up at the window to see her standing at it, her head cocked and a puzzled expression on her face. Then the corners of her mouth twitched up when she recognized me, and she added, "Although perhaps I should give it some reconsideration."

I blushed and gave her a weak half-smile and an embarrassed wave. She moved away from the window.

"He was chosen," she continued, "because he knows the most about the new plan, and we need someone with an analytical and organized mind like his to carry it out. He was the man who solved the murder, remember? Besides, he's trustworthy, discreet, and can be trusted not to go snooping where he shouldn't. Plus he has no self-interest in this. He's a company man."

At first I was embarrassed, now I was perplexed. Was it wishful thinking on her part, or did she have me confused with someone who cared?

"Of course," Opperman said with a huff.

"Besides," she said softly, so soft I almost couldn't hear it, "I'm sure the construction crew can find something else to do for a few hours. It won't cost us anything and look at all the goodwill we'll be creating."

He was at a loss now, and I could imagine him wringing his hands, eyes scanning the room as he pressed for something to say to regain conversational control. Michelle knew it, too, and wisely gave it to him on a platter.

"It's your call, Jerry. But I suspect the police are aware of the inconvenience to the park. Lieutenant Brown said he would hurry it along as fast as he could."

What's this? I thought. Why would Theo have called her? But before I could analyze the meaning behind this—if there was any—the door flew open, and Opperman emerged. I was caught off guard: he hadn't said good-bye or made a closing statement or anything. As quickly and quietly as I could, I backed away and faded around the corner of the trailer, holding my breath. I let it out only after I peeked around the corner to make sure he had gone the other way.

"What are you doing here, Gil?"

The voice suddenly behind me made me jump.

FIVE

I spun around abruptly, almost falling down in the process and sending a sharp spasm of pain up one side of the back of my neck. Michelle stood on the rear steps to the trailer, her private entrance that I had forgotten about. Opperman had used the salesmen's door. How she opened the door without me hearing it, I'll never know. Perhaps I was losing my touch.

"Uh, truth is," I started slowly, "I was just walking by when I heard Jerry in there yelling at you, and I . . . uh . . . I'm sorry, Miss Yokoyama. I shouldn't have been listening."

"Michelle. And, no, you shouldn't have," she said sternly. "But then, anyone walking outside could have heard, so it's not like you were snooping. Besides," she smiled sweetly, "it's part of your cop sense, your second nature, I suppose. That's what makes you so good at detecting." She didn't sound patronizing.

"Who says I'm good at detecting?" I asked. I wasn't fishing for a compliment, although in retrospect I realize it probably sounded that way. I was just curious to find I had a fan.

"Lieutenant Brown, actually."

"Oh. Well, thanks. But it gets me in trouble now and then, especially when I'm not actually detecting anything. I ought to control myself a little better."

"Well, a little more discretion might not hurt," she admitted. "Come on in." Then she added, "If you have a minute, that is." Always the lady.

"As a matter of fact, I have plenty of time." I told my stomach to shut up and go to sleep, and mounted the stairs.

56

When we made ourselves comfortable, Michelle got right to the point.

"So just what is going on out there?"

I told her what they'd found, what they were doing and why, and that they'd work as quickly as they could but would take as long as necessary.

"I was given the impression the remains were ancient Native American bones. Is that not true?"

"No, it's not. Is that what Jerry told you?"

"Yes."

"Rest assured, the skull is very modern. I imagine the rest of her, if there is anything else to be found, will be also."

"Just the skull, you say? Why wouldn't there be the whole thing?"

"Just the skull so far. I would guess there's more, but sometimes in cases like this the killer doesn't bury the whole body in one place."

The look on her face told me she was beginning to understand—and didn't like the idea.

"Spare me the details," she begged. "I'll take your word for it." Her dark, perfect eyebrows knit themselves closer together, creating a single, faint wrinkle in the clear ivory skin between them. It was hard not to notice natural beauty like hers.

"So this is a homicide?"

"Unless the park sits on what a decade ago was a cemetery, I'm sure of it."

"Is Jerry aware of this?"

"Absolutely."

"He didn't let on."

"Well, I understand he's concerned about the delay. But we told him this was serious. How much information leaked into his peanut brain, I can't say." I suddenly remembered who I was talking to. "Oops. Sorry about that."

Michelle narrowed her eyes slightly but let it pass. She knew what Opperman was like, she had to deal with him daily.

"I know the woman heading the dig," I said. "She's thorough, but she's quick. She won't waste any time. I wouldn't be surprised if she gets done tonight."

"Well, that's certainly good news." She sighed, then said in a breath almost as an afterthought, "It's about time I heard some good news." She stared out the window.

"I beg your pardon?"

"Oh, nothing," she said, her face flushed. Embarrassed, she smiled wanly.

"Anything I can help you with?" I ventured.

She dropped her head and took a breath. "No . . . oh, I might as well tell you."

"Please, not if you don't want to."

"It's okay. I need to get this off my chest." She took a deep breath. "You remember the trouble I was having with my husband a few months back?"

"Yeah." Who could forget a black eye on that face?

"Our divorce was final yesterday."

"I'm sorry."

"Don't be."

"No, I mean I'm sorry you had to go through that. I'm sorry anyone has to get a divorce."

"Oh, that's right. Theo told me you're a Christian and don't believe in divorce."

Michelle and Theo were doing a lot of talking these days.

"Well, it's not quite that simple," I said. "The Bible's clear that God hates divorce, and in most cases He views it to be wrong. . . ."

"How about in spousal abuse cases? Does the Bible address that?"

Yes or no would not have sufficed here. This is one of those complicated issues that requires a look at the intent of scripture and the circumstances of the people. But I didn't believe God meant for any woman to sit around and let herself be beaten up. Or any man, for that matter. But if both parties professed to be Christians, then divorce was not part of the solution: repentance was. But in her case? I decided to keep my opinion to myself.

Instead I said, "Still, you seem troubled by the divorce."

"Not so much by the divorce as by everything it entails. I imagine it's not unlike having your spouse die."

"I wouldn't know," I said quietly. "I've never been divorced."

There was a brief, awkward silence, then I said, "Uh, look, I better get back to work. When I find out more about how long this'll take, and what it's all about, I'll let you know." I stood.

"Okay, Gil. Thanks." She got up. "Maybe in a couple days we can get together again. I'll show you some of the new merchandise that's been proposed. And we need to start looking for a cartoonist, someone who can give the little dinosaur some life."

"What about the folks in Design and Planning?"

"They're good, but they're not cartoonists. We need someone with fresh ideas. Some new blood."

"A transfusion."

"Yes," she said. "Breathe life into the old place."

"Well, I'll think about it. I don't know anybody off hand." I thought for a moment. "Listen, does the little fellow have a name yet?" I asked.

"We've tossed around a few. I take it you have some ideas?"

I smiled. "Just one. It would be awfully nice if we could honor his creator."

"Everett?"

"Fits well, don't you think?" I said.

She smiled. "Suits me fine. Everett it is."

"Thanks," I said. "Trish will be pleased." I added my condolences, saying I hoped things would work out for her. I really did. She was a classy lady. I couldn't imagine how anyone could smack her around.

I waved as I left, conflicting emotions vying for my attention. I was glad she had consented to call the dinosaur Everett but bothered by Michelle's plight and my inability to do anything about it. I wondered if she had filed charges against him. I made a mental note to ask Theo.

Intending to finally get something to eat, I headed back toward the Frontier Oven. As I went through the gate, Trish was coming out.

"So, there you are," she said. "What's going on?"

"Could you be more specific?" I suggested.

"Well, I was referring to Lucy. What else are you doing?"

I decided to wait to tell her. This wasn't the time or place.

"Right now I was going to have some lunch. I don't have any news yet about our mystery woman."

"Forget lunch," Trish said. "For now, at least. You're wanted in the pit. I've been trying to find you."

I sighed audibly. Another meal missed.

"You'll live, Mr. Beckman." She glanced briefly at my stomach and grinned. What she meant by her comment I have no idea.

"Join me?" I asked.

"No thanks. You can tell me about it later."

She smiled a teenage smile, and I wished, not for the first time, that I was nineteen.

The pit was abuzz with activity. Two youngsters (college age kids are youngsters to me now, I realized painfully) stood over an elevated, wood-framed screen, sifting dirt for small particles; others crouched in the hole they had made over the place where we thought the rest of the skeleton might be; Judy inspected something at a table; others were moving wheelbarrows full of dirt to a location out of the way. The place was cordoned off with a maze of sticks and strings.

Judy saw me and waved excitedly, motioning me to come down into the hole, while she got up from her table to meet me there. When I arrived at her side I smiled. They had uncovered the remains, a complete skeleton, leaving the bones in the position they were buried in, and I was a little surprised by how much soft tissue remained. It wasn't enough to cover the bones completely, but it was enough to be a little disconcerting to the uninitiated.

She—Lucy, that is—was not completely unearthed, only uncovered. Her bones were still partially imbedded in the dark soil. She wore slacks, which for the most part completely covered her legs, but there was no sign of a blouse. A few wires over her exposed ribs were probably all that was left of her undergarment. He arms were folded over her abdomen as she lay on her back. Either she had been purposely placed in that position, or the hole was narrow when she was interred and there had been no room for them at her sides.

"Is Theo coming?" I asked.

"I'm here," said a voice behind me.

He looked bad.

"No nap?" I asked.

"Are you kidding?" he grumped. But he said no more about it. We both knew how it was, and Theo wasn't the kind to elicit sympathy from others.

"What do you think?" he asked Judy. "Five feet tall?"

"In the lower five-foot range, I think," she said. "It's too soon to judge accurately. She's all bunched up."

I asked her about the absence of a shirt, but she tossed it back at us. Always the teacher.

I deferred to Theo but he only shrugged and said, "She wasn't wearing one when she was buried."

I leaned over and pointed to a small white button sticking out of the dirt. "No, I think she was fully clothed. Why would the killer remove her blouse but not her bra? Probably, the blouse was a hundred percent cotton, which would disintegrate. Her pants are polyester. Non-biodegradable."

"Very good," Judy said. "What else do you see?" She looked at Theo for this one.

"Some soft tissue."

"Okay. Why would there still be soft tissue, if she's been down here for several years, as we can assume, based on the type of clothes she has on and the age of the structure she was buried under?"

Theo thought for a second. "Damp soil delays decomposition?"

"Excellent. Do you see the adipocere?" She pointed to the greasy substance, the soap, that was evident on all the bones just as it had been on the skull. "It's the result of a chemical change in the soft tissue when bodies are buried in moist or damp earth, or immersed in ponds, that kind of thing. Because of her current state, with much soft tissue gone, I'd say there was likely some change in the moisture of the earth here recently, and her rate of decomposition increased as the dirt began to dry. They've found tissue like this on exhumed Civil War soldiers, and I've seen remains buried three, four years with facial features that were nearly identifiable by sight alone."

"Like mummification?" Theo asked.

"Very similar."

"Can you date her death by it?"

Judy shook her head. "It so depends on the soil conditions over the whole period of burial, there's no way to accurately gauge how long she's been there. There are other more reliable means."

"What about a clay reconstruction of her face?" I asked. "Are you going to try that?"

"It's certainly possible, but we won't do that unless absolutely necessary. There are more reliable means to identify her we need to exhaust first."

"Dental records, missing persons reports, teletypes to other agencies," Theo clarified. "You know the routine. It's expensive to try the reconstruction. Fitzgerald doesn't like to let go of money . . . unless it's for an administration perk."

"So what do you make of it so far?" I asked Professor Ellison. "Any theories?"

"Not yet. To be honest, I've been too busy to do any speculating," she admitted. "What do you think?"

"Well, it's obvious she was placed here. She didn't fall. The suspect dug a hole or used an existing one and put her in it carefully, almost respectfully."

"With love," Judy suggested.

I kneeled down. "I don't see any obvious broken bones. I'm sure you'll check for knife nicks and such. This is just a guess, but I believe it's probable she was either dead or unconscious when buried."

"Oh, come on, Gil," Theo objected. "How can you tell that?"

"She looks like she's resting comfortably, not trying to claw her way out. If she wasn't already dead, she was knocked out and unable to protest, and as soon as her face was covered with dirt it only took a few seconds for her brain to run out of oxygen."

"Okay, I'll buy that. But what does that mean?"

"Who knows? You're the detective. When you catch the guy, ask him."

"Come on," Judy urged. "You have a theory."

I grinned. "Okay, but remember, you asked. If she was alive but unconscious when buried, I don't think the killer knew it. He thought she was dead. If that's the case, I don't think he meant to kill her. It was an accident, and he panicked."

"Then he would not have preplanned to bury her but used what was available," Theo said, picking up the thread. "She was killed right here—or close by."

"If she was just unconscious when buried," Judy reminded us. "And there's no way to verify it. Don't get so hung up on one scenario that you lose sight of the other possibilities. But your theories make sense. Good ideas, Gil."

I had continued to inspect the remains while she spoke, my curiosity getting the better of me. I tried not to touch anything but the trousers obscured Lucy's pelvis, and after getting a nod from Judy I gently peeled them back and peeked inside. Only the elastic from her panties remained. What I saw below that stopped me cold.

"Look at this," I said quietly.

Professor Ellison and Theo both leaned in.

"What in the—"

"Oh dear."

We were looking at a perfect little skeleton, about six inches long, resting on Lucy's pelvic bones. It was distorted from the pressure of the dirt that had been above it, but Lucy's semi-sideways position had allowed her pelvic bones to protect it somewhat.

Judy said solemnly, "Looks like our little lady was pregnant."

SIX

I drove the yellow behemoth out of the employee lot and turned left toward my favorite restaurant. It had been quite a day, what with the discovery of Lucy and her baby, and the capture of Amber's abductor. Just before I left, Theo told me they found all the usual things in his van—porno magazines, implements of torture, empty and full booze bottles—plus some Polaroid photos of other children, some in the act of being molested. It would take some doing but the police would try to identify them all. Theo feared—reasonably so—that some or all of them had subsequently been harmed or killed, their bodies buried or otherwise gotten rid of. These were logical assumptions. Mr. Greaseball fit the profile, and killing was a part of the pleasure for them, the sense of power they held over their victims, the absolute control over their lives.

Knowing that, do you now understand why I wanted him to resist?

The only consolation was that he had been stopped. Frankly, I don't believe there is a punishment man can think of that is too cruel or unusual for people like him. I also believe—despite the lack of scripture to support it—that God has prepared a special hell for child molesters.

Where does this fit in with the Christian's duty to love and show mercy? I don't know, frankly, but I believe in justice, and I believe that you can forgive someone and still punish them. God does it that way. Just look at the life of David. God forgave him, but David still lost the son he had by Bathsheba. And God forgave Moses, but he didn't enter the land of promise.

It had been the mother of all days, and I was tired and starved and didn't feel like going home and waiting on myself, so I let the van have its head, confident it knew where to go.

Hollie's Hut, the greatest restaurant on the planet, all things considered: price, service, menu, place mats. . . . It was just about the only place I ever ate, aside from my own living room.

The Ford's inline-six coughed as it bounced with creaks and groans into the parking lot, then the motor smoothed out again. I let it idle for a moment after docking it, but the motor continued to purr so I shrugged it off and went inside.

Melody at the register and Pedro busing tables greeted me by name as I found my own way to my usual booth. Hollie had stopped waiting tables since her mom died a few months back, and she took over running the place. She renamed it after herself—at my suggestion. I knew she'd feel more like it was hers than just the caretaker of a hand-me-down.

She was at the back booth pouring over some sheets of paper when she saw me sit down, and I thought she grinned a little. She set her pencil down and brought the coffee pot over herself. No one else had even bothered to do it, knowing how it was between us.

No, not like that. It was strictly a waitress-customer relationship. She enjoyed pouring coffee, and I enjoyed letting her. We'd known each other for years but, oddly enough, had never seen each other outside the restaurant. We talked a lot and had given each other good advice from time to time. Frankly, I considered her a good friend, no more, no less. It was a limited partnership: I could tell her things and get a woman's viewpoint without the risk of runaway emotions.

Hollie was thirty-five or so, dark hair in a ponytail, with chiseled features and a twinkling eye. When she smiled, one side of her mouth curled up more than the other, making her look slightly mischievous. She'd been married, but her husband was killed during the Gulf War. Since then she'd devoted herself to her mom's restaurant and her ten-year-old daughter.

Funny thing, I didn't know it was her mom's place until she died, and Hollie took over. Hollie'd never mentioned it and never acted like the boss's daughter. But it explained why she took such good care of her customers. They really were *her* customers. She was building the business, making sure it would continue to thrive after her mother was gone.

"So, how's it going, big shot?" she asked as she poured the coffee. Hollie was great at keeping people from getting too big a head. "What's happening at the park?"

"You wouldn't believe it if I told you."

She produced another cup and poured herself one, and sat down across from me, something she had never done before.

"Try me."

I smiled. Why not? It wasn't a secret.

I filled her in on Lucy and Amber, watching her animated face respond with delight, disgust, interest, and awe at all the right times. She stayed even after my food—chicken parmesan—was delivered by Angela, a new girl. Hollie watched me eat, enjoying my tale of the day. I even found myself enjoying the roll of raconteur, gesturing and using volume and inflection to add interest to the telling.

I never gave a second thought as to *why* she had been so absorbed. After all, we were just friends.

It wasn't until I had left the parking lot later and was headed home in the dark that I reflected on it, seeing in her eyes what I had missed when I was across the table from her.

I shook my head. No, I'm just a good storyteller, I told myself. And lonely. But the idea that she might have more than an entertainment-interest in me caused a flutter in my stomach, no matter how unlikely the possibility.

Frankly, I had trouble accepting the potential as a reality. That a female might actually think of me as something more than a friend was hard to accept. I mean, I hadn't had to think about it for years, as long as Rachel was still alive. And even after her death I didn't think about it, not on purpose. I couldn't. Rachel had been the world to me.

True, I had taken Sally Foster out a few times. Had a great time with her, too. It was nice that I had known her from church and work for a couple years first. Made it easier to spend time with her, already being friends. But . . . well, she might have known Rachel, and I . . . well, to tell the truth, I hadn't even kissed Sally.

I was a teenager trapped in an grown man's body.

I was snapped out of my self-reflection when I passed by a group of male juveniles trudging up the sidewalk. I thought I recognized one of them. Three wore baggy, gang-style clothing, the fourth wore surf apparel—although the distinction between the two styles was lessening. They were talking, laughing, and I didn't like what I was seeing. Nothing I could articulate, but they just looked like they were up to no good.

The surf dude was my little probationer friend, Joey Duncan. I had arrested him back when I was a cop, and now I was making sure he got through the last six months of his probation without messing up.

I don't know why I cared, to be candid about it. He was just another punk kid with a dysfunctional family (the politically correct word for rotten), and he listened more to his peers than to all the grown-ups he had ever encountered. Kids like him were a dime a dozen.

Maybe God saw something in him I didn't. I'm sure that was the case, because I saw nothing. I don't even understand, in retrospect, why I stuck my neck out for him.

But I had, and now my reputation was on the line. I drove past them and parked around the corner. When they caught up to me, I was leaning casually on the street lamp standard, my arms crossed.

Joey was laughing when he recognized me, and his reaction was straight out of a cartoon. His eyes popped, his mouth fell open, then his eyes darted from side to side as he tried to think of something to say, some excuse for hanging out with these ne'er-do-wells, which he knew was a violation of his probation.

"Get lost," I told the three boneheads.

"Who do you think you are?" one of them challenged.

Although not a man of violence, I wasn't going to be intimidated by these jerks. I flashed my security badge just quickly enough so they could see what it was but couldn't read it—hoping Joey wouldn't say anything—and repeated my directive.

"I don't say things three times, homeboy."

"Better do it," Joey said. "He's nuts."

I smiled inwardly, but wasn't quite sure just how Joey meant that. I gave the three geniuses one of my patented wide-eyed stares and they began to move away; slowly, to make it look like they were doing it because they wanted. I didn't care how fast they evacuated, just so long as they split. Let them keep their machismo intact. One thing police work had taught me: There will always be another day.

"I'll remember you," the spokesman said.

"I doubt it," I disagreed. "You probably have trouble remembering which house you broke into last."

He flashed me a sign of his esteem but kept walking.

"Aw, isn't that sweet," I said to Joey. "He thinks I'm number one." Joey gave me a glare but quickly looked away and shoved his hands deep into his oversize pockets.

"What's the deal, Officer Beckman? Why'd you want to go and embarrass me like in front of my friends?"

"Those weren't your friends, Joey. They use people like you and cast you aside when they're done. Besides, you know you can't be hanging around with gang members."

"They're not gang members . . . any more. They got out."

"Nonsense."

"It's true. They told me."

"Look at the facts, Joey. They dress like gang members, they associate with the same guys they hung with when they were gang members, they act like gang members, smell like gang members, talk like gang members. . . . Get the picture?"

"Yeah . . . so now what? You gonna bust me?"

I looked hard at him, squirming in place, his hands still deep-sixed. His hands. . . .

"Let me see your hands, Joey."

"Huh?"

"Don't play dumb. Your hands. Those things you use to scratch yourself. Pull 'em out."

He obeyed, slowly.

"That's what I thought," I said, noting the blue and black spray paint on his right index finger. "You've been tagging."

"No way!" he protested.

"Ah, come on Joey. Those guys don't go anywhere without leaving their graffiti. Shoot, I've seen them try to spray a chain link fence. Let's not have another battle of intellects and wills."

"Okay, yeah, I was tagging," he said, "but not the way you think."

"What other way is there? Were you looking in a mirror over your shoulder? Were you doing trick tagging?"

"I don't mean that. I was at the beach wall. I have a permit."

"The beach wall?"

"Yeah, you know, the retaining wall at the beach below the parking lot. If you get a permit from the city, you can tag. It's like art. Here I'll show you."

"I don't care what you call it, it's not like art," I said while he pulled out a crumpled slip of paper and thrust it at me. "Shoot, Picasso's not even like art as far as I'm concerned." I read the slip and handed it back to him. "Okay, you got a permit. But you're still not gonna hang with those guys, got it?"

"Yeah, I got it. Listen, what's the deal with you anyway?"

"What do you mean?"

"Why do you care what happens to me? Why can't you leave me alone? Okay, so you took me out to lunch a few times and to that holy meeting at the stadium. I don't owe you nuthin'."

"Maybe, maybe not. I'd say you owe me your freedom right now. As you'll recall, you were arrested for the murder of Everett Curran. Seems to me, I had something to do with getting you off the hook."

"How long you gonna hold that over my head?"

"As long as I need to."

"Why do you think you have to pal around with me? Is it that religion stuff of yours? Do you have to be my buddy so you can go to heaven?"

"No, I don't. And being your buddy isn't a piece of cake, either. For the life of me, I don't know why I care, but I do. And I stuck my neck out to guarantee you'll make probation. I'm just protecting my investment. Somehow, Joey, I think you've got some potential in you. You're smart. . . . Let me rephrase that: you're intelligent, you don't have any smarts yet. You could be something, though. We just need to find out what it is. Okay, fine, I'm not your pal. Suits me. Think of me as your gym coach. Hate me, if you like. But remember that I'm trying to help you, not hurt you. Whatever you do, don't forget that. I'm not the enemy."

He pawed the ground and looked away, blinking rapidly. Whether his eyes were tearing up or not, I don't know. I looked down at my hands until he was ready to talk.

"Go on home, Joey."

"That's it? You not gonna make me ride with you?"

"You want a ride?"

"No."

"Okay. See ya."

I abruptly turned and went back to my van, and he slowly crossed the street, never looking back. I wondered what would ultimately happen to him, how long I could keep pressing him like this.

I checked my watch. It wasn't quite nine, and I didn't feel like going home just yet. You know how it is when you've had a fun or exciting day: You don't want it to end. Once you go to bed, it's all over, everything's back to normal.

But where to go? I didn't want to bother anyone. Theo was probably asleep already, Trish was out of the question, Sally was . . . well, that would be presumptive and uncomfortable. We'd had a few dates, yes, but I couldn't drop in unannounced.

There was one place I could go, a place I was welcome anytime, my home away from home.

The Currans'. The murder victim's parents. Ever since I helped them finger their son's killer, they'd kind of adopted me. I don't know whether they thought of me as a substitute for their son, or just liked me. It didn't matter.

As I drove slowly up their street, my van sputtered again like it had at the restaurant. Maybe tomorrow I'd give it a tuneup. Might have a plug going bad.

I parked by the curb and was let in immediately after I knocked. They must have seen me. Mrs. Curran—Estelle—smiled as she held the door open.

"Look who's here, hon!" she called to her husband, sitting in his easy chair reading *Field and Stream*.

He looked up and nodded.

The place hadn't changed since my first visit. The same photos on the mantle, same knick knacks and figurines and spoon collection, same doilies. . . . It was a mighty comfortable place.

"Grab a seat, Gil," Harold Curran said. "I was just thinking about you."

"Good or bad?" I asked.

He chuckled. "Good, of course."

"Trish was here for dinner," Estelle explained. "Told us about what happened at the park today. You really get into it, don't you?"

"What do you mean?"

"You know, solving mysteries and catching criminals. Makes me wonder why you're not back with the police department."

"Well," I said lingeringly, "truth is, they won't take me back."

"Why in heaven's name not?"

"It's kind of complex, but when someone leaves, most police administrators take it personally. They think it's a sign you're not a loyal employee, so they have a 'no rehire' policy. It's probably more involved than that, really, but you get the idea."

"What about somewhere else?" Mr. Curran asked. "Someone'd be happy to have you, with your experience."

That gave me pause. I'd never considered that, not seriously anyway.

"I don't know," I said. "It's not like private industry, where you can be hired right into a top spot. In law enforcement, your seniority doesn't follow you. I don't really want to start over, pushing a patrol car around on graveyard for the next five years. Besides, I'm doing okay at the park for now."

Both the Currans *hmmm'd* out loud, then Harold said, "Say, not to change the subject, but the reason I was thinking about you was, I wondered if you've got a vacation coming up."

"Not right now, what with all the construction going on. But in a few months maybe. Why?"

"That's perfect. I'd like to take you fishing up at my son's resort. You'd love it. Great fishing for rainbows and browns, world's most magnificent scenery. All the Pop Tarts you can eat. What do you say?"

"Sure!" I said. It was the Pop Tarts that decided it for me. Frosted brown sugar cinnamon Pop Tarts. Heaven on earth.

"You can bring that kid along, too, the one you're keeping

an eye on. Do him good to get away from here for a bit, see that there's more to life than surfing and crime."

I'd told them about Joey, and solicited advice from them on dealing with a teenager . . . from a parental standpoint, that is. I knew how to bust their chops already. But when he suggested Joey come along on the fishing trip, well, I have to admit my first reaction was disappointment. But I immediately checked myself as I realized God had probably prompted the suggestion. I still didn't like it, but I was being selfish, and I knew it.

"Sounds good," I said, wanting to mean it but not feeling generous about it yet. "I'll try to talk him into going."

"Fair enough," Harold said.

I got up to leave. "Well, thanks. I'll see you later. I've got to get up for work in the morning."

"Leaving so soon?" Mrs. Curran wondered. "Won't you stay and have some brownies?"

"No thanks," I declined in an amazing display of willpower. Her brownies were addictive, and I needed to drop a few tons.

"I'll get you some to go," she concluded, heading for the kitchen.

"Okay," I protested. "Just a few." What else could I do, I didn't want to hurt the poor woman's feelings.

Three brownies and a cold glass of lowfat, negative-calorie-brownie-counteracting milk later, I stretched out on my bed with a good book; actually *the* Good Book, God's Word. I leafed through the thin pages with no purpose or intent, pondering my existence, asking God what He had in store for me.

Not that I expected Him to answer. Out loud, I mean. I'm quite sure God puts thoughts into our heads, impresses us with the directions we are to take. That's why we need to pray, to meditate on God. That's when He "speaks" to us, that's when He gives us direction and comfort.

My problem—okay, one of my problems—is remembering that it's God's way and according to His time schedule and not my way, Frank Sinatra's accomplishments notwithstanding.

Those were the last thoughts I recall from that night. I woke the next morning to the ringing telephone with the Bible open on my chest.

SEVEN

"Hello," I mumbled.

"You still asleep?"

I craned my head to the side and tried to focus through puffy, swollen eyes at the digital alarm clock.

"I must be. It's only seven-thirty, and this is Saturday."

"Yeah, I know. Sorry about that. But I thought you'd want to be in on this."

"Who is this?" I asked finally. I was about to ask who I was, but I'd just remembered.

"It's me, Theo."

"Oh. Just a second." I set the receiver down beside me on the covers and rubbed my eyes open but didn't sit up. "What's up, Theo?"

"Professor Ellison's going to have the body all laid out for us today, give us a preliminary report so I have something to work on. I thought you'd want to be there."

"I do," I said. "What time?"

"Noon."

"Noon? So why'd you call this early?"

"I wanted to make sure I caught you before you took off."

Yeah, like I have somewhere to go, I thought.

"Okay, fine. I'll be there. Her lab at the university, right?"

"Right."

"See you there. Oh, and thanks for being so thoughtful." I hung up before he had a chance to realize I was being sarcastic.

I stretched back out, but it was no good. I was awake and

going to stay that way, so I got up, showered, had a leisurely breakfast of ham and eggs and coffee, and sat down to read the paper.

Sports and funnies, then local news, and the front page—that's the usual order. But it was a dull sports day the day before, none of the funnies were funny (I imagined how Everett's little dinosaur guy would look in the paper and thought he'd liven up the page), and I couldn't get past the local news section; when I read a brief blurb about the bones, I threw the paper down in disgust.

Normally I get mad at the paper because of the numbskulls that put it out: the writers who think "objective" means writing with a specific purpose, not from a central, non-opinionated, impartial point-of-view. By their choice of words, or emphasis, or what they choose *not* to print, they slant the "news" to suit their own opinion.

Even the headline writers do it. Recently, a cop in another county accidentally shot his partner, killing him. The widow, when interviewed, said she had spoken to her late husband's partner and was praying that he would be okay. She knew he was devastated.

She told the reporter about her phone call with him. The headline stated: "Widow Prays For Killer."

Well, excuse me, but *killer* carries the connotation of *murderer*. Even the newspapers' own stylebooks, the guidelines editors go by, say killer is to be used to apply to suspects, people who kill with malice, not to those involved in accidents. Nonetheless, there it was on the front page. Another police officer maligned by the "objective" news media.

This morning, though, it wasn't the newspaper that set me off but the person they were quoting. Unless, of course, they misquoted him, but I didn't think so because the comment was in character.

Jerry Opperman told them the "artifacts" were early Native American and were being processed by Professor Ellison at park expense in the interest of science and as a goodwill gesture to the local Native American community.

Oh brother.

I retired to the garage to putter around and get my mind off things. My eyes lit on my van, which needed a wash. I hated to do it, though—it would just get dirty again—and easily talked myself out of it. I was restless, almost nervous; anxious, perhaps, would better describe it, although I didn't know why. I was looking forward to the meeting with Professor Ellison, but that wasn't the cause. Something else was making me feel uneasy, and not being able to pin it down intensified it.

Standing in the garage with my hands on my hips, I tried to understand my feelings but couldn't. Something was just beyond my grasp, some important fragment was not there. Like a jigsaw puzzle with one piece unaccounted for. You are done. You know what the picture looks like, but it's just not right. It's not really a whole thing, not really finished until that irregularly-shaped little hole is filled in.

And you have no idea where it is.

I used to feel this way when I investigated a case that appeared complete but still had a loose end or two that just didn't add up, didn't quite fit with the rest of the puzzle.

Deep down I suppose I knew what was bothering me now. I had a Rachel-shaped hole in me. Someone with whom I had shared all my adventures, someone who had listened to my tales without me having to buy dinner. Someone who made me a complete person. But I'd never be complete now, because she was missing from my life.

Missing. The missing person Theo'd asked me to check personnel files on. I'd forgotten. Maybe that's what was bugging me. I hate leaving things undone.

Jumping in the van, I drove to the park and hurried to the security office. I was surprised to see Sally at the console. She was strictly a Monday through Friday dayshift type person, especially since her promotion to be Harry Clark's secretary.

"What's up, Sal?"

"Oh, hello Gil."

"Working dispatch and on a Saturday? What gives?"

"Melinda's sick, and I needed the hours."

"The pay, you mean."

"Yes. The pay."

"I don't mean to pry, Sally, but . . . anything I can help you with?"

"No." She shook her head demurely and didn't offer anything else. I took the hint and dropped it, and Sally changed the subject.

"How about you, Gil? What are you doing here?"

I wanted to tell her it was to see her, but I knew she'd see through it. And if I said it as a joke . . . well, that would have done more harm than good.

"I need to access some personnel files for Lieutenant Brown. He's got a missing person case, a guy who works here for ride maintenance."

"Oh? What's his name?"

"Russell Albright."

"Sounds familiar." Sally's fingers flew over the keyboard and in less than a minute the laser printer began to hum, and several pages glided out. She checked them quickly, then handed them to me.

"Not much to help you," she said.

I leafed through the pages. "What do you mean?"

"He's a long-term employee. Anyone who's been here over five years doesn't have everything in the computerized files. Things like their application, transfers, promotions, anything that happened before they set up the new computer system can only be seen by looking in their hard file, which is locked up in Human Resources. We can't access it. Whoever set up the system was lazy, didn't want to put in the old stuff."

"Okay," I said. "Well, the lieutenant will just have to make-do with this. Thanks."

There was an uncomfortable silence as I considered complimenting her and whether or not I should ask her out to lunch sometime. I didn't want to push myself on her, especially if she wasn't interested, but I didn't want to act like I hadn't enjoyed being with her, either. That's what I get for marrying my only girlfriend: no social graces, no knowledge of how to balance friendship and interest while avoiding pressure and indifference.

"I . . . uh. . . ." I struggled for the right words.

"Yes Gil?"

The squawking radio gave me a reprieve, but it was sort-lived. In a moment, she was looking up at me expectantly again.

"Listen, Sally," I began slowly. "I . . . uh, just wanted to tell you how much I enjoyed our . . . uh, dates." I groaned as soon as I said it. It sounded like a kiss-off. Thanks, but no thanks.

Her face fell, but she remained gracious.

"Thank you, Gil. I had a good time, too."

Her reaction encouraged me. If she was disappointed at my comment, perhaps she had been hoping for more. My palms began to sweat, and I hoped I could recover from my near-fatal error.

"I'd like to do it again sometime." No good, Gil. Too vague. Her eyebrows raised slightly.

"So would I."

"Good. I'll give you a call." The radio barked again, and I checked my watch. "Oh, got to go. Theo's waiting for me."

Sally smiled and waved as she answered the radio, and I backed out, irritated at myself. On the one hand, she deserved better treatment than I had just given her. One the other, I wasn't sure I wanted to commit to anyone or anything, or make her think I was committing. Not that dating some was committing, but I was afraid I'd maintain a relationship I didn't really like just to avoid hurting someone's feelings.

I had no reason to believe I wouldn't enjoy a relationship with Sally, that was the crazy part. Our first date had come about in a rather bizarre fashion, but it really had been something we both wanted.

Hadn't it?

I shook it off—or tried to, at least—and guided the Ford to the university.

Theo and Professor Ellison were already there, ready to go, when I walked in. I was late, but neither of them seemed upset. I handed Theo the file on his missing person, explaining its deficiency.

"That's okay," he told me. "If you can get the rest on Monday, that'll be soon enough for me. I've got this to worry about right now." He jerked his thumb toward the table on which Lucy's bones were arranged.

"Are you ready?" Professor Ellison asked cheerily.

We nodded and moved over to the table. Theo switched on a portable cassette recorder and set it on the table next to Lucy's ribs.

The remains were arranged as if she was on her back with her arms down at her sides. The clothing had been carefully removed. She emitted a faintly foul odor but not any worse than corpses do in an autopsy. The dirt had been brushed away, and we were left with a brown skeleton partially covered with leathery tissue. The skull was resting on the table where it belonged, at the top of her shoulders.

"Let's start at the cephalic region," Judy said, and when Theo gave her a funny look she added with a smile, "The head."

"I'll never understand you medical types," he said. "We've got perfectly good, simple words to describe things that everyone understands, and you use the most obscure ones you can find. It's like you're trying to keep us all in the dark."

She chuckled. "Lieutenant, I went to school for eight years at great expense to learn those words, and by golly, I'm going to use them!" She winked. "But for you, I'll try to use the simple ones too."

"Thanks. Gil thanks you too."

"Speak for yourself, buddy," I protested. "I know the big words."

Judy ignored us and proceeded.

"Okay. The skull as you have noted is small, without pronounced brow ridges. The mandible is more pointed than square. This is most likely a female based on that alone, as you know, but there are other confirmations we'll get to later. The skull sutures are closed but still visible, as is the joint between the sphenoid and occipital, so we have a post-teenager. The teeth have a few fillings, Theo, so dental records to verify identity should be available somewhere."

"Needle in a haystack, Doc. I'll check all our local dentists, but what if she wasn't from around here?"

"Always a problem, to be sure." she admitted. "Now, there

are no signs of trauma to the skull, no fractures, broken teeth . . . but, if we move down to the throat. . . ." She pointed to a tiny horseshoe-shaped bone resting on the spine, then to an X-ray mounted on a viewing screen on the wall. She switched on the light.

"See there?" She pointed to the apex of the curved bone. "There's a tiny fracture."

"What is that? What's that mean?" Theo asked.

"She was strangled," I said.

"Very good, Gil," Judy said.

"I knew that," Theo mumbled.

"This is the hyoid bone," Judy explained. "It supports the tongue and its muscles. Not all strangulations fracture it, but a fractured hyoid is almost always an indicator of strangulation. Seldom does it mean anything else."

"Cause of death?" Theo ventured.

"Strangulation very likely is the manner of death," Judy said. "Asphixiation would be the cause. There is adipocere in the break, indicating it was fractured before she was buried."

She clicked off the light and returned to the table.

"There are no other signs of struggle, no cuts, nicks, fractures, bullet holes, anywhere on the remains. She was indeed pregnant, about three months' worth, based on the size and formation of the baby's skeleton. This was to be her first child."

"How do you know that?" Theo asked. I opened my mouth, and he added, "Shut up, Gil."

Professor Ellison pointed to the pelvic bones, at the area of the birth canal. "See how smooth these planes are?" She ran her finger down the edge of the bones at the birth canal location. "Once a woman has given birth, they will be pocked or pitted from the stress. By the way, the width between these bones are another indicator of sex, even if she hadn't been pregnant. Men don't give birth, so their pelvic bones are closer together. "

"What about a previous C-section?" I asked.

"Good question. She had enough tissue left to check for that. There's no evidence of scarring. I'd say she was in her early twenties, pregnant, and barely showing, if at all, was strangled by someone and placed—not dumped, but carefully laid—in the excavation before the ride was built on top of it."

"Or while it was being built?" I offered. "She was pretty deep. I doubt someone would go to the trouble of digging a hole that deep."

"The hole was already there," Theo concluded.

"And the killer knew about it. He worked there."

"That narrows it down," Theo said. "What do you think, Gil? Boyfriend? Father of the child?"

I nodded solemnly, my gaze fixed on the tiny bones of the child. Even at that early stage of the pregnancy it looked completely human, although not in proportion to what it would have been at birth. I couldn't help but wonder how any doctor on the planet could scoop a baby out and throw it away and pretend it was just non-viable tissue, or use the tissue of an aborted fetus for medical experimentation.

"I need to know precisely when that ride was built," Theo told me. "I mean to the day. I need the builder's records, the day they dug the hole, the day they filled it in—"

"Could it be she was already there, before that ride was put in?" I asked Judy. "After all, she was deep. I don't believe the Starcoaster needed a foundation that deep.

"Don't even think it," Theo said. "It's going to be hard enough as it is."

"I don't think so," Professor Ellison said. "The moisture content would have been different, her rate of deterioration greater, had she been in there much longer than a decade. I won't rule it out, but I think it's safe to proceed on the assumption that she was buried just before the hole was filled completely in and the ride built.

A lightbulb went on over my head.

"Speaking of moisture content. . . ." I said. I told them about the new pump system and the high water table.

"That would account for the recent, accelerated decomposition," Judy explained.

"I'll try to get a history on the location," I said to Theo. "Including what was there before the Starcoaster. We'll see how far back the previous ride, or whatever it was, goes. It might have been a parking lot, or an empty field. And maybe we'll get lucky, and the Starcoaster contractor will still be around."

Suddenly a thought struck me, one I hadn't considered before. In fact, it was so obvious, I wondered why we'd missed it.

"Theo, what about the construction crew themselves?" I didn't need to explain in any more detail. He got the point.

"Almost makes more sense," he said. "They had a greater opportunity, access to the equipment, and wouldn't be worried about someone stumbling on to her."

"They'd know right where she was, where they could put her so she wouldn't pop up unexpectedly."

"I'll work on them as soon as you get me the name of the company," Theo said.

I thanked Judy and took one last glance at Lucy, wondering what she had looked like. She would be near my age if she had lived, maybe a little younger. And if she was a local girl, there was even a chance I knew her. Not well, of course, or I'd've missed her. I shuddered. What was I doing when she was murdered and her body dumped?

I stepped out into the bright afternoon.

I spent that afternoon working on my van. I gave it a good wax job with that stuff that removes oxidation, surprised at how good it looked. The yellow paint job was brighter than I'd realized.

I also gave it a tune-up, replacing the plugs, points, rotor, and all that stuff. When I started it up, it settled into a pleasant, quiet idle. I was disappointed it didn't sound any better than it had before, but at least it wasn't running rough.

I went inside, showered, heated some spaghetti leftovers, and sat down in front of a blazing fire with a Louis L'Amour western. I had already found out about a stolen herd of cattle and a family of squatters who were brutally murdered when the phone rang. I thought about letting the answering machine get it, but couldn't go through with it. I'm always afraid it'll be the most important phone call of my life, and by not answering in person, I'll miss a golden opportunity.

So far it had always been a wrong number, or people trying

to get me to subscribe to the local newspaper, or worse, some-one calling me into work on my day off. But maybe this time. . . .

I switched the answering machine off and picked up the receiver.

"Hello," I said cleverly.

"Gil?"

"Were you expecting someone else to answer?"

"This is Theo."

"No kidding."

"Am I interrupting anything?"

"No, I was just sitting here, hoping you'd call."

"I mean, am I interrupting anything important?"

"I was just about to find out whose side the ranch owner's daughter is really on—"

"Huh?"

"No, I'm not doing anything. What's up?"

"Just thought you'd want an update on your missing employee, Albright."

"Did he come home?"

"Not yet."

"What then?"

"They found his car out in the desert. Not in the desert itself but in a town out in the desert. The outskirts of Santa Vista."

"That all? Just his car? Maybe it broke down, and he's in some cheap motel out there, waiting for parts."

"He'd have called work, don't you think? And what would he have been doing there in the first place? Besides, it had the key in it, and it runs fine. Listen, there's more."

"What?"

Theo paused for a moment for effect.

"Go ahead," I urged. "I can take it. I'm sitting down."

"There was blood in the car."

I hummed the theme from Twilight Zone.

"Looks bad," Theo said, ignoring me.

"So what do you think?" I asked. "Albright was kidnapped, murdered, and dumped in the desert after a crazed matron had her way with him? Was there a circular burn nearby where the spaceship landed? What?"

"Something more ordinary, most likely," Theo said, disregarding my sarcasm. "He probably picked up a hitchhiker who killed him for his—"

"For his car but forgot to take it? I don't think so, Theo. And he didn't appear to have anything else worth stealing."

"That's why we call these mysteries, I guess," Theo sighed. "Endless speculation will get us nowhere."

"But it sure is fun."

"His car's being brought in. It'll be checked for prints. We'll go from there."

"Anything else?"

"No, that's all for now. Just thought you'd like to know."

"I do," I admitted. "Thanks. See you Monday."

"Okay." He hung up.

Well, what could this mean? I wondered as I put the receiver back on the hook and switched on the answering machine. Two mysteries at the park at the same time.

Attendance would skyrocket when word got out.

I poured a cup of coffee and returned to the beanbag by the fireplace where the rancher's daughter was waiting for me, her flame red hair spilling onto the shoulders of her gingham dress. . . .

EIGHT

Church the next day was ordinary, nothing much different than previous Sundays. Same people in the same pews. Same snotty kids running around between services. Same folks at their respective stations: information booth, greeting at the front doors of the sanctuary, making fifty-gallon drums of coffee and cutting muffins in half to feed the five thousand at the between-services-meet-the-visitors muffin table on the patio.

Not that ordinariness and sameness are bad things. It's beneficial to be able to count on people to complete certain essential tasks so the elder board doesn't have to concern itself with the routine functions of the weekly operation of the church and can concentrate on bickering about their personal agendas. And sameness can be comforting; things like occupying a familiar pew gives a person less to adjust to so they can concentrate on worship, just so long as one doesn't get possessive about it.

Concentrating on worship was what I was trying to do but having some difficulty. I found my mind wandering during the announcements, and my singing was perfunctory, not really paying attention to the all too familiar lyrics. Truth is, I had three women on my mind.

Two of them dead.

Who was Lucy? Who had killed her? And why? Confident that Theo would identify her soon—there was a strong likelihood, in my estimation, that she was a local, although I was in no way certain about it—I was anxious to learn her history.

I guess you could say I'd bonded with her, but I think it was

84

just plain old curiosity and intrigue. These kind of things get my attention, which is probably why I'm a history/mystery buff: historical mysteries, like Jack the Ripper and Amelia Earhart, and visiting real American West ghost towns.

As I sat there, dropping my wallet into the offering plate—they took out what they needed then sent the wallet back—I suddenly realized, with a wry grin, just how many women I was dealing with currently. Wendy, Sally, Rachel, Lucy, Judy, Trish . . . to the uninitiated, I would seem like quite a ladies' man. If they only knew.

I hadn't seen Sally that morning. Perhaps she had been asked to work again for the sick dispatcher or was ill herself. But since we aren't in the same Sunday school class, and worship service was so crowded I would have had to stand on my chair to see if she was there, I decided to put her out of my mind and concentrate on the sermon. After all, there's nothing I could do about it now. I opened the Word and settled in to listen, learn, and be convicted.

After the benediction I filed out of the sanctuary with the rest of the cattle—sheep, I suppose, would be a more accurate term—to the strains of the organ, shaking hands with the pastor and his wife and a sweet little old lady who thought her spiritual gift was knowing who was there and who wasn't. Looking my dapper best, I hung out around the muffin table, half-heartedly scanning the multitude for Sally, although I hadn't considered what I'd do if I found her.

Five minutes was all I gave it before talking myself into going home. As I was heading across the parking lot for my van, someone behind me called my name. I turned to see Joyce Stevens, my deacon's wife, waving and smiling at me like she had just found the "old time religion." An alarm should have gone off, but my guard was down, being at the Lord's house and not expecting treachery.

"Gil, wait a minute. Don't rush off."

I hadn't, I thought to myself as she pattered up to me. I've been hanging around.

"Joyce!" I said. "How's Lewis?" *And Clark*, I said under my breath. I liked the Stevenses, a couple of really old folks. They were nice, sincere people, always well-meaning, even though they occasionally tended to go overboard.

"Oh, he's fine. He's locking up. He'll be right out."

"That's nice. I take it his gout isn't acting up?"

"No more than he is!" She laughed at herself. "Listen, Gil, we wanted to know if you could join us for lunch? We're going to the Rib Rack. There's a group of us."

She knew I liked the Rib Rack. No, she knew I *loved* the Rib Rack. I loved barbecue, regardless of the cut of meat or the type of animal that had been sectored. Shoot, why not go? I didn't have anything else to do.

"Be happy to."

"Grand! The others are already on their way there. We'll meet you."

"Okay."

I headed out in the beast for the Rib Rack, catching myself humming on the way. It would be nice to spend some time with good, Christian people for awhile, eating mountains of God's creatures whacked into edible portions and covered with messy sauce. The Rib Rack was one of those all-you-can-eat places, the way God intended.

Halfway there, it let me down. My van, that is. Although it idled fine, under acceleration or load the roughness came back and didn't leave. It choked out a couple times, and I couldn't go over thirty. I thought more than once about turning around and going home, but since the Rib Rack was closer than my place, and I had friends there if I needed anything, I pressed on, nursing the accelerator and praying out loud. When I finally struggled into the parking lot, the Stevenses' car was already there.

I went inside and found my group, and the whole insidious plot became painfully, excruciatingly evident.

The only empty seat around the table for ten was next to Sally. They'd invited her, too.

Her back was to me when I walked in, and when one of the party hailed me, I saw her stiffen and turn slowly in her seat, also aware now of the conspiracy. She smiled but looked as uncomfortable as I felt.

The dear, sweet brothers and sisters, led by the nefarious Bonnie and Clyde Stevens, were trying to play matchmakers.

I grinned like a trooper, apologized for being late, spread personal greetings around the table, then took my assigned seat. While I adjusted my napkin, I leaned over to Sally and whispered, "Hi, Sal. Long time no see."

The corners of her mouth curled up uncomfortably while she stared at her table service. We both knew what was going on, we were both uncomfortable about it, and we both realized the other was innocent of being a part of the scheme. In that, we were united.

Their plan having succeeded thus far, our hosts and hostesses were now engaging one another in conversation, talking about grandkids and retirement and quilts and golf, leaving Sally and me pretty much out of it.

You know, there's nothing that can kill a romance quicker than someone else trying to orchestrate it. Even if we wanted to get serious, I didn't want these well-meaning but misguided folks to take credit for it. The fact is, at this point Sally and me getting together would be in spite of their efforts, not because of them.

"Sorry," Sally said quietly. "I didn't know."

"Me either," I replied.

Although we were both uncomfortable, we were nonetheless friends and had no trouble conversing. It was what we didn't talk about that told the tale—us. Conversation was restricted to work topics, church, anything non-personal. I told her what was going on with Lucy and Albright, and she volunteered to help me the next day to find what I needed. She said Harry would be in meetings all day, and she'd have the time.

The dinner itself was great, which is another reason I was a little disappointed Sally was there: I couldn't pig out. Despite everything else, something inside me still wanted to make a good impression.

I even forgot about my van until I started it up to leave. I gazed about the parking lot to see who could follow me home in case I broke down. Only Sally was left. She had noticed I was just sitting there and came over.

"Are you okay?" she asked.

"Yeah. I'm having car trouble. I thought I took care of it yesterday, but it's not running right. It'll run, just not very well. Would you mind following me home?"

I could feel the blood pounding in my head.

"Sure. No problem."

"Just in case it takes a powder," I added, patting the dashboard.

She smiled and retreated to her Toyota. It took awhile, but we got there okay. I wanted to ask her in but didn't know if she wanted me to, so I didn't. I'd rather not ask than ask and be turned down. I waved and said thank you, and she drove off, slowly. I'm not sure, but I think she watched me in her mirror.

I finished off Louis L'Amour that night. You'd never guess, but the rancher's daughter fell in love with the drifter, who avenged the squatters, brought back the stolen herd, captured the bad guys (killing the really bad ones when they asked for it), then broke the girl's heart by moving on.

It has to end that way; there's no secret about it. They all end that way. What's interesting is how the hero does it, and how he can do it differently each time. You'd think, with all those beautiful ranchers' daughters and pioneer women—all of whom can cook—falling in love with him all over the West, that soon his old horse would start to look kind of ugly.

Would I leave my beloved van for the love and cooking of a woman with freckles and sun-darkened skin and deep brown eyes and a handsome figure packed into a calico dress or blue jeans?

Faster than Wile E. Coyote on Acme rocket skates.

I leaned back in the beanbag by the fireplace and thought about my situation. Rachel had been gone several years now, close to four. She wasn't coming back, I knew that. At least, intellectually I knew it; emotionally, I still had an attachment. Memories are one thing, I told myself. To allow myself to act as if she was just on an extended vacation and would be coming back was quite another matter.

It was probably unhealthy.

Did I love Sally? No, I couldn't honestly say that I did. Could I, if I let myself? I had to admit it: probably. She was everything a man could want in a Christian wife, as far as I knew. And she appeared to have an interest in me.

That was the difficult part. I couldn't think of a good reason for her to see anything in me. Oh, I was attractive and witty, sure. And humble.

Seriously, I had no idea how women saw me. It never mattered before. . . . Did it matter now?

As I stared into the fireplace I came to realize it apparently did matter. That's why I was spending so much time thinking about it.

I sighed and went to bed.

NINE

When I got to work the next morning I had a message to call Theo. I phoned him just before lunch during a lull in my work.

"What's up, Lieutenant?"

"I called early this morning," he complained. "Where've you been?"

"I've got work to do. I'll get to your stuff after lunch. I had to get the construction guys back on schedule, Design and Planning showed me some renderings of the new ride, I had a meeting with Michelle—"

"What about?"

"What do you mean, what about? Park stuff. She's my boss, remember?"

"Oh, yeah."

"Well . . . what'd you want?"

"I got an interesting call this morning, from a gal who says she used to be Albright's girlfriend. Saw the article in the paper about his disappearance. Said they went together a couple years, then one night he kissed her goodbye, said he'd see her later, and never came back. Didn't call, didn't write, nothing. Six months later she goes by his apartment, sees him coming out with another girl. She left, never saw him again. She figured he was just one of those guys. She learned her lesson."

"How long ago was this?"

"Five years."

"No warning, no explanation, he just cut off all contact with her," I snapped my fingers, "like that?"

"Yep."

"Did she ever figure out what might have happened?" I asked.

"Not really. They weren't planning on getting married or anything, just dating regular, never fought—"

"No indication at all?"

"None."

"Why'd she call?"

"She said she didn't know, thought it might help us, though she didn't know how."

"That's interesting," I mused. "What do you make of it?"

"Nothing. So he dumped a girl five years ago. What's that got to do with his disappearance now?"

"Nothing, I guess. Except maybe he's not as reliable as we thought. That it?"

"Yeah. Don't forget the file," Theo said.

"No, I won't," I assured. "Right after lunch."

Following a delicious repast of beef stew and coffee, I checked in at Personnel, cleverly entitled Human Resources here at the politically correct park. Why we didn't have a Nonhuman Resources Department or Subhuman Resources I couldn't say. We certainly had employees in those categories. Personally, I was offended at being referred to as just a resource. Hey, I'm a person!

Most of the time, anyway.

I showed the secretary Theo's business card.

"The lieutenant is investigating a missing person, an employee named Russell Albright. He asked me to pick up Albright's file for him. The lieutenant's busy on a homicide, and since I used to work with him he thought. . . ." I gestured with open hands to complete my sentence, leaving her to figure out what I was trying to say without having to pound her on the head with it.

"Yes?" she said.

Oh yeah, I reminded myself, this is the park. I glanced at the door to see if that's where she'd checked her brain on the way in.

"So could I see the file?"

"Just a moment, please." She took Theo's card and disappeared into an office, to return a moment later.

"Mr. Gray will be right with you."

"Excuse me, Miss . . . "I scanned the desk for her nameplate but there wasn't one. She just looked at me with a smile. "Excuse me, Miss Resource, but I don't want to bother Mr. Gray. I just need to see the file, please."

"Mr. Gray will be right out." She went back to her work, leaving me no choice but to wait.

He was out in five minutes, just a few seconds under my patience threshold.

"Come on in, Lieutenant Brown."

"I, uh . . . okay. Thank you."

I hadn't said I was Lieutenant Brown, Miss Resource just hadn't been listening. But since the mistake was theirs, well. . . .

"Why do the police need this file?" he asked after we'd been seated.

"It's not all as sinister as it sounds," I assured. "Mr. Albright has vanished. Poof. Kaput. Although he doesn't seem the type to just take off, there is no indication of foul play and the pol—uh, we were thinking that there might be a clue to his whereabouts in his file. Relatives, things like that. We don't know for sure, but it's worth a try."

"I could look in it for you. Just tell me what you want."

"You don't understand, Mr. Gray. You're not a trained investigator. Besides, we don't exactly know what we're looking for, that's the whole point. Sometimes we don't know until we see it."

"Well, you see Lieutenant, there's a problem. The files are confidential."

"I understand, Mr. Gray, under normal circumstances. But this is a matter of some urgency."

"Well, if you can get a written note from Mr. Albright . . . otherwise, it's privileged information."

That did it. The color and the pleasant looked drained quickly from my face and I leaned forward, my teeth clenched. I spoke low but with some force. "Mr. Gray, if we could get a note from Albright none of this would be necessary because he wouldn't be missing, now would he? And as for privileged information, that only applies to someone's spouse, lawyer, or doctor. Which one of those are you to Mr. Albright?"

"Well, I—"

"I appreciate that you're trying to protect the employees here, Mr. Gray, but I don't think you even understand what you're protecting Albright from. I am not a prospective employer trying to see his work record. He's not a suspect in anything, he's a victim. We're trying to help him. I could get a court order, but I don't have the time, and frankly, I don't have to!"

I knew I was getting a little red in the face, so I forced myself to calm down. What was making me so upset? I guess it was his pompous attitude, that sense of importance he had no right having, that so many people in management positions here—and everywhere else, for that matter—tend to acquire when left in a position without accountability long enough. When I was at the P.D., we had a group of patrol sergeants who got that way. It took a blanket party with one of them to change things.

A blanket party is one of those cop rituals where the offender is confronted leaving the station by having a blanket thrown over his head so he can't identify anyone, and then the daylights get beat out of him. He's not injured badly, just has the message driven home. I didn't participate, but I can't say I wasn't happy with the result. It woke the administration up. They were scratching their heads about why it happened until they began asking questions.

A common occurrence in police departments? Too common, I'm afraid. But you'll never hear about it in the media. It's just a little in-house attitude adjustment.

I didn't have a blanket right then so I decided to try another tactic, now that I had Mr. Gray's attention.

"If you'd like, I'll call Michelle—excuse me, Miss Yokoyama—and have her give the okay, since you don't seem to have the authority to do so."

Gray cleared his throat. "There's no need for that, Lieutenant. Here." He handed me the file across the desk. It was already out, which could only mean he'd intended giving it to me all along. I guess he just wanted me to beg.

Didn't work.

"We just have to be careful, you understand," he continued.

Good job, I thought. *You didn't even confirm my identity.*

"I must ask you, though," he said, "not to remove it from the premises. You can copy whatever you like, but the file stays here."

I thanked him and took the file out to Miss Resource's office where the copy machine was. I didn't bother looking through it, just copied the whole mess. It took about fifteen minutes, then I took it back into Gray and set it on his desk, thanking him.

"You're welcome, Lieutenant. Uh, have we met before? You look familiar."

"Perhaps we have," I said smiling. "Maybe I gave you a ticket once."

I left him pondering that and breezed out of the office with my trophy.

I didn't really have an office of my own. That was one of those things that had so far been overlooked. They weren't quite sure what to do with me, since I was actually still listed as a security officer. I'd put it to Michelle that perhaps I could use John Hayes's old office, since it was vacant, and she said she'd look into it. So far, though, all I had was a desk in an unused corner of a warehouse. It was too cold in there to get much work done most of the time and at other times was too noisy. It was seldom private.

So I took the file with me to security to read it. I was going to have it there for Theo to pick up anyway—I couldn't do any extra running around with my van on the fritz—plus I needed Sally's help digging up the construction records.

Her desk was in a small windowed office—more like an alcove, actually—outside Harry's office, with barely enough room to walk around it to access her chair. The window faced the hall—there was none to the outside—so it was like working in a fishbowl. Other than the desk, it contained a bookshelf, a chair for guests, and a coatrack. But Sally never complained. I think she was grateful just to be out of dispatch.

She was also better at being content than I was.

Sally was gone for lunch when I got there, so I made myself at home in the guest chair and read the copies of Albright's file.

Nothing jumped out at me. His application listed the usual personal information, former addresses—all local—and prior job experience. There was no one listed in the space for emergency notification. Parents were deceased, no other close relatives. He had worked for several years for an engineering company in Harrisburg, Illinois. I thought it odd that he hadn't listed an Illinois address, but, after all, he had just been applying for a job at an amusement park, not with an aerospace firm doing secret government contracts. The park didn't run checks on people, not into their prior living arrangements, at least. Come to think of it, I hadn't listed my previous addresses either. It was none of the park's business.

Just the same, I made another copy of the whole thing, including the photo, for myself and left Theo's with Wendy in a manila folder.

"So, are you excited?" I asked Wendy as I dropped the folder on the desk and wrote Theo's name on it. "About the P.D., I mean."

"Yes," she admitted, beaming. "It's going to be fun. I can hardly wait."

"It's going to be hectic and stressful," I corrected. "You'll be answering phones, answering the radio, talking to people at the front counter, running teletypes, typing logs, processing reports. . . . Everything you do now, times ten."

"Yeah," she said dreamily.

"Like I said," I shrugged, "it'll be fun."

One person's angst is another person's ecstasy, I guess.

The door opened. Sally had returned. She came into dispatch.

"Every time I see you, you're hovering around Wendy," Sally scolded. "Leave the poor girl alone, she's got work to do." She smiled, but I detected an uncharacteristic edge to her voice.

"Sorry," I said. "I'm a victim of circumstance. I was just

dropping off a folder for Lieutenant Brown of the police department."

"Likely story." She walked down the hall to her office without looking back.

"That's silly, to think we'd be. . . ." Wendy started to say. "You're almost twice my—"

I turned and gave her a look of disdain. She was right, but I didn't like hearing it just the same.

"I didn't mean it like that," she blushed.

"It's a good thing you're cute, and I'm a gentleman," I said, then added, "Am I really almost twice your age?"

She shrugged sheepishly. "Nearly. I think you've got me by nearly sixteen years."

"Oh my. In that case, it's all over between us."

"You know Gil, she really likes you."

"Who?"

"Sally, of course."

"Aw. . . ." I tried to wave her off but what I really meant was *tell me more.*

"Do something about it," Wendy urged.

"Okay, we'll see," I said, because I didn't know what else to say. "And thanks for calling Lieutenant Brown for me."

"No problem."

I retreated to Sally's office. She looked up when I knocked on the open door as though she hadn't seen me in a week, a surprised smile on her reddened face. The look she wore reminded me about Rachel's periodic bouts with emotional ups and downs. It had been a long time since I lived with a woman, and I'd lost the finely honed edge to sense things like that. I forgave her odd behavior—in my mind only, of course; I'm no dummy—and returned her smile.

"Come in Gil, what can I do for you?"

"I need to get some info on old construction here. About ten years ago."

"The Starcoaster?"

"Precisely. How do I go about it?"

"That stuff is probably in the archives. Design and Planning files their stuff there as soon as they're through with it."

"Where are the archives?"

"The files are kept in a room in the old building where Jerry's office is. You have to go through his secretary to get in."

"Old Lizzy Borden Potter? The ax murderer secretary? The Dragon Lady? She who must be feared? She who has been here since before the world was formed?"

"Elizabeth is a very nice lady."

"Depends on your definition of nice, Sally. If you like the rack and enjoy bamboo shoved up under your fingernails, I suppose, in comparison, she's nice. Even the owners are afraid of her."

"She's been here longer than anyone. In fact, she was the one and only secretary to Mr. Golden."

"Mr. Golden, as in Old Man Golden, the founder?"

Sally nodded.

"I heard he died in his office, and she didn't tell anyone for two weeks."

"Nonsense. He died at home, in bed, with a nurse sitting there."

I slapped the desk. "I told them that wasn't true. So, do you think the dear sweet woman will help me?"

"Not if you patronize her like you do everyone else around here . . . especially Wendy."

"What do you mean by that?"

"You're a little too nice, don't you think?"

"I'm not often accused of that."

"That's what makes it so obvious. You practically drool when you see her."

My neck reddened. I hoped Sally wouldn't notice, but I couldn't hide it. I shrugged. There was no defense I could raise. "I didn't realize," I said. "I'll try to keep my tongue in my mouth next time."

"Don't be offended, Gil. I tell you because I'm concerned about your reputation. I know you don't mean anything by it, but other people don't. You just need to be careful, that's all."

Sally seemed sincere so I took it at face value. "Thanks, Sally. And will you help me? Get the files, I mean." I deftly changed the subject.

"I'll handle it." She picked up the phone and punched in an

extension. "Elizabeth, this is Sally. Just fine, thanks. You know Gil Beckman, don't you? Yes the good-looking ex-cop that solved the murder and . . . He did?" She covered the mouthpiece and whispered to me. "She says you monkeyed with Jerry's chair once." To Elizabeth: "It did? For a whole week?" Sally laughed. "Well, Gil needs to get into the archives to inspect some old construction records. The Starcoaster. Yes, that's right, he's in charge of tearing it down and putting up the new one. Could you—you will? Oh, thank you. Yes, he'll be right over." She hung up.

Sally grinned at me.

"How'd she know it was me?" I asked.

"She's smarter than everyone thinks. That's why she's still here. She makes it her business to know about people."

"Yeah, but—"

"Why don't you ask her, if you're so curious. She thought it was great fun. Said Jerry left her alone for a whole week, he was so upset." Sally paused, then added, "And don't worry, she didn't tell him it was you."

"I best be on my way, then."

"You owe me now, Gil Beckman."

"I'm in your debt," I said, avoiding the question of exactly *what* I owed her. I got up with a smile and retreated down the hall, not realizing that I'd left my copy of Albright's file on Sally's desk.

Mrs. Potter was waiting for me.

I had approached her door with caution, not wanting to run into Opperman, but I noticed his parking place was empty. He must have been on an extended lunch: an every day occurrence, not that anyone cared. When I opened the door and went in, she was already staring in my direction, her face with that *I'm sizing you up, you whippersnapper* look to it.

She wasn't a large woman or threatening in her appearance. In fact, she was downright tiny. And old. She reminded me of every schoolkid's nightmare: that really ancient, spinster teacher in the sixth grade whose job it was to make sure you hate her so much you'd be sure to pass so you could go to seventh grade even though you were afraid of junior high, just to get away from her. She was the rock, junior high was the hard place.

Elizabeth Potter the teacher would have had one of those giant rulers that you would swear, because she was so tiny, was at least fifteen inches long; the kind with the metal blade down one edge that you were afraid would chop off your hand if she ever held it wrong when she smacked you with it.

Elizabeth Potter the president's secretary smiled sweetly, shattering my impressions immediately.

"Good afternoon, Mr. Beckman."

"Good afternoon, Miss Potter. Thank you for helping me out."

"My pleasure. You know, that was a good thing you did, catching Mr. Hayes and Mr. Brito for. . . . Oh, it's so terrible, I can't even bring myself to say it."

My fame had preceded me, once again. "Well, thank you for saying so. I didn't—"

"You know, I always thought there was something wrong with him."

"Brito?"

"No, not him. I didn't know much about him. Mr. Hayes, I mean."

"Something wrong like what?"

"He had that look in his eye, that shifty used car salesman look. I never trusted him. He's the kind that would get other kids to throw spitballs then tattle on them."

I knew it. She used to be a teacher, way way back. "Well, if you never trusted him, Miss Potter, how did—"

"How did he get to be vice president?" She stood up—her head barely higher than when she was sitting down—and pattered over to me. I scanned her hands quickly for the presence of a ruler. She arrived empty-handed. "People think I run the place, or used to, at least. I know what they say. I hear them. Well, once upon a time that was nearly true. Mr. Golden used to consult me about everything. I was more than a secretary to him, you know. Get that look out of your, Mr. Beckman, I don't mean it that way. You young people think everything revolves around sex. I mean, I was more like a business partner to him than a secretary. You know the ghost town? That was my idea." She tilted her head up proudly, then broke into a smile. "Of course, it was new when I was young. Wasn't a ghost town then."

She cackled at her joke, then continued her trip down memory lane. "Mr. Golden, may he rest in peace, didn't make any decisions near the end. He was too senile. But no one knew it, not for sure. When he died, they brought in Mr. Opperman, didn't even consult me. The new owners, I mean. They were all the major stockholders. He had no relatives. Married to the park, he was. They kept me around because they were afraid I had the goods on them. Did, too, although I'd never use the information. Skulduggery was never my bailiwick, Mr. Beckman."

She sighed as she recollected, then went on. I wasn't about to stop her; this was all too interesting.

"His first big project was the Starcoaster." She rolled her eyes. "Big deal! A Tilt-A-Whirl in a dark building. When I was a kid, we used to swing each around in circles until we threw up; that was much more fun than the Starcoaster. Suddenly, he's a big genius. Between me and you, Mr. Beckman, he's got a screw loose. You know that. That's why you monkeyed with his chair."

I had to ask. "How did you know it was me?" I didn't see the point in playing innocent with Miss Potter.

"Easy. No one else working at night had the moxie. You were older, an ex-police officer . . . Need I tell you that cops are great practical jokers? I knew a few in my day." She winked. "Don't worry though, he doesn't know. Never will, either." She scrunched up her face for a moment, like she'd eaten something distasteful.

"Aw, I'm boring you," she said.

"No, not a bit," I assured. "But I am a little curious; why tell me all this?"

"You policemen, always with the questions. I like Sally, that's why. And she likes you, otherwise she wouldn't have sent you here. I'm not going to be around forever—I know what you're thinking: I already have."

I couldn't suppress a smile.

"I'm going to retire pretty soon, and I needed to tell someone. I figured I could tell you. You have a nice face, you're smart, and I don't take you for a blabbermouth. Besides, play your cards right and you'll move up quickly here."

"I don't see how," I said. "I don't have any skills that—"

"Doesn't take skills. It takes being in the right place at the right time, knowing the right people. Mr. Opperman's worried, Mr. Beckman. He hasn't said what about, but I suspect it's you and the way you're running things right now. Mind yourself, though; he'll cut you out if you give him a chance. He won't do anything criminal, I don't think—but then, I didn't think Hayes could murder."

"He couldn't," I reminded her. "That's why he recruited Brito."

"Ah, yes. That is so." She smiled and patted my hand. "Well, you keep doing good work. I'd like to see you make it some day."

That stung, although I didn't think she meant it to. But it was true, I hadn't made it yet. And I was approaching forty, and picking up speed. But, then again, what difference did it make? I was never goal-oriented. I just wanted to serve God to the best of my ability. Didn't I?

"The archives are back there." She pointed through the doorway at the rear of her office and down the hall while handing me a key ring. "When you're done, lock it and slip out the back way. Leave the key with Sally, I'll get it tomorrow. Mr. Opperman could return at any time. We don't want him asking questions, sticking his nose in police business, do we?" She grinned.

How'd she know it was police business, I wondered.

"How'd I know it was police business?" she continued without a pause. "I know you found someone out there, under the Starcoaster. Mr. Opperman hasn't stopped complaining about the delay and the way you sidestepped him." She winked. "I doubt he'd be too happy to see you here."

She returned to her desk and went back to work, her arthritic fingers flying over the keyboard of her typewriter. I was trying to suppress a surprised grin.

"Uh, Miss Potter?" She stopped typing and turned toward me.

"Yes?"

101

"Excuse me, but I just wanted to say I think you're a really neat lady, and I'd like to thank you for helping me, but. . . ." I couldn't phrase the question.

"You want to know why they call me Lizzie Borden Potter?"

I could only nod self-consciously.

"I started that myself, many years ago. I'm small—as you may have noticed—and I didn't want folks thinking they could take advantage of me. Self-preservation, that's what it was."

"Surely somebody knew you were a sweetheart."

"A few people knew what a peach I was—and still am, mind you. But they keep it to themselves." She opened her desk drawer and pulled out a giant ruler, which she held threateningly. "If they know what's good for them."

We laughed, and I left her humming at her desk. She'd had as much fun as I had.

I retired to the archives to find a windowless room lined with file cabinets. In the center was a small table with an unpadded wood chair next to it. It didn't take long to find the "S" file, and the folders marked *Starcoaster*.

I sat down in the chair and began leafing through the pages.

TEN

The security office was nearly deserted when I wandered back in a couple hours later. The day was winding down, and I wanted to talk to Sally before she left, maybe even ask her out.

Her office was dark. I checked my watch. After five. It'd taken longer than I expected to go through the files just to extract a couple dates. It was akin to an investigation all by itself, just to pinpoint the possible days when the construction of the Starcoaster would have progressed to the point where the pit was still open but about to be filled in and concreted over. But I'd done it. I'd gotten it down to four days when it could have been done.

Four days, ten-and-a-half years ago. Not much to go on, but Theo'd have to be satisfied with it. If he hadn't picked up Albright's file yet, I could add this—

Albright's file. Where was my copy? I had that same sickening feeling you get when you reach for your driver's license at the request of the motor cop, or a twenty dollar bill to pay for dinner, and it's not there.

Where had I left it? I checked in dispatch, but the nighttime dispatcher didn't know. She did have a clue, though.

"Did you get the note Sally left on her door?"

"Note?"

"Yeah." She chomped her gum, making me wonder how they could understand her over the radio. "She said to be sure and tell you to get the note. So I'm telling you."

"Okay, Emerald, thanks." Emerald Stone. Could there be

any doubt her parents had been hippies during the sixties? I hurried down the hall and there it was, taped to the glass window set into Sally's door.

"You left your folder in here," I read. "I didn't want anyone else seeing it, so I took it home. Call when you're on the way, and I'll have dinner ready." It was signed *Sal.*

Things were looking up.

"Sorry, Sally," I said sheepishly when she opened the door. "I didn't mean for you to go to all this trouble."

"It's no trouble, Gil. Come in." She held the door wide and took my coat.

Her place was neat as a pin, as usual. She hadn't picked up; she kept it that way. It was a warm, homey apartment; tasteful, light furniture in pastel colors and natural wood. Plants and flowers everywhere, paintings and prints of Americana and still life. Everywhere the feminine touch. Not feminist, feminine. Two entirely different things.

The place was so feminine, I stuck out like a two-day growth of beard; like armpit hair on a ballerina.

The glass dining table was set for two with white china and delicate silver tableware. Her coffee cup was a fragile-looking piece with handpainted flowers and a matching saucer. For me, she had set out a heavy, large mug with a picture of a cowboy on it and a handle so hefty I could have grabbed it with a catcher's mitt.

I wondered, had she bought it special, or did she have it sitting around for occasions like this? I decided that I didn't want to think about it.

"Dinner's almost ready. Your folder's on the coffee table."

"Anything I can help with?"

"No thanks. I've got it. Make yourself at home." She disappeared into the kitchen.

Despite her invitation to make myself at home, I left my shoes on and controlled my urge to belch. Sitting down on the sofa, I thumbed through the folder slowly, thinking more of my hostess and the smells billowing from the kitchen than I did of the contents. We conversed between rooms, inconsequential small talk about work and the weather.

Nothing about Albright's past jumped out at me. Maybe he had some connections in Illinois. It was possible, since he'd worked there. I'd call tomorrow. There was nothing else to go on that I could see.

"Soup's on," Sally called softly. I jumped up and met her at the table, standing behind my chair. "Please, Gil, go ahead and sit down. You don't have to be so formal. I want you to relax. Okay? Feel at home."

"Maybe you should have used paper plates," I explained. "The last time I ate off stuff like this was on prom night, and the meal set me back two hundred dollars—including tip. I'm afraid I'll break it."

"Nonsense." She uncovered a steaming dish of homemade chili. Large, meaty chunks of beef and pork, a thick reddish-brown sauce, tomatoes, several different kinds of beans. . . .

Wait a minute, I knew this chili. I'd had it at one of our frequent potlucks at church. My mouth commenced watering, the memory of it still fresh in my mind.

Sally was looking at me.

"What?" I asked. "Am I drooling?"

"No," she laughed. "It was just the look in your eye."

"A combination of hunger and recognition. I've met your chili before." I hoped she be impressed with my memory.

"I know," she admitted quietly.

Parry and thrust. A plot.

"How's that?" I asked.

She blushed. "I watched you go back for seconds at the last church dinner."

What could I say? It was my turn to blush, and I tried to hide it behind a quick smile.

"Uh, shall I say grace?"

"Please."

I obliged and we ate, peppering the meal with casual, comfortable conversation. I imagined what it might be like to do this every night and every morning, to be with her all the time, and I liked it. But would she feel the same way? For that matter, would I always feel the same way? What if she had intensely foul breath in the morning, or left her underwear all over the place. No, that described me. Surely she had some bad habit I would find distasteful. Rachel used to—

I cut off my own thought. That wasn't fair to Sally. Rachel was gone, gone for good. I had to stop thinking about her.

Dinner over, I volunteered to help with the dishes, but she said no, much to my relief. We retired over flavored coffee and homemade cookies to the living room. I was suddenly nervous—for the first time since my first date with Sally—but I wasn't sure why.

Yes, yes I was. The old animal instincts were stirring. Mine at least. Time to go. I thanked her for the dinner and for rescuing the Albright file and told her I had some things to do before going to bed. Like reading the Bible and praying. She was gracious and said she enjoyed my company.

Later that night when I went to bed it was with mixed emotions. Mixed-up emotions, that is.

Jurassic jungle vines clutched at my face and clothes as I picked my way through the dense undergrowth, the chill of the thick air, even at the middle of the day, heralding the coming Ice Age.

I stopped at the edge of the clearing and listened. The clicking and chattering of insects; the distant screech of a pterodactyl that circled afar off; the rustling of large blue and orange leaves; the gurgling of a lava flow and the occasional hissing of a boiling geyser. The only odor was that of sulfur and triceratops droppings and grease.

Then a mechanical hum, oddly out of place here but subdued, probably unheard except by my ears trained for the noise—came to me before the source was in view: a contraption vaguely reminiscent of H.G. Wells time machine, as portrayed in the classic movie, glided out from an unseen tunnel, occupied by a family of wide-eyed bipeds.

As they approached, a twig cracked to my right and a raging tyrannosaurs charged out from its hiding place, roaring as it opened its gaping jaw to reveal rows of irregular, sharp teeth. It lunged at the primates, useless upper arms dangling comically, yet no one laughed at its handicap. No, they screamed, screamed what could have been their last scream as they saw the yellow saliva dripping from the mouth of the mottled, blotch-skinned beast, whose iridescent, bumpy, cracked skin, the color of a film of oil in a puddle of water, quivered with the flexing of its powerful muscles.

But technology won out as the time machine whisked its occupants away to safety in the flickering light of a time transfer, and the bewildered T. Rex retreated to its hiding place to await another less resourceful victim, its hunger unsated.

The improvements to the Time Machine ride were remarkable. Without enlarging the dinosaurs that much—there was precious little room in the building for that—the designer had succeeded in making it truly scary. My hat was off to the late Everett Curran.

I retraced my steps back through the employee sneak-in into the workshop of the dino ride and gave the Rides Department head, Dave Whelan, a thumbs up. He smiled.

"Looks great!" I told him. "All the dinos are great, and the carts are ten times better than those giant eggs we had before. It makes sense now."

"I'd say we're on the move," Whelan said. "Let's hope everything else comes out as good."

"It will," I assured him. "It will."

I left him with his crew and headed back toward the warehouse where I had my "office." As I moved past the Moonraiders site—the decade-long gravesite for Lucy and baby—I was waylaid by my assistant.

"There you are," Trish said breathlessly. "Why don't you carry a radio so we can call you?"

I shrugged. "Too cumbersome. No place to put it in this suit." What I didn't say was, *because then you'd be calling me all the time.* "What do you need?" I asked.

"Harry Clark wants you in security."

"I am in security." I fished out my badge and showed her.

"He wants you in the office, I mean." She started to walk away.

"Why send you? He's got security officers all over the place."

"Shoot, I don't know. Why ask me? I just do what I'm told." She heaved a sigh. Either she was bored or something was wrong. Usually she'd take my bait and let me lead her into a pointless discussion.

"What's the matter, Trish?" I grabbed her hand to stop her and only let go when she turned to face me. She looked at me then away from me, but didn't say anything.

"Everett?" I asked.

She shook her head. Of course his death still bothered her, but it was something else getting her down right now.

"What then? Come on, don't make me guess. I'm no good at that. Who do you think I am, Sherlock Homeboy?"

She stifled a laugh. "My parents," she said slowly, "are moving to England. They told me last night. Dad's been transferred by the company to open their office in London."

"England, huh? Sounds exciting. I'd like to go there. Maybe they'd settle for me, let you stay."

"No, you're too much trouble. Dad would never go for that. And besides, I can't believe you'd up and leave right now in the middle of all this."

"I see your point," I agreed, "but if you wear a hat no one will notice."

"What's that supposed to mean?"

"This sounds like a great opportunity, but if you'd rather stay. . . . Are they making you go? You're an adult, you know."

"Yeah, right." She sniffed. "I don't want to leave now, but I feel like I should. They still pay for everything—"

"You make good money."

"I'm saving it. Daddy and I have an agreement. If I stay here, I'll probably have to pay my own way, mostly. But I so want to continue Everett's work. On the other hand, everything reminds me of him, and I keep thinking what things might have been if. . . ." She broke down and leaned into me so I put my arms around and held her as she cried, figuring as I did it that Sally would probably choose this moment to walk by.

A construction worker nearby saw us and whistled. I shot a

glare over Trish's shoulder, but he was too far away to see. He continued to catcall, so I broke off and led Trish away.

"I don't know if this'll cheer you up any," I said when we were away from the construction, "but I had a talk with Michelle, and she and I agreed on a name for the little dinosaur character."

"Everett wanted to name him Solomon," Trish reminded me.

"Yeah, I know. But I think we need to do something to honor his creator, don't you?"

Wet, expectant eyes stared up at me.

"We're going to call him Everett," I said. "Is that all right?"

The corners of her attractive mouth curled up in a bittersweet smile as she blinked a tear onto her cheek. She nodded.

"It's a fitting tribute," she agreed. "Although it will also be a constant reminder."

"In time, the pain will diminish."

"How long does it take?"

"I don't know yet," I admitted. "It's been almost four years since Rachel died, but I was with her since we were in junior high."

"Does it still hurt?"

"Only when I'm awake." I forced a grin.

She sighed. "Four years is a long time."

"Not when you're having fun."

"Are you having fun?"

"Yes. No. Sometimes."

"Gil . . . ?" She looked up at me doe-eyed. Uh oh, something was coming.

"What, hon?"

"Are you going to see Sally again?"

"Oh yeah. In fact, I'm going to see her in about five minutes."

"You're evading the question. You know what I mean."

I gave her a fatherly smile. "I'm thinking about it, Trish."

"Is there something special you're waiting for?"

I chuckled. "A vision from God."

She patted my arm. "I hope you get it soon. You're not getting any younger."

"Respect your elders," I cautioned. "And by the way . . . shouldn't you be getting back to work?"

"Yes sir," she replied with a salute.

As we began to go our separate directions, I called her.

"I'd really like you to stay on with me here. But if you go with your parents, that's okay too."

She smiled. "Thanks."

Harry Clark was waiting for me in his office. Sally, from her office, motioned for me to go on in.

"Sit down, Gil," Harry directed, his open hand indicating which chair. "Sorry to bother you. I know you've got a lot to do now, but I need your expertise." Suddenly I had expertise. He always knew I used to be a homicide dick, but now, since I solved the Curran killing, I'm suddenly valuable. "I called Michelle," Harry continued, "and she gave the okay."

That's nice. Didn't I have any say in the matter? Now I knew how professional athletes feel. *Lefty, I checked with the owners and they said it's okay, so you're being traded to the Cleveland Indians. We need a right-handed reliever and, well, they need someone with your expertise.*

It'd be funny if police departments worked the same way. *Officer Beckman, we've appreciated your many years of service, and, well, with your stats slipping as they have all year long now, we've decided to trade you to the sheriff's department for a rookie and two dozen doughnuts.*

This was getting funny, really. I was officially a security officer, on loan to Design and Planning (with a hefty raise) via the former Vice President of Merchandising, who was loaning me back to the Director of Security for . . . for what? For something that required my expertise? An investigation of some sort? Suddenly I was being paid management wages to work inside my hourly wage job classification.

What a cool job!

"How can I help you Harry?"

"This is very hush hush."

"Okay. Shall we lower the Cone of Silence?"

"Huh? Oh, *ha ha*. That's a good one. No, just keep this under your hat."

I nodded, refusing to make a joke about not having a hat. Hey, I have my principles. I waited for him to fill me in.

"We're missing some valuable stuff." He coughed. "Some gold bars."

"Gold bars? What gold bars?"

"From the museum safe."

"The one in the American West Museum? The one they got rid of?"

"Yeah."

"Wait a minute," I said, leaning forward and lowering my voice, caught up in the gravity of what he was saying. "Those gold and silver bars were real?"

"Quite. So were the coins."

"Are they gone too?"

"No, the coins are still here."

"Wait a minute. Start from the beginning."

"Okay. To make way for the new ride, the. . . . What is it?"

"Moonraiders."

"Yeah, Moonraiders. We had to tear down the museum, as you know. Well, we sold most of the stuff inside to New Laramie Movie Town, in Arizona, including the old Wells Fargo safe. But before we packed it up, we took out the gold and silver and put it in the main safe in the bank."

The bank Harry referred to wasn't a bank downtown but the park's own bank, where all the money was processed and counted before being transferred in an armored car to the bank downtown. It was underground, near the main gate, and at any time might contain a million or two in cash, more on a heavy day.

It was apparent Harry wasn't through, so I waited patiently as he took a sip of water. He was beginning to sweat again, only this time he hadn't been running.

"We've got a better safe in storage, and the new museum's going to be much larger."

"Wait a minute, Harry," I said for the third time in as many minutes. "What's the park doing with bullion? I thought only the government could have it."

"Mr. Golden—funny name, now that I think about it—he got permission way back to have a little for display. It's about two hundred thousand worth is all. That's why we're not making a big deal out of this."

No, I thought, that's not the reason. It's an inside job, and probably by someone high up in the organization. Bad press, that's why you're keeping it quiet. Embarrassment. A security system so lax that the only bullion outside of Fort Knox gets up and walks away. No wonder Harry was sweating.

"So what's the deal?" I asked. "What happened? Did someone in the bank walk out with it?"

"That's what we think. It was checked in and signed for—"

"Then disappeared."

"Not exactly. The box it was packed in is still in the bank's safe, but. . . ." He opened his drawer then dropped a heavy gold bar about six inches long and an inch-and-a-half wide on the desk. It was shaped roughly like a parking block.

"Is this a confession Harry?"

"Looks real, doesn't it?"

"Isn't it?"

"Nope. This is what was in the bank safe when they checked this morning. It's painted lead."

I picked and hefted it in my palm. It looked and felt pretty good to me, but then I had never seen bullion before, except in pictures. I doubted the bank employees had either. I imagined it would pale in comparison to the real thing. When I turned it over, I saw where some paint had been scratched off.

"Who at the bank had access to it?" I asked, handing it back to Harry.

"Just about all the bank employees. That's what we want you for. You've got good interrogation skills, according to Lieutenant Brown. He says you could squeeze a confession out of a nun."

"They're easy," I said. "They don't lie. Let's say I could get a T.V. preacher to cop out."

"We set up an interview schedule for tomorrow and the day after, if necessary. Eight to five. That okay?"

"Sure. But first I need some background on the people I'll be rubber hosing, so I know what I'm up against."

"I'll have it this afternoon."

I stood. Harry did likewise and extended his chubby hand. "Thanks, Gil," he said quietly. "Look, I . . . uh . . . I know we haven't utilized your abilities as much as we should have. When you get back to security full time, I don't think you'll be shaking doors on graveyard again."

"I'd appreciate that," I said. What I thought was, *I've heard that before and I'll believe it when it happens.* But I just smiled and left.

I returned to my office space in the warehouse to think, distractions or no distractions. Besides, I really didn't like total silence. It's so . . . silent. You know, like when you lie there at night in the dark, there's no outside noise, and you can hear yourself blink.

The warehouse, even in the middle of the night, had the constant hum of the florescent lights and the scraping and popping of the enormous metal shelves as they contracted. Not enough to bother me, as it wasn't a regular noise, like a clock ticking, and not potentially interesting like a radio on a volume too low to understand what's being said and you find yourself concentrating and straining to make it out.

I leaned back and put my feet up. There was suddenly a lot going on here at the park, and, as usual, I was in the middle of it. The building of new rides and refurbishing of old ones; the missing employee, now possibly a kidnap or murder victim; the finding of human remains under a decade-old thrill ride; and now the newly discovered theft of bullion.

The disappearance of the bullion didn't bother me much. Embezzlement happened all the time, in any business. Even if I couldn't get a confession from the guilty employee, I was sure I'd be able to discern who did it, at least well enough to satisfy management. A quick run through of all the bank employees, all of them who have access to the safe—

But what if the bullion never made it to the safe? We're assuming the switch was made after it was signed for. What if the phony bullion had been slipped in before the box arrived at the bank? The fake stuff looked good enough to fool the uninitiated, especially if it had been packed in a box, perhaps with some saw-dust or shredded newspaper filler, maybe with the real gold coins thrown in on top. Could that be why the coins hadn't been taken too, to provide a camouflage?

They'd have been looking at some gold and silver bars, three or four. What's to count? They look in, yeah, they're here, sign for it, that's it, into the safe. Until someone checks them later at monthly inventory.

That would mean—if that's what happened—that whoever took them to the bank might be the guilty party. I dialed Harry's number.

"This is Gil. Does your list of suspects include whoever delivered the bullion to the bank, and the person who signed for it?"

"No," he said. "The bank checked it and signed for it. We figure it had to happen after that. Besides, Dave Whelan himself dropped it off, and the bank director, Raul Torres, signed. Neither of them needs to steal."

"Well, Harry, you should know that need has nothing to do with why people steal, usually. Nonetheless, I'd like to talk to Whelan and Torres first. Think you can swing it?"

"Shouldn't be a problem. They'll be expecting it, actually."

I hung up. Okay, so much for the theft. Now, what about Lucy? Who were my suspects for that?

All male employees and construction workers. Let's see, Theo had the construction records I gave him. That left me with the employees. Who worked there then, during those months the ride was under construction? Could I narrow it down to those all important four days when the dumping of her body was likely to have occurred?

As for the missing Russell Albright, that wasn't really a park problem since he apparently was abducted off property or was simply a grown-up exercising his right to act like a child. I'd done all I could for Theo on that.

I checked my watch. Five o'clock. Time to get some dinner.

ELEVEN

Bert Gibson was manning the receiving gate, the port of entry and exit for backstage vehicular and foot traffic. He was a good kid, a gifted musician, and I hoped he'd get a shot at using his talent in a more constructive way than checking delivery trucks in and out.

Not that he minded working for security. He got to sit in his little booth for eight hours jotting down license numbers and handing out passes for them to stick in their windshields, listening to music, thinking. It was a virtual paradise for philosophers or bums or people like Bert who needed an income while waiting for something better to come along.

I made a mental note to see if I could use my influence with Michelle Yokoyama to get him an audition with the entertainment folk.

"Hey, Bert."

"Gil," he nodded, turning his FM radio down a notch.

"Still pickin' and grinnin'?" I asked.

He showed me his pearly whites to confirm at least half the answer. "How about you? You like your new gig?"

"Yeah, it's okay."

"It's okay," he mocked. "You're one of *them* now."

"Not really. It just looks that way."

"Undercover, eh? Some costume."

"Like it?"

"Nice threads, man."

"Thanks. So I see you finally got off graveyard."

"Nah, I'm doing a favor for Eddie," Bert said. "He wanted the evening off, big date or something. He'll work my shift tonight."

"After a big date?" I shook my head. "I hope you brought an extra large Thermos of black, strong coffee."

Bert shrugged. "I don't care one way or the other. All I've got to do is sit here, bone up on my rock and roll, or listen to the insomniacs call up the all night talk shows and make us think they represent mainstream America with their worthless opinions. It's pretty cool sometimes. Hold on." He leaned over to the radio and turned it up. A hot guitar solo came on.

When it was over he turned it back down, his expression was distant.

"You could do that," I said quietly. "You're better than that guy."

"That was me," he said. "Three years ago."

"No way."

"Yeah, I was goofing off at a studio a buddy of mine worked in while those guys were recording a demo. They didn't have a record deal yet. Well, they got into a big tiff about something—you know, creative stuff—and the guitar player walked out. My buddy says to them, 'Bert can fill in. You can at least get the rest of the song down, put in the guitar later when he comes back.' They said they didn't care. So I filled in. They didn't say anything at the time, but they never rerecorded the lead. They left it in."

"You're kidding. So did you get any credit or anything? A mention in the liner notes?"

"Zip. My buddy accepted some hush money, too, so I couldn't prove it. Of course, once the album came out and I heard my guitar playing, he was no longer my buddy. Since then, I've never done anything but play for my own enjoyment."

I took a hanky out and started to cry. "That's the saddest story I've ever heard."

Bert grinned. "Knock if off, Gil. I'm not asking for sympathy."

"I know. I'm just saying you should do something about it instead of letting one little incident like that sour you completely."

"Seems to me I'm not the only with that problem," Bert noted.

"I'm not sour about anything."

"You got a girlfriend?"

"Well. . . ."

"Why not?"

"Okay, you made your point. Here's the proposition: I'll get a girlfriend if you get a job playing your guitar." It was a bet I had no intention of trying to win.

"It's not that easy," Bert complained.

"I know, but I'm willing to risk it."

"No, I mean getting a guitar job isn't as easy as getting a girlfriend."

"It'll never happen sitting out here in the booth, that's for sure. Tell you what." I told him I'd get him an audition with park entertainment. That way, if it didn't work out, he could slip right back in the security booth and that would be the end of the experiment. I only hoped I could live up to my end of the deal.

"Deal," Bert said. "Loser buys lunch. Say, what's all the hub-bub I've been hearing about? All the cops here the other day? Eddie was telling me about it but he didn't know any particulars. We have another one?"

He was alluding to the murder of Everett Curran. Bert had helped catch one of the bad guys as he tried to drive past Bert's booth without stopping, and Bert tossed his stool through the windshield.

"Not exactly," I said. "They were digging for a new ride where the Starcoaster used to be, found some skeletonized remains."

"Like, a human?"

I nodded.

"Cool!" he said, genuinely impressed. "You know, with Hayes and Brito croaking that kid, you getting to work with the big shots, and now them finding some dead person buried under a ride, this is starting to be a pretty cool place to work."

What could I do but smile? He was right.

"If you only knew what else was going on. . . ." I said mysteriously. "But if I told you, I'd have to kill you."

"Go ahead, man. Working out here in the booth, I doubt I'd notice the difference."

I recalled the fake bullion as I alluded to the theft and the lead the phonies were made of.

"Say, Bert, maybe you know. . . . Do they use lead here in large quantities for anything?"

He thought a minute. "Yeah. It comes in a couple times a year in large blocks. I think they use it for counter weights on some of the rides, and on the trains for ballast or something. Yeah, for sure on the trains."

"So they keep it backstage? In the train barn maybe?"

He shrugged. "Probably. Why?" He raised one eyebrow in suspicion.

"Just curious."

"Yeah, right." He grinned. "When it's over, will you tell me about it, whatever it is?"

"Sure."

"Let me know if I can help," he offered. "Force 'em to come this way, I've still got my stool."

I laughed and waved as I walked away shaking my head. Bert was definitely bored.

And I was definitely coming back later, to take a ride on the Reading.

I barely made it to Hollie's Hut. The old gal—my van, that is, not Hollie—coughed and sputtered and gagged and finally wheezed her last as I coasted into the lot.

No doubt about it, I needed another car. I didn't think the van was worth fixing . . . too many problems. Wouldn't you know it? Right after I spend a day cleaning and polishing it, making it look good.

At least it could have an open casket.

I took off my coat and tie, replacing them with a pullover sweater, and traded my suit pants and dress shoes for a pair of denims and white leather basketball shoes I kept for emergencies, dressing quickly in the rear of the van. I grabbed a couple flashlights and took them with me, as well.

I thought of walking home after eating and possibly having

the van towed in the morning to the shop—just in case it was something simple and I could squeeze a few more months out of her—but I'd still need a ride to the park tonight. I could have asked Hollie, I suppose, but we weren't that close, and I didn't want to give her any ideas that I wasn't willing to follow up on. Not that she wasn't nice plus attractive. But she wasn't a Christian, to my knowledge. Nor was I particularly attracted to her. She was a casual friend, that's all. But, given the right—rather, the wrong—circumstances. . . .

Temptation is a powerful force, and my way of escape in this case was to head it off at the pass.

I couldn't call Theo for a ride, either. He was being overworked because of all this and needed whatever rest and relaxation he could get. I didn't really want to call anyone from the church, although I'm sure someone would have been happy to do it. You know how it is; they all have families, or activities to attend, and you feel like you're putting them out.

The dayshift guys from security were young and had their own agendas; the swingshift guys were working, and my old crew, the graveyard slugs, were sleeping.

I smiled. That left Sally. I entered the restaurant—I could find my way blindfolded, following my nose like they do in the cartoons when a wafting, waving white smoke of odor lifts them off the ground by the nostrils and reels them in—and headed for the pay phone.

Sally picked up on the second ring. I explained my plight to her, apologizing profusely.

"Sure, Gil, I'd be happy to. I have to go to the library anyway and return some books. Do you mind?"

"No, of course not," I confirmed. "Sally, have you eaten?"

"No."

"Why don't you come on down now, I'll buy you dinner then go to the library with you. I've always wondered what one looked like."

"Okay. Be there in a little bit. Is casual okay?"

"Maybe you could put on an evening gown, black with a sequined bodice, sleeveless with black gloves up over the elbow, a single strand of dainty pearls tight around the base of your neck—or jeans, your choice."

She said she thought she could find a pair of jeans and hung up.

I took my usual table and told Angela I was waiting for someone, that coffee would be all for now. She brought a whole pot.

"You got it, big boy," she said, smiling and winking.

I grinned back, but after I thought about it, I wondered if she had meant anything by it. Nah, probably just my imagination. I'd gone from never thinking about women to thinking about them constantly. That realization led to thinking about Hollie. Where was she?

I wasn't long in finding out. I hadn't had two cups of coffee when she wandered out from the back office and spied me, making her way over with a smile.

For the first time, I saw her with the eyes of a male companion, not just a business acquaintance. I have to admit, I liked what I saw, but knew, deep down inside, it was a dead end.

"Hi Gil."

"Hey Hollie."

"Not eating tonight?"

"Huh? Oh, yeah. Later. I'm waiting for someone."

"Oh?"

"Yeah. . . . Friend of mine . . . from work."

Well, it was true.

"In fact," I said, looking toward the restaurant lobby, "there she is now."

At the word *she,* I could have sworn Hollie's face flickered, but I couldn't tell whether it was disappointment, surprise, or just some feminine acquiescence, whatever that is. She just reacted; no more, no less.

"Friend from work," Hollie repeated with a bittersweet grin. "Yeah, right." She got up.

I stood and waved, and Sally came over, somewhat tentative when she saw Hollie.

"Sally, this is Hollie. She runs the joi—the restaurant. Best food in town."

"Best *restaurant* food in town," Hollie corrected, more sensitive to Sally's feelings than me.

"That's what I meant," I said weakly in self-defense. "Hollie, this is Sally."

They greeted each other and shook hands in that limp, womanly way that I always find fascinating, being old-fashioned. Women ought to nod their heads and smile, or if they know each other they should hug or something. Handshaking just seems so . . . male.

So sue me. I'm a chauvinist, okay? And proud of it.

"You look familiar," Hollie observed.

"I come in all the time," I said.

"Not you, Gilbert. I was talking to Sally."

"I've been in before," Sally explained. "Usually at lunch time. My boss likes it here."

"Who's your boss?"

"Harry Clark, from the park."

"Clark from the park," I sang.

"Harry," mused Hollie.

"A little bald guy with the cheesy clothes," I prompted, drawing a look of benevolent disdain from Sally. I ignored it. "How come bald guys are named Harry?" I asked no one in particular.

"I think I know him," Hollie said.

"Didn't you used to. . . ." Sally started to ask Hollie, but faded out when she couldn't come up with the right term.

"Wait tables? Yeah. Up until my mom died. Now it's mine."

"I'm sorry," Sally said. "About your mom, I mean."

"Thanks. Listen, you two are probably hungry. We could stand here all night and chat. I'll have Angela come right over. Nice meeting you, Sally. Gilbert . . . a pleasure as always." She turned and disappeared into the back.

When we had settled in, Sally locked eyes with me. "You nervous about something?"

"Why?"

"The way you acted when she and I were talking. Like you were trying to sabotage the conversation."

I shrugged. I couldn't lie so I acted ignorant. "Sorry."

"She's nice," Sally went on. "Attractive, too."

"Think so?" I said, turning around in my seat as if to look at Hollie again like I hadn't really noticed her before.

Sally ignored my acting. "I saw her sitting with you when I came in. Known her for long?"

"Oh, we go way back. I've eaten here for years, even before I came to the park."

"I hope my arrival wasn't premature. I mean, I hope I didn't interrupt anything."

Picking up my menu without expression, I said: "No, not at all. She often sits down with me, at least now that she's not waiting tables any longer."

Sally glanced over at Hollie, who was talking to Melody at the register.

"She's . . . tall."

"Huh? Oh, yeah, I guess she is." I knew Sally meant more than that but didn't let on. I suspected this was some kind of test, some woman competition thing. I changed the subject.

"So, what'll you have?"

"Just a salad, I think."

Angela saw me nod and came over, pen in hand, and we ordered. While we waited I told Sally about the bullion and explained what I was going to look for in the train barn.

"I'd like to find the secret warehouse, too," I said. "You know, the one where they've stored all the really neat stuff they're going to put in the new museum."

"Why?"

"Partly curiosity, I guess. And partly because it's a secret. Since I'm going to be in there skulking around, I might as well have some fun."

"I'm not so sure—"

"It's official business, this time," I assured her.

"Well, unless it's in a basement somewhere, there's only one place it could be."

"Which is . . . ?"

"Somewhere in the middle of the old building, where Jerry Opperman's office is. It used to house Design and Planning, the carpenter shop, all the offices. It was the only building here when Mr. Golden started the park."

"But where's the door? There'd have to be a door large enough to move things in and out easily." I thought about it. The park was nothing but facade and illusion, why should the backstage be any different?

"You know, I bet it's hidden," I concluded. "Behind a false wall or something."

"What do you think is in there?"

"I don't know, but it must be important or it wouldn't be such a secret. Maybe even some gold and silver bullion."

She gave me a funny look. A serious, funny look. "Are you saying. . . ."

"That it might be an insurance scam?" I kept my eyes on her while I took a sip of my coffee. "It crossed my mind."

After I'd paid for the meal, Sally went out to her car while I retired to the men's room. Coming out, I met Hollie in the hall-way.

"I watched you two," she said quietly.

"Oh?"

"Yes. Sally's got her eye on you, Gil. But I suppose you knew that or you wouldn't be here with her. You two serious?"

"No, we're usually pretty lighthearted and fun—"

"You know what I mean."

"Well . . . I wouldn't—"

"You should be."

"What makes you say that?"

"The way she looked at you when you weren't looking. She's in love with you, Gil. I'd bet the restaurant on it."

I didn't know what to say. That was an exciting thought, albeit a scary one. But I didn't want to react too much in front of Hollie. I don't know why, I was just uncomfortable.

"Do you date?"

"A few times."

Hollie put her hand on my arm. "Get with the program, Gil. Rachel's gone. You loved her deeply, still do. But your life goes on. Look at me, honey."

I had been inspecting my shoes, but obeyed.

"I was all primed to make a play for you, Gil. You're a sweet guy. But she's more your type, and I think you'd be great together. Now go on, do something about it before I change my mind."

With that she kissed me lightly on the mouth and disappeared into the kitchen.

"You okay?" Sally asked when I got in the passenger side of her Toyota.

"Uh . . . yeah, why?"

"I don't know. You look kind of funny. Your face is flushed."

"Hmm. Uh . . . no, I'm fine. Just excited about tonight. Going to the park, I mean. Skulking around always makes me this way. I enjoy it." It was true, and I didn't think she needed to know about my conversation with Hollie.

She pulled out of the lot, past my crippled van. I watched it sadly as we drove slowly by.

"You still okay about the library?" she asked.

"Huh?"

"The library."

"Oh . . . yeah. Sure." I was still having trouble thinking. My lips were tingling.

"You can wait out here if you like," Sally said as she pulled up in front of the library. "I'll just be a second."

"No, that's okay. I'll come with you."

While she attended to her business I dawdled near the checkout counter and looked around at the place. There was quiet talking going on, and no one was shushing anybody. The librarians were all younger than I remembered them. Still older than me, but younger than they used to be. And none of them wore buns or had scowls lining their faces. A bank of computers had replaced the old card file. This was not my father's library.

Another video display inside an attractive wood box sat off by itself on a counter. There was no keyboard in front of it, and I wandered over out of curiosity and touched the screen. It blinked on, surprising me. I stepped back and looked at my fin-

124

ger, not realizing I looked for all the world like I'd just come out of a coma after twenty years.

A touch control screen. This could be fun.

COUNTY RECORDS the screen proclaimed. Below that it had several lines of titles, things like FICTITIOUS BUSINESS NAMES, PROPERTY RECORDS, and BIRTH CERTIFICATES.

I touched BIRTH CERTIFICATES. The screen flashed and changed, and the alphabet appeared in two rows at the bottom. The instructions said to touch in *last name [space] first name*, then the birthdate in six digits, like 010165. I wasn't born in the county so I thought a minute and entered ALBRIGHT RUSSELL 061149. Then I touched the word ENTER.

The screen went blank. I thought I'd broken it and started looking for my escape route, then it blinked back on.

> RECORD LOCATED.
> COST $5.00
> DO YOU WANT A COPY?
> [YES] [NO]

Sally came over.

"What are you doing?"

"Having fun, mostly." I touched [YES]. The screen flickered and said THANK YOU, then went blank again and stayed that way.

We stared at it a few moments, then Sally said, "A fool and his money."

"I didn't put anything in it."

"Over here." The hushed voice came from behind us. I turned and a pleasant-faced librarian behind the checkout counter motioned us over.

"I . . . uh . . . ," I started to explain.

"It takes a few minutes. What did you order?"

"Birth certificate."

"Okay. That'll be five dollars."

I paid her, and in a few minutes she came out of an office with a fax.

"Thank you, Mr. Albright." She held it out.

"Uh . . . thank you," I said, taking it from her. It was a digitally transmitted copy of Albright's birth certificate.

"What're you going to do with that?" Sally asked after we climbed into her car.

"I don't know. Maybe Theo can use it to call the parents or something."

Without comment, Sally started her car and headed to the park. We left it in the employee lot and carded our way past the night guard, even though he knew us. Rules were rules, and you never knew when a supervisor was hiding in the bushes.

Bert was still at the receiving gate.

"Eddie didn't show, huh?" I asked.

"Evening, Gil." He noticed Sally. "That's not fair. Our bet can't start until I get off work at least. Evening Sally."

"You snooze, you lose," I said. Sally was perplexed, but I had no intention of explaining it.

"Eddie called," Bert went on. "Said he had a flat tire. He'll be here later."

"I'll bet he had a flat."

Bert smiled. "And I believe in the tooth fairy, too."

"Listen, Bert, do me a favor."

"Name it."

"Don't tell anyone we're here, okay?"

"Sure. What'cha up to?" He held up his hand. "Don't say it. I know. Tell me later." He shook his head with a grin. "As a matter of fact, maybe it's better I don't know." He smiled at Sally. "He'll get you in trouble."

"I'm finding that out," Sally said wryly.

I led the way, Sally alongside, to the train barn. It was wide open, as usual, but empty, as all the trains were inside the park, which was now closed. They were only brought back here for painting and maintenance. We wandered around the barn, using the flashlights I'd brought. After only a few minutes, Sally called me.

"Over here. Is this it?"

I picked my way around the clutter to her. "Yep, that's it."

In the corner was a pile of large, lead fragments: used wheel weights, scraps, and assorted odds and ends, next to several large bricks of shiny new lead.

"How do you think he did it?" Sally asked.

126

"It'd be easy enough," I said. "A small mold made out of wood, or plaster, pour molten lead in, wait a few minutes, *voila*. Clean it, paint it, instant gold or silver bullion."

"How'd he heat it?"

"Simple. Lead is soft, has a low melting temperature. You could do it on your stove. Sets quickly, too."

"What'd he paint it with?"

"Paint, most likely."

"I mean—"

"I know what you mean. I was joking. Let's look around some more."

We had just started to move when I heard tires on the gravel outside the barn, then an engine.

"Hide!" I whispered.

We ducked behind some 50-gallon drums and held our breath. A spotlight swept past us, and I could see Sally shaking. I put my finger to my lips, and she nodded hesitantly, while Bert's warning ran through my mind. Sally's too, I'll bet. In a moment, the car went away.

"Security mobile unit," I told her as I helped her up. "Routine checks. He won't be back any time soon."

"How would we explain this?" she asked.

"Not a problem. Harry commissioned me to investigate this, remember?"

"You, not me."

"That's why we're sneaking around. Hey, you could have waited in the car."

"Sit in the cold, dark car for who knows how long? No thank you."

"Come on, then. Back to work." I took her hand—for the first time ever, I might add—and led her across the train barn to a workbench, letting go reluctantly when we got there. I have to admit, I felt a slight tingle when we touched. Yeah, I know. That sounds corny. But it's what I felt.

I shined my light around, searching, finally coming to rest on a shelf. There were rows of spray paint cans.

"Look here." I pointed to a can of silver and a can of gold, next to each other. They were mingled with others—blue, flat black, copper—but they were the only two colors I was interested in.

"How do you know these are the cans he used?" Sally asked as I took them carefully off the shelf and dropped them into a small box I'd found on the floor.

"I don't. Theo can have it analyzed and compared to the paint on the fake bullion. That'll tell us for sure, but it seems likely he'd use what was available."

As soon as I'd said that, it was like a veil has been lifted, and I stopped.

"What is it?" Sally asked.

"It seems like a veil's been lifted," I said. "Everything the thief used was readily available here. I don't think this was necessarily pre-planned. It could have been a spur-of-the-moment thing."

"What does that mean?" Then she added when she saw the smirk start to form on my face: "And don't explain *spur-of-the-moment*. You know what I'm asking."

"It means, Sally, that whoever got the idea to steal the bullion had to have known the lead and paint were accessible, in addition to having free access to the gold."

"Which means . . . ?" she prompted.

"Whelan," I pronounced. "He delivered it to the bank, and he's in charge of all this." I swept my arm in a wide arc. "No one would question him being in here, anytime of the day or night."

"Are you taking those cans to Theo?"

"Not directly. I've got a friend at the P.D., forensic specialist. She'll check them for prints for me. It's a long shot, maybe, but. . . ." I shrugged.

As we walked through the yard toward the old building I stopped.

"You up to looking for the warehouse?"

"The secret one?"

"Yeah. It'll be fun. Like Indiana Jones."

"We don't have keys."

"I'll borrow Bert's."

"I don't know. . . ."

"Wait here."

I hurried off before she could protest, telling her to keep in the shadows and not move. I came back a few minutes later with Bert's keys and without my box of spray cans, which I'd left in Bert's booth with instructions not to touch them, not unless he wanted to become a suspect. I didn't tell him of what.

Sally was still reluctant, so I grabbed her hand again, this time not letting go until we were at Jerry Opperman's door.

I let us in, looking both ways, locking the door behind us.

"You know," I said slowly, "Miss Potter told me Opperman's first project was the Starcoaster. He was awfully upset when we found Lucy. He wanted her dug up quick and carted off. I wonder if that's because he knew about her."

"You mean, like he knew ahead of time she was there?" Sally's eyes widened.

I nodded solemnly. "Like maybe he had something to do with it. The timing is right." I unlocked his office door.

"What are you doing?" Sally was aghast. "This is why you wanted to come in here, isn't it? You didn't just think about Opperman, you suspected him all along."

"Not all along, just this afternoon. Honest."

"Still, we can't go in there."

"Why not? Security does it all the time."

"Not to snoop."

"Look, Sal, this is how we catch crooks. It's how we nailed Hayes and Brito."

"You go on," she said.

"Okay. Wait here."

"Where would I go?"

I clicked open the door and went in, closing it behind me. In about three seconds, she knocked lightly. I opened it, and Sally joined me inside. When I gave her a quizzical look, she grinned sheepishly.

"It's spooky out there."

I smiled and began rummaging around while Sally, intrigued by all the talk about Opperman's chair, sat down in it. When she accidentally turned on the Vibramassage, she yelped, and jumped out. I clamped my hand over her mouth and flipped the switch off.

"Don't touch," I suggested in a whisper. She nodded obediently.

There was nothing to find, and after fifteen minutes I gave up. I left, fighting the urge to fiddle with his chair, Sally close behind. Outside in the hall, I considered the doors.

"That's the archives, that's a conference room, that's his private potty. . . ." I pointed to each door in turn. "That's the only one I don't know what it is."

It was labeled SUPPLIES.

What supply closet did you ever see that had not one, but two dead bolts? I tried all the keys but could only get one dead bolt unlocked.

"Wait a minute," Sally said. "If you were them, how would you protect this room?"

"Guard dog?"

"Did you read *The Hobbit*?"

"A guard dragon?"

"No, remember how the entrance was disguised?"

"Okay, they did that. It looks like a supply cabinet."

"What about the key?"

"Give the key to the person most likely not to lose it."

"Someone who would always be around."

"The person least likely to be asked for it."

"The most trusted and unapproachable person in the park."

I smiled, and we both said, "The Dragon Lady."

We retreated to Miss Potter's office and checked her cabinets. Sure enough, on a hook under the well of her desk, way at the back and out of sight unless you were under the desk, was a lone key marked SUPPLIES.

"Could this be it?" Sally said, holding it up to me.

"If it's not, I'll be suppliesed," I said.

It fit, but didn't turn easily. I didn't think it had been used in a long while, which would preclude anything germane to the theft being in here. But I wasn't going to stop now, even if the room had nothing to do with the missing bullion. I pushed the door open slowly, a musty odor rushing out to greet us. Feeling for a light switch, I flipped it up, and several overhead bulbs flickered on. One of them immediately burned out.

This was certainly no supply closet but a surprisingly large room filled with boxes and crates and huge irregularly-shaped objects covered with sheets and tarps. A pair of wood-spoked wheels with skinny black tires peeked out from beneath one tarp. Pulling up the bottom edge, I shined my light underneath and whistled low. I was looking at a brand new Model T Ford.

"Holy cow," I breathed, wondering what other treasures could be in here. Did the owners know what they had?

We walked down a narrow aisle slowly, almost reverently. I wouldn't have been surprised to find the Ark of the Covenant and reminded myself not to touch it if I did.

"Look here," Sally said in a half-whisper. It was in a glass case. A mask. A gold mask of a human face, a young man, with blue horizontal stripes on the headpiece that hung down behind the face like hair. He wore a hat with a snake on it. We looked at each other.

"No way," we both said. We covered it up, not wanting to know any more.

I uncovered a large box, four-feet-long, four-feet-wide, by a foot deep, made out of plexiglass and mounted on a pedestal. Inside was what appeared to be a large diorama. I blew the dust off it.

Sally sneezed. "What is it?"

"A large diorama." It was of a portion of the park, with scale buildings and trees and people and litter. Whenever they build a new ride, they have a model built to show what it will look like. They use them for promotional things and news releases and such until the ride is opened. I didn't know they kept them, but figured, if that was the case, they had the whole park here in model form.

"Looks like the Starcoaster," Sally said.

"Isn't that the receiving gate, right next to it?"

Sally nodded. "Looks like it."

"Who worked the gate at night ten years ago?" I wondered out loud, not expecting a response.

"That's easy," Sally said. "Fred Billings. He worked there for years before they stuck him out in the employee lot." She looked at me, the possibility becoming clear. "You think he might have seen the man who buried Lucy?"

"It's been a long time, and the odds are against it. Not even a bad novel would have the solution to the mystery solved by a coincidence like that. Besides, even if he did see someone, I doubt he'd remember." I sighed. "Oh, well. At least we solved one mystery. We found this room."

"Yes," said Sally, "but we can't tell." She held up the key. "Miss Potter."

The wind blew. A dog howled. A chill ran up my spine.

TWELVE

I was late for the interviews.

I'd had the yellow behemoth towed from the Hollie's Hut parking lot to a shop. The mechanic just stood there, shaking his head. Rebuild the engine, he said. Fifteen hundred dollars, he said. But I'd still have an old vehicle and things would keep going wrong with it, he said. I said, you don't happen to own a car sales lot, do you? He laughed and said no, that he could get it running for about two hundred but couldn't guarantee it would last very long. I said go ahead, and he gave me a ride to work.

Raul Torres was first, and his interview proceeded without a hitch. He was relaxed, forthright, and I believed he was telling the truth—he didn't look away when answering, didn't fidget or play with the paper clips I left on the table in front of his chair.

He told me he received a phone call from Whelan saying the bullion was on its way. Whelan arrived about fifteen minutes later with a box. He opened the flaps for Torres who glanced in, saw several gold bars and one silver, and a small canvas sack of gold coins. The box was then sealed with strapping tape, placed in the main safe, and Torres signed for it.

No, Whelan hadn't appeared nervous. He didn't say anything about the bullion in particular, hadn't tried to keep Torres from taking the bars out and inspecting them—and Torres hadn't done so, having not thought about it. He didn't know what bullion looked like anyway, had no reason to be suspicious.

When I asked what caused them to open the box a few days ago, he told me it was routine. He wasn't there, and the on-duty supervisor was curious.So during an otherwise standard accounting of the other contents of the safe, he departed from procedure—sealed bundles aren't supposed to be unsealed except just prior to a transfer—and pulled a bar out in the presence of two others. When he turned it over he saw what appeared to be a drip with a partial fingerprint in it. That looked odd to him so he scratched at it and the color came off. That's when they found out it was painted lead. He put it back and called Torres.

When Whelan came in for his turn on the hot seat, I recalled our meeting in his office during the Curran investigation. He seemed composed now as he had been that day, but with himself as the subject of this interview, he soon began to sweat.

To his credit, though, he looked me in the eye throughout. If he was lying, he did a good job of it.

"Mr. Whelan," I said solemnly after we'd been at it about a half-hour. I leaned toward him and crossed my arms on the table in front of me. "Do you know where we keep the lead around here and for what purpose?"

"Of course. In the train barn. We use it for weights and quick molding jobs."

"And spray paint. Is that kept on the premises?"

"In every shop and maintenance shed we have—for quick touch-up work."

"I assume you've gathered that that's how the fake bullion was made."

"I suppose it's possible."

"Do bank employees have access to it?"

"Not in their regular course of business. But employees wander all around backstage. They could come in at night and do it."

Whelan was now imagining how someone else could have committed the crime, a classic dodge. Innocent people usually just shake their heads, they don't know. The guilty tend to think up ways others could have done it, "helping" the detective look in another direction rather than toward them.

"Possible," I conceded. "But not very likely. When you delivered the box to Mr. Torres, he checked it then taped it. Is that correct?"

"Yes."

"Did you know that when it was opened the other day, there was no evidence that the tape had been disturbed?"

"How could I know that? What are you getting at?"

"This: The bullion was replaced before you turned it over to the bank. The bullion you delivered was fake."

"Are you accusing me? I thought we knew each other better than that."

"No," I said truthfully, "I'm not accusing you. I'm just telling you the facts I have to deal with. How long after the bullion was taken out of the old safe did you deliver it?"

"I don't exactly know."

"No? Well, did anyone watch you remove it?"

As I said this, a strange look came across his face, as if he'd just come to the realization of a great philosophical truth.

Whelan cocked his head slightly, perplexed. "I thought you knew," he said. "I didn't take it out myself. I delegated the job."

"To whom?" I asked.

"Russell Albright."

I sat in Harry's office across the desk from him, studying his face as he pondered the implications of this news with animated eyebrows and puffing cheeks. We canceled all the other interviews, at least for the time being.

"So, Albright took the bullion and disappeared, eh?" he said after a few minutes of contemplation.

"That would be the obvious conclusion," I agreed, "but I don't think it's necessarily that simple."

Harry looked intrigued. "Oh?"

I shook my head. "There's other factors to consider. First, it seems he has met with foul play. You know about his car being found . . . with blood in it."

"Of course," Harry said curtly.

"Until now, that didn't make sense. He had nothing for anyone to steal, that we knew of. But if someone did kill him for the bullion, that would almost surely mean they knew about it in advance. That would point to an accomplice."

"Whelan?" Harry asked apprehensively.

"Possibly, but I tend to doubt it. Murder for money doesn't

seem like Whelan's bag. I'd be more inclined to think it was a co-worker of Albright's. Call me prejudiced, but I tend to suspect people with less to lose first, unless there's evidence of gambling debts, that kind of thing in Whelan's life."

"Who then?"

I shrugged. "No clue. But there's another possibility, too—one that could involve Whelan." I paused, just to make sure Harry was listening.

"Go on."

"Whelan could have pulled it off alone and is setting up Albright to take the fall. Whelan's not dumb, he could do it."

"Yes, he's smart enough. But murder? You just said that wasn't Whelan's—"

"I don't think Whelan could have discovered that Albright took the bullion, then killed him for it and dumped his body—or at least his car—in the desert. I think, if there is an accomplice, they were on the lam with Albright and decided to pull a double-cross. As for Whelan, he's smart enough to have stolen the bullion and made it look like Albright took it. After all, who told Albright to unload the safe? Besides, Albright had no way of knowing in advance he would be unloading it."

"I see what you mean. But could Whelan kill him to keep him silent?"

"I'll admit, that part of the theory bothers me. But you were a cop long enough to know very few people can be absolutely predicted. Did you ever hear of anybody who wasn't surprised when their normal-looking neighbor turned out to be a killer?"

He shook his head, not in disagreement but acknowledging the sad truth. He knew I was right.

"But you keep saying you don't think Dave could kill, then you explain how he could have pulled it off," Harry pointed out.

I smiled. "I like Dave. I want to believe he wasn't involved. But too many of the possibilities point to him. Except one. Albright did it on the spur of the moment, alone. If that's the case, though, what happened to him?"

We were both silent at that sobering thought, each in our own way trying to think of an answer, trying to put the pieces of the puzzle together. We couldn't. There were too many pieces still missing.

"So what now?" I asked. "We've got to tell the cops."

"No."

"What do you mean, no? They're already investigating Albright. Lieutenant Brown will be seriously peeved when he finds out we kept this from him."

"This is still a park matter. Until there is some connection between the theft of the bullion and foul play to Albright, you're to keep it to yourself. Besides, I'm under orders."

"Whose?" I had no right to ask that but couldn't help myself. Normally Harry wouldn't have told me. He'd just give me a look and ask if there wasn't something I was supposed to be doing. But apparently things had changed between us—not a lot, but by a degree or two—although I wasn't sure when or why. No longer was I the lowly door-shaker, and he took me into his confidence.

"Opperman."

I groaned. I should have known.

"With all due respect, Harry, this now transcends Opperman's personal motivation for saving the park's face. This could be material evidence in a homicide."

Harry pretended he wasn't listening.

"Look, you don't need to say a word. I'll handle it."

The corners of his mouth curled up slightly.

"In the meantime, do you want Whelan tailed or anything?" I asked.

"No. We'll sit on it for now, let the police investigate the Albright case. If it looks like Whelan might be involved—but only to the extent that he's somehow tied in with Albright—we'll do a full disclosure. Can you live with that?"

"You know me, Harry." I stood.

"What's that supposed to mean?"

I winked. "Better you don't ask."

I returned to my warehouse office, did a little paperwork, made a few phone calls regarding the Moonraiders construction, checked on how Trish was faring in D and P, and made myself a cup of hot tea.

As I sipped the orange pekoe, I ran the Albright affair through my mind for the umpteenth time, trying to find a clear path through the maze of fact and conjecture, the known and the guessed at. I likened it to a U.S. Marshal tracking an outlaw by following trail sign: a horseshoe print, a bent blade of grass, a small cloud of dust in the distance.

Best guess. That was all I really had. But that was a starting place, a springboard for which direction I—rather, Theo— should go to collect the facts that, when woven together, would answer the riddle.

I put my hand on the receiver to call the lieutenant but stopped myself before completing the dialing process. A phone call or two, perhaps clearing up some issues and saving the busy detective valuable time, wouldn't be unwarranted. After all, Albright was an employee here, I told myself.

His file—my copy of it, at least—was in my drawer. Would the contents mean something to me now that there was a possibility Albright was involved in the theft of the bullion? I retrieved it and extracted his application. My first question—and Theo's, once he knew about the bullion—was whether Albright had any history of theft from his employers.

I dialed the number of his former boss in Harrisburg, Illinois, as listed on his application.

"Sparta Engineering," said a female voice.

"Mr. Lyle Webber, please."

"One moment." Easy-listening music by Kenny Rogers entertained me while I waited for about thirty seconds.

"Webber."

"Mr. Webber, this is Gil Beckman." I told him who I represented.

"I've heard of your amusement park," he said. "Never been there, though. Maybe some day."

"We'd love to have you. Listen, I'm doing a routine check on an employee. He listed your company as his last job.

"Sure. What's his name?"

"Russell Albright."

There was silence in Illinois for a few seconds, then Webber said, "Are you sure that's the name?"

"Yes, I'm sure. It's been a long time since he worked there. Fifteen years."

"Fifteen years?"

"Do you know him?"

"I've worked for this company for twenty-five years. I'm president now. I don't recall the name offhand, but let me check."

"Thank you."

A haunting saga by a female singer had replaced Mr. Rogers. I heard most of the song by the time Webber returned.

"No sir, Mr. Beckman. We've had no one work here by that name, ever."

"Okay, thank you."

"I hope I was a help. I don't know why someone would say they worked here when they didn't."

"He listed you by name as his supervisor."

"He did? That's really bizarre. What's this guy look like?"

I gave him Albright's description.

"Sounds pretty common," Webber said pensively. "Doesn't ring any particular bells, you know what I mean?"

"Have you had any employees that quit or were fired for theft? Or for that matter, have you ever had a major employee theft or a problem of any sort?"

"No, no thefts. There's been no real problems here—well, except for one guy, and that really had nothing to do with the company. One of our employees, Lloyd Mercer, was murdered. Left a wife and three kids."

"Did they catch the killer?"

"No, never did. The guy's body was dumped in the Wabash."

"The Wa-what?"

"Sorry, I forgot you weren't calling from around here. The Wabash River. They never solved it."

"Any other employees suspected?"

"Oh, no. No way. We were all questioned, of course, but I could vouch for everyone. We were all here at work when it happened."

I thought for a second but didn't have any revelations, so I thanked him and hung up. So, Albright had lied on his application. But why? And what, if anything, did that mean to us now? I fiddled with Albright's file, and my eyes landed on the birth certificate I'd gotten from the library. It'd been forty years, but it couldn't hurt to try.

Directory assistance provided the phone numbers for an Alvin Albright, in town. The likelihood of it being the right Alvin Albright was slim, but there are people who never move, who stay in their hometown for life. Maybe he was one of them. He answered on the fifth ring, an elderly man with a gravelly voice, the kind damaged by years of smoking and liquor.

I identified myself and explained my dilemma.

"One of our employees is missing. He disappeared, and there is a possibility of foul play. His name is Russell Albright and I obtained a copy of his birth certificate. It lists a man with your name as his father."

"Well, that's mighty strange," Alvin Albright said slowly. "What's the man's birthdate?" I told him, and the mother's maiden name, and I heard him suck in a raspy breath. "There must be a mistake," he said. "That's my son's birth certificate, but he can't be your missing employee."

"Why is that, sir?"

"Because my son died when he was six months old. Crib death. They call it SIDS now, I think."

Instead of clearing things up, the more I found out, the muddier the waters became. Every piece of information was another stir of the stick. Was this just a really weird coincidence? Was Albright born somewhere else on the same day as another Russell Albright was born here? Possible, I suppose, but too coincidental for me to be comfortable with.

Boy, this was nagging at me. An obscure past, a mysterious disappearance, a former employer who never heard of him. . . .

I dialed Illinois again and got Webber on the horn.

"Hi. Gil Beckman. Sorry to bother you again, but there's a new wrinkle to this that's really bugging me." I explained about the birth certificate, then asked, "Why would this guy pick your company, and how would he know you?"

"I'm sure I don't know."

"Could it be someone who'd applied there and didn't get hired?"

"Could be, but I have no way of checking."

"Are you sure the description doesn't sound familiar?"

"It's so general. A lot of our employees fit it. It even sounds the same as the guy who got murdered."

"And they found his body in the Wabash."

"No, I never said they found his body. I said he was dumped in the river."

"How do you know that if they didn't find his body?"

"That's just what the cops concluded. He left work one day, early as I recall, said he wasn't feeling well but never made it home. About three, four days later they found his car, parked in a clearing off a dirt road on the top of a bluff overlooking the river. The window was broken, and there was blood on the seat—his blood."

"Did they drag the river?"

"Yeah. They found three bodies," Webber said with a chuckle, "but none of them were his. They explained that the current could have dragged him anywhere downstream before he popped up to the surface, or he could have gotten caught in something underwater and never come up, or been picked up somewhere else and never identified. He was declared legally dead. His wife and kids still live in Pankeyville, south of here. Two older kids are married, of course, and gone on their own."

"When was this?"

"Fifteen years ago."

"Do you have a fax machine?"

"Yes sir," he said and gave me the number.

"Okay," I said. "I'll fax you a photo, then call you back in about fifteen minutes." I hung up.

I raced to security and slipped Albright's photo into the fax machine, then ran back to my office and called Webber again. He picked up before the first ring had finished.

"It's him, Mr. Beckman, it's him! This is a picture of my murdered employee!"

THIRTEEN

"A re you certain?" I asked.

"Well, he looks a little older here, but I'm sure it's him." He paused, and I could imagine him, stunned, looking off into space as the reality hit him. He was thinking about the wife and kids Albright—or rather Lloyd Mercer—left behind, who for fifteen years have believed him to be dead, brutally murdered.

The shock that he was not only alive but apparently had abandoned them . . . what would that do to them?

Then again, maybe he was now really dead—no, wait, the irony was too great to accept. Fifteen years ago he disappears, his vehicle is found in a remote area with blood in it, body never recovered. And now he disappears again—only under another name—his vehicle found in a remote area with blood in it . . . and we're missing two-hundred-thousand dollars in gold bullion.

I thanked Webber and told him I'd get back to him later with more details and asked him to keep quiet about this until we could confirm it. He also gave me Mercer's wife's name and number.

I pressed the disconnect button without hanging up and punched in Theo's number.

I left work that evening feeling pretty good. Although I couldn't say I'd solved the case of the missing bullion—there were too many unanswered questions and other viable possibilities that hadn't been ruled out, such as whether or not Mercer had an accomplice—I did feel we'd taken a giant step toward the solution.

But what a solution. Out of nowhere—Pankeyville, Illinois, to be precise—a fifteen-year-old unsolved murder turns out to have been a scam perpetrated by the victim for reasons unknown, who then fled across the country adopting the identity of a dead baby who would have been approximately his age, to begin a new life, only to repeat the scenario again, possibly embezzling thousands of dollars in gold and silver bullion.

If he took the bullion, of course, but it seemed likely he had.

I exited the employee lot in the aging behemoth, which had been chewing gummed and bailing wired together, and headed home. I thought of going to Hollie's Hut for dinner but decided against it. I would've taken Sally out, but she had some ladies' deal going on at church.

I hadn't gone two blocks when I witnessed something that made the bottom of my stomach drop about a foot. Pulling the car quietly over to the curb, I watched Joey Duncan put the finishing touches on a cinderblock masterpiece.

I had to admit, it was a work of art. Not the hasty scrawl of names, but a multi-colored design with caricatures of people, complete with shading to give it a 3-D effect. The proportions were excellent, as good as I've seen from many professional artists. But I couldn't admire it, as I remembered it was defacing someone else's property.

Disgust, disdain, depression, helplessness, anger—all welled up within me at once, coursing through me and fighting for dominance. How could he, I thought, after all I'd done for him? I stuck my neck out for the ingrate, and he so much as spits in my face.

Then I realized I was sounding like a self-righteous mother and swallowed it, taking a long breath to cool my jets.

I could have just driven off and washed my hands of him, but I'm a glutton for punishment. He was my project, and I couldn't give in so easily and admit defeat, admit that I'd been wrong. That I'd had no effect on him.

Something I'd done—maybe everything I'd done—hadn't

worked. But I was going to give it one more try; only this time take a different tack.

If only I knew what that was.

While still chewing on this, I saw in the distance a black-and-white moving towards me in a hurry but with no siren. The cop had his roof-mounted rear-facing amber light flashing—what cops calls their "excuse me" light that they use to let everybody they've just passed at high speed know they're going to a hot call and not the doughnut shop.

He was on his way to catch a tagger.

I gave my horn a light tap, and Joey jerked around, threw down the can of paint and coiled to sprint away, then recognized my van and froze, not knowing what to do next. Running wouldn't help, he'd been nailed. I leaned over and opened the passenger door and shouted.

"Cops are coming, Joey. Get in."

He hesitated, not knowing my intentions. For that matter, I wasn't sure of my intentions right at that moment. I hate tagging—gang-style graffiti perpetrated with abandon on the property of others—and I didn't plan on helping him get away with it. But I at least wanted to be involved in the situation rather than let him run and risk injury to himself or the cops who would give chase.

Reluctantly, deliberately, he moved toward me, lifting his feet as though they weighed a hundred pounds each.

"Hurry up!" I yelled.

He glanced both directions and got in, closing the door but keeping a loose grip on the handle.

"Nice work," I said dryly. He looked at his art, then down at his hands, and said nothing.

We watched the police car approach.

"Aren't we going to take off, or are you throwing me to the wolves?"

"What do you think I should do?" I asked, tossing it back to him.

He shrugged but said nothing.

"It's up to you, guy. I gave you your last break already. You chose to keep tagging. And by the way, this isn't the beach wall."

144

"I wasn't lying, if that's what you're thinking. I really was at the beach wall the other day."

"Yeah."

"Man, you don't understand. It's just something I've got to do."

"Joey, life is full of little desires we just have to learn to control. We can't do everything we feel like doing," I said, remembering the other night at Sally's apartment.

The police car arrived. We watched it slow down, the amber light and the headlights blink off, and the car suddenly veer right and drive away from us, up another street. He hadn't been coming here. Joey exhaled audibly.

"You'd a given me up, wouldn't you?"

"I don't know," I said truthfully, glad it hadn't come to that. "Joey, believe it or not, God's trying to send you a message."

"God? What's He got to do with this?"

"I can't explain it, Joey, but He cares. He cares about you, He cares about me. . . . We don't deserve it, that's for sure. None of us do. But it looks like He's giving you one more shot, which is more than I would have given you. Do you think it was coincidence I happened to drive by and see you?"

"You have a vision?" he mocked. "Did God speak to you?"

"You've been watching too much TV. He doesn't speak to us in an audible voice. He speaks through His word, the Bible. Sometimes He puts thoughts or ideas in our heads—sometimes we recognize that it's God, sometimes we don't. And often He just uses the circumstances of life. Like tonight."

"What are you saying?"

I smiled at him. "You hungry?"

He stared at me. "Yeah," he said quietly.

"Let's go eat. You can come back tomorrow and clean this up."

I drove him in silence to my place, with him staring at me most of the way, trying to figure me out. When we got there, I ordered a pizza. While we waited for delivery, I talked to him about God, about how He created a perfect world, and how Satan got man to mess it up and that broke off our relationship with the Creator. It had to be put right because our attempts to get back on His good side by being really good people always fell short, no matter how righteous we thought we were.

"So how'd He do it?" Joey asked, almost in spite of himself.

"You know how," I told him. "He sent His Son, Jesus, to take the rap for us. He got what we deserve. He was the sacrifice for our sins. You remember how the Jews had to kill a perfect lamb? Christ was the perfect lamb, the sacrifice for all humanity."

"Then isn't everyone saved?"

"Only those who believe in Jesus as their Lord and Savior. He didn't save anyone so they can go on living like they always lived before. He saved us to a life of obedience to His word."

"We have to give up everything that's fun."

"No, just what's bad."

"I'm not sure about this. . . ."

"Don't expect you to be," I said. "I'm not asking you to decide anything tonight."

"You're not trying to save me?"

"I can't save you, Joey. God is salvation. We can't force Him to save someone. The important thing is that you not shut Him out. I've got some books for you to read if you want. Or we can talk, answer questions you might have. It's up to you."

"No pressure?"

I shook my head. "No pressure. It's between you and God. And it's not a pie-in-the-sky issue either. Becoming a Christian doesn't immediately solve all your problems, won't make you rich, and may totally disrupt the life you've come to know."

"You don't make it sound too appealing."

"Life is just a blip on the time line of eternity, Joey. What's important is where we go when these bodies give out."

The doorbell rang.

"Speaking of bodies giving out," I said. I paid for the pizza and scraped the newspapers off the coffee table so we could eat in front of the TV. I didn't want to overload him with doctrine, just give him enough to get him thinking.

I found an old western movie, and we watched in relative silence. I was more interested in it than Joey, who seemed to not be seeing the screen he was looking at. A good sign. When the credits rolled by, I noticed it had been filmed at New Laramie Movie Town.

"Look there," I said, pointing to the screen with a slice of sausage and pepperoni. "That's where the park's old museum stuff is going."

"Where?"

"New Laramie Movie Town. That's where they filmed the movie."

"Oh, yeah," Joey said casually. "The park used to own that place."

"Really? I didn't know that."

"Yeah. Some of the ride operators and maintenance guys used to work there. The park sold it a couple years ago. They said it was too far away to manage properly, or something like that. I dunno."

"Must've been before I came to work here," I concluded. "Where is it?"

"Middle of nowhere in Arizona. Not too far from Mexico."

"How'd you know about it?"

"It's not a big secret," Joey said. "It's just no big deal." He shrugged it off.

I turned off the tube with the remote and picked up the empty pizza box.

"Now what?" Joey asked. "You gonna turn me in?"

"Why would you think that?"

"After that big lecture on sin and stuff."

"That's not why I told you about that. Like I said, tomorrow you're going to the people who own that wall and take care of it yourself, on your own." I could tell by his body language he wasn't happy with that.

"What about forgiveness, man?"

"You can be forgiven for the deed but still have to undo it. Repentance doesn't release you from responsibility. The convicted murderer can be forgiven, but he stays in jail. He can die in the electric chair, then go to heaven. It's not the body that is saved, but the soul. Besides, I haven't heard you doing much repenting."

"You've got an answer for everything, don't you?"

"I wish. Joey, the issue is, what are you going to do with your life? You're close to crossing the line. You can still salvage yourself."

"I'm trying," he protested. "I just like to draw, that's all. What else is there to do?"

As he said this my eye fell on the pile of newspapers on the floor. They were open to the funnies.

"Just a minute," I said. I hurried out of the room, a perplexed Joey Duncan watching me leave, and came back with some blank paper, pencils, pens, and a couple sheets of sketches. I plopped them on the coffee table in front of him.

"What's this?" he asked.

"Can you draw that? On paper, I mean."

He glanced up at me with suspicion then leafed through the sketches.

"Yeah. no problem." He sat back and sipped his Coke.

"Prove it," I challenged. "And don't just copy what's there. Fill the pages up, vary it, give it some action, different costumes. Interpret."

"Why should I?"

"Consider this payment for not turning you over to the police."

"What's this about?"

"Your future, Joey, your future."

I took Joey home a couple hours later, sticking his drawings in a large envelope to give to Michelle Yokoyama the next morning.

As I was walking out the door to go to work, sipping my second cup of coffee, the phone rang. It was Theo.

"Good morning, Gil."

"You sound terrible," I observed.

"Been up since three."

"Oh? What's up?"

"Albright—I mean Mercer—is no longer missing."

"Found his body, did you?"

"In a manner of speaking."

"Come again?"

"He was still in it, Gil."

"Huh?"

"He's alive."

"I'm not surprised. What happened?"

"Hold onto your hat. A couple of phone company security guards found him laying at the side of the road outside Yuma—"

"Yuma? As in Yuma, Arizona?"

"The same. He was near the perimeter fence to their microwave station and hadn't been there thirty minutes before, the last time they made their rounds. And get this: He was barely conscious and a little undernourished and dehydrated, but he was otherwise uninjured."

"Uninjured?" I repeated. "What about the blood in his car? Whose is that?"

"Don't know yet. What's really weird is, he was clean-shaven and, in general, looked pretty good."

"How does he account for it?"

"There's the rub. He claims he doesn't remember anything of the past few days. He told Yuma P.D. he was on his way to work, stopped for gas, and that's the last thing he remembers."

"Do you believe it?"

"No."

"When are you going to talk to him?"

"He's in a Yuma hospital for a day or two, then will be allowed to come home. Rather than confront him there and face an extradition problem if we get something to charge him with in the bullion theft, I thought I'd wait till he comes home. Michelle Yokoyama told me the park would arrange to have him brought back."

"Sounds reasonable."

"In the meantime, I thought I'd take a drive out to Santa Vista, see if there's anything or anyone out there who can shed some light on this. Maybe someone saw his car being dropped off or something."

"Would you like some company?"

"Sure. You can buy lunch. Will they let you go?"

"This is park business. Besides, if I don't ask, they can't say no. If they get upset later, I'll apologize and promise not to do it again. Let me clock in first; pick me up at the receiving gate at 8:30."

I hung up with a wry grin on my face. This was getting more interesting by the minute.

"Just like old times, eh Theo?" I said as I settled into the passenger seat of his unmarked Chevy.

He smiled. "You miss it, don't you?"

I nodded. "I can't deny it. Being a detective—especially a homicide detective—is probably the best job in the world, next to being president of an amusement park, perhaps. It's the most interesting, at least."

"If you don't mind wading through the scum . . . the private affairs and sordid details of people's lives, not to mention exploring the insides of their dead bodies. I'd think you'd have a problem with that, being a Christian and all. You guys like to be happy all the time and praise the Lord and stuff like that."

I looked at him like he'd just eaten a bug. "Au contraire, Theo. You know me well enough to know I don't have a problem with it. And the reality is, Christians are more aware of man's sinfulness than anyone. Hedonistic and humanistic mankind—and that's just about everyone, including you—believes people are basically good and occasionally do bad things. Christians believe people are basically bad and occasionally do good things, and that no one can be saved on the basis of their own merits."

"I resent that."

"What?"

"You saying I'm basically bad."

"Not you, everyone. Even me."

"What about Mother Theresa?"

"She was born in sin, just like everyone else. If she's saved—if she puts her faith in Christ and is obedient to His word—then her eternity in heaven is secure. But all the good she does is not what saves her. She does it *because* she's saved, not to *get* saved."

"Come on, Gil, you don't really believe all people are basically evil, do you? If they were, the crime rate would be in outer space. We'd never pass laws."

"Laws are passed to protect us against each other," I

explained. "Peer pressure of the highest order, that's what laws are. Even evil people have to interact with each other. As a rule, pirates work together toward a common goal. The notorious Vikings worked together to prey on others outside their circle. There's a sense in society of the need to control extreme behavior for the benefit of everyone. Take away the restraints, however—the possibility of capture and punishment—and more people will cross those lines we call laws to satisfy their egos, their personal desires."

"You can't prove that."

"Oh yeah? Remember the riots in L.A.? The burning and the looting? Did you see the photos? The videos? People who would never under normal circumstances consider committing a burglary were out en masse, going into stores and carting off sofas and televisions and clothing. And why was that?"

Theo shrugged.

"Because the restraints had been removed. The laws were still on the books, but they couldn't be enforced, and people knew it. They saw an opportunity to satisfy a hedonistic or materialistic desire without risk. The fact that it was illegal or immoral was irrelevant. Thus, they were revealing their true selves, unencumbered by societal restraint."

"Interesting theory," Theo admitted, "but it still was a relatively small group of people."

"Law enforcement regained control. If things had been allowed to continue to digress, more people would have joined in and pretty soon there would have been total anarchy."

"You can't prove that."

"Again with the 'you can't prove that.' Well, maybe not to your satisfaction. But it happened once before, and only eight people survived."

"Huh?"

"Noah and his family. God destroyed the world and all the people in it."

"Because they looted and burned?" Theo smirked.

I chuckled with him. "Among other things. And he destroyed two whole cities because of gross sin. Sodom and Gomorrah. Read it for yourself."

"Is that in Hezekiah too?" He narrowed his eyes and glared at me. I laughed out loud.

"You tried to find it, I take it."

"It's not there."

"You must have the Unauthorized Version. The U-V we call it. Like UV light, there's nothing there you can see, but it'll still burn you."

Theo only grunted, which is how he reacted when he didn't know whether or not I was serious.

"I still don't know how you can conclude that all people are basically bad. Look at all the good people in the world."

"Oh, yeah, right. All the good people and all the wonderful things they do. Most of what we see in the papers and on television is done for their personal gain, to get publicity or something, usually with greed as their ultimate motivation. Look, Theo, I don't conclude people are basically bad, the Bible says it. And mankind continues to prove it. Besides, if you want to grind it down to the nub, understand it this way: those people who do many good things . . . even if their motive is only to receive God's approval, then everything they do is not really for others, but for themselves. That's self-interest in the extreme. It may not be 'wrong' as our society views it, but in God's eyes it's worthless."

"Your God is mean."

"My God is a loving father, who wants our love in return. He made the world, He made us, and He determines what's right. It's all in the Book."

Theo made a guttural noise that told me he was thinking about it, then switched on the radio, his signal that the subject was closed. That didn't bother me, I was done. For the time being, at least. The seed had been planted.

"Did I tell you I called Mercer's wife?" he asked presently— using Albright's true name—as the desert stretched out before us.

"How'd she take it?"

"She was okay. Actually, she called me. I'd had one of the local cops break it to her in person. In fact, I called the detective who'd investigated the case fifteen years ago. He's chief now."

"What'd he say?"

"He wasn't surprised. It was something he suspected but could never prove, so he never said anything."

"Wow. What's Mrs. Mercer say? Is she still Mrs. Mercer?"

"Yeah, she never remarried. She ID'd him. I think she was still in shock. She's going to come out in a few days, with her kids . . . once she pulls herself together."

"She's not hoping for a happy reunion is she?"

"I don't think so. She got his life insurance money eight years ago. It's long since spent. My guess is she wants to ask him the big 'W'. . . . Why?"

"I bet she changes her mind, once she thinks about it, and doesn't come out. For her, he died fifteen years ago. I think she'll wish him well and blow him off."

"Maybe the kids will still want him."

"They'll want a piece of him, you mean."

"Because of their inherently evil nature?" Theo asked, somewhat sarcastically.

I just smiled.

"So, Lieutenant, what do you figure his motive was?"

"For which offense?"

"The only one we can prove right now: leaving his family in Illinois."

"Who knows? Probably to get a new start, but only Mercer can say why he wanted that. Do you think he took the gold?"

"I think he's as good a suspect as anyone right now."

"How do you figure it?"

"Well, fifteen years ago he decides to start over, so he fakes his murder and splits. Obviously, he can't handle responsibility. He's a runner. Couldn't even face his family, tell them he didn't love them any more. Now it looks like he's done it again. Only this time, he decides to clean out the park first. Or he cleans out the park then decides to split, or maybe he thought up both schemes at the same time."

"Crime of opportunity, maybe?"

"He couldn't have planned it in advance. He didn't know Whelan was going to ask him to clean out the safe. And the fake bullion was made with readily available stuff. Maybe he needed the money and took it, thinking he would get away with it by doing what worked before."

"Faking his own murder."

"But something went wrong this time."

"What?"

"Ask him. I'm just a security guard."

Theo took an offramp in the outskirts of Santa Vista. "Here we are."

He made a few turns, consulted his map book, and turned onto Williams Street, stopping by the curb just short of the intersection of Williams and 7th, a few blocks off the main drag and away from the center of town.

It was a completely unassuming place; a vacant lot on one corner, a used car lot proclaiming *Manny's Fine Autos—Se Habla Español* on the sign on the opposite corner, a vacant business on the third, and an independent gas station on the fourth. The only pedestrians were a Hispanic woman pushing a baby in a stroller with her toddler walking several steps behind. The car lot and gas station were open but without customers at the moment. The air was still and thick and dry, and no clouds filtered the intense desert sun.

At the dealership, a salesman in a loosened tie and rolled-up shirt sleeves watched us from the steps of the small portable trailer which served as his office as he thoughtfully sucked a cigarette, probably sizing up whether we were potential customers or not. No, on second thought, in this neighborhood we stuck out like broken toes. We exuded *police*. He was just watching the cops.

"It was right here," Theo said, pointing to the curb in front of the vacant lot. He stood with his hands in his pants' pockets, just looking around as though the insight would find him if he stood still long enough. I leaned against the car and waited. After all, this was his gig.

"You got a picture of him?" he asked.

"I didn't bring it with me."

"Okay. I've got two." He handed me his extra, made in the police photo lab.

"I'll take the gas station," he said. "You can get the car lot."

We split up. I waited for an old pickup to pass then walked across the street toward the car dealer. The salesman, figuring I wasn't a paying customer, made no move to greet me when I stepped onto his property. He finished his smoke and ground it out on the carpeted step but waited for me to go to him.

"What can I do for you?" he asked casually, perhaps a little suspiciously. "You guys are cops, right?"

Without directly answering his question I said, "We're investigating a missing person. His car was found abandoned across the street the other day. Over there." I pointed toward the vacant lot.

"Oh, yeah," he said, suddenly interested. "I saw the cops swarming all over it before they hooked it up. I just figured it was stolen."

"Did you see anybody in or around that car? Besides the cops, I mean."

He shook his head. "Nope. Sorry, man. You know how it is, customers and all."

Wishful thinking, I thought. I showed him the photo of Mercer, the one taken when he was Russell Albright.

"Have you seen this man?"

He took the photo and held it out at arm's length. "No, I don't believe I—wait . . . wait a minute. This is the missing guy?"

"Yes. Have you seen him?"

"Seen him? I sold him a car."

FOURTEEN

I immediately turned and whistled for Theo. When he looked up, I waved him over.

"Are you sure?" I asked the salesman.

"Positive. He paid cash. Real cash, I mean, not a check or anything."

Theo came up at a jog, puffing. "What's up?"

"He bought a car here, for cash."

"When?" Theo asked.

"Week ago," said the salesman.

"Do you have any paperwork on it?"

The salesman hesitated. Theo took out his badge and ID card and let the man inspect them. "Okay, Lieutenant. Had to make sure, you know. I'm Manny Gomez." He stuck out a yellow-fingered hand that Theo accepted.

"Let's go inside," Gomez suggested. "See what I can find."

We followed him into the trailer, a dingy, poorly lit affair with dirty carpets and a small swamp cooler rattling in the window, vainly trying to circulate the stale air. The only art on the wall was a calendar, the kind given by realtors with their name and address imprinted on them. There was no one else inside the trailer. Manny's Fine Autos was apparently a one-man operation. He sat down behind a small, littered desk and opened a drawer. It stuck until he hammered it with the heel of his hand.

"Let's see . . . okay, here we go." He pulled out a file folder and opened it. "He bought a Chevy Impala. Two thousand. Got a good deal. I had it stickered at twenty-four. Radio, heater, good rubber, low mileage. But . . . he had cash, you know, so I cut him a deal. Lost my shirt on it." He grinned, but it soured when we didn't return it.

"What name did he give you?" I asked.

"Let's see . . . Patterson."

"Clyde Patterson?" I guessed.

"Yeah. Is that his name?"

"No," Theo said.

"No? Then how'd you know he used it?" Manny asked me.

"Yeah," Theo parroted. "How'd you know?"

I pointed to the calendar on the wall behind Gomez. Courtesy of Clyde Patterson, Patterson Real Estate.

Manny chuckled uneasily. "I thought that name sounded familiar."

"What's the color and the plate?" Theo asked sharply.

"Blue. Robin's egg blue. Four door. The plate? . . . Here it is."

Theo copied it down. "Can I use your phone?"

"Yeah, sure. Go ahead." He turned it around to face the detective.

Theo punched in the number of his department.

"This is Lieutenant Brown. Put out a teletype to all southwestern states." He gave the person he was talking to the plate number and vehicle description. "Just say it may be involved in a grand theft and a missing person. Yeah, put Russell Albright's info in it, and his AKA. Oh, and give me a 10-29 on that plate. No, I'll wait."

He started to light a cigarette, but Manny pointed to a No Smoking sign on the desk. Theo flipped the cover back up on his lighter, leaving the cigarette dangling from his lips.

"What's that?" he said, slowly reaching up to pluck it out. "Okay, give me the number. Yeah. Three-four. Got it." He hung up.

"Car's been impounded already," he told me. "In Yuma. Used in a robbery."

Manny whistled low.

"That was quick," I noted.

Theo picked up the receiver.

"Uh . . . excuse me, lieutenant. . . ." Manny said slowly. "I support law enforcement but not quite in this way. This is a small business—"

Theo hung up. "Sorry. I've got one in the car. Thanks." He put down a dollar for the first call, and we returned to Theo's plain unit. Climbing in, he grabbed his cellular phone.

"Yours or the department's?" I wondered.

"Are you kidding? If it was mine I'd be making this call on a pay phone." He turned his attention to the phone. "Hello, yes. Robbery division please. Thank you." Again on hold, Theo attempted once again to light up, but I tapped the dashboard and shook my head. The city had a no-smoking-in-the-buildings-or-cars policy. This time he threw the cigarette out the window.

Someone must have picked up because Theo identified himself. "You guys arrested a couple of dudes for robbery a few days ago, impounded their car, a blue Chevy Impala four-door. Yes, that's the one. Well, I'm investigating a theft and a missing person—who's no longer missing. . . . Yeah, that's right. The guy you found out by the phone company microwave station. Russell Albright, that's right. Anyway, my missing—when he was still missing—ditched his car in Santa Vista and purchased that Impala. From there the car went to Yuma and into your hands, but somehow my guy got separated from it. I'd like to know more about your two guys, how they got the car, what's in the trunk, that kind of thing. Yeah, we're missing some property, all right. Gold bullion."

Even from my seat on the other side of the car, I could hear the Yuma detective's swear words of awe. Theo jerked the phone away from his ear for a second.

"Yes sir," he continued. "Would you ask them about it? And could you fax a copy of the reports of their arrest to my department?" He gave him the fax number and the number of his cellular phone.

"I understand. Good, I'm glad they're still in custody. Yes. I should be back at my office by then. Thanks." He punched off.

"Well?" I prodded.

"I'll tell you over a burger."

It was quite a tale. Briefly, these two guys had gotten a ride from Mercer west of Yuma, decided they liked his car, and drove off in it when he stopped outside Gila Bend to relieve himself beside the side of the road. They drove into town, robbed a convenience store by simulating a gun but were spotted driving off by a patrol officer, who took them down without a struggle.

That was all Theo knew so far. We drove home, both of us excited, discussing the possibilities but getting no closer to the truth, at least as far as we knew for sure.

Theo dropped me off at the receiving gate.

"I'll call you when I hear more," he promised as I got out.

I nodded and waved, then returned to my little cubicle in the warehouse, collapsing into my chair.

Just under an hour had passed when Theo phoned.

"What'd you find out?" I asked groggily.

"You been sleeping?" Theo asked.

"None of your beeswax," I rejoined, having no defense.

"Those guys are a couple of losers, that's for sure. They said they didn't hurt Mercer, just drove off without him. He didn't tell them where he was headed, or what he was up to, and they didn't ask. They said Mercer hardly said a word the whole time."

"Why would he pick them up?" I wondered. "That doesn't make any sense."

"Not if he had the gold with him, but apparently he didn't. They swear they never saw any, and never looked in the trunk. One of them told the Yuma detectives, 'Would we rob the 7-11 if we had a trunk full of gold?' You've got to admit, that makes sense."

"You can't spend bullion. They would've needed capital, no matter what they were planning. For that matter, how do we know they're telling the truth about how they got the car? Makes more sense to me that they overpowered Mercer at a rest stop or something. I can't imagine he'd picked up a couple hitchhikers."

"Could be," Theo agreed.

"Well, at least we can be reasonably sure Mercer wasn't kidnapped on this end. But I'd say he has a partner who still has the bullion somewhere."

"If he's in on it all," Theo said. "We still don't have anything but circumstantial evidence."

"Yeah, but it's smoking gun circumstantial. What about the partial print in the paint on the fake bullion?"

"As soon as Mercer returns to town, we'll be able to check that. Illinois has no prints of his on file."

"So that's about it then," I mused. "We're left with more questions unanswered than when we started."

"Yeah, looks that—oh, say, I almost forgot. We've identified the remains."

"Lucy?"

"Yeah. Dental records did it. She's Stephanie Taylor, a reported missing from town here."

"Name sounds familiar."

"Guess who took the missing report."

"No way."

"Yep. Patrol officer Gil Beckman."

"Small world. Does the report list any boyfriend?"

"No, but she did work at the park, according to your report."

"Not surprising. So now what?"

"So now starts the routine stuff. Checking out her family, her acquaintances. . . . You know the routine."

"Yeah. Do you think I could get a picture of her?"

"I suppose. We've still got the one the family gave us when you took the report. I'll fax it over. Uh, any special reason you need it?"

"No," I admitted. "Sentimental curiosity, I guess. I don't remember her, and now that I've seen her at her worst, I'd like to see her with a face. Sort of a memento, I guess."

"Yeah, I can understand that," Theo sympathized. "I've got a few of those."

When the fax came in, Sally brought it out to me.

"Is that her?" she asked.

I studied the photo. Medium length, thick, wavy hair, plain face, certainly not model quality but pleasant enough to warrant a second look; thin lips parted to reveal the teeth I had already inspected at close range.

"Yes," I said quietly.

"She looks a little better there."

"She was having a bad hair day when we found her."

"All over." Sally's smile faded quickly. We joked, but our hearts weren't in it. "So have you figured out what happened yet?"

I shook my head and put the fax photo of Stephanie in the desk drawer. "She was strangled, probably by someone known to her, then buried. Motive unknown."

"Well, don't let it get you down. I'm sure Theo will figure it all out."

"That's part of what bothers me," I admitted. "Not that Theo will solve it but that I won't be in on it. Besides, this one is ten years old. Her killer could be long gone or dead. The likelihood of this being solved is a million to one."

"You miss it, don't you."

"What?"

"Police work."

"Some of it."

"Go back."

"Can't. Not here, at least."

"Then go somewhere else."

"Easier said than done. Besides, I'm too busy to be putting out applications and interviewing. I don't want to start over. Police departments aren't like civilian jobs. New hires start at the bottom, regardless of qualifications, unless they are specifically hired for a ranking position. And nobody gets hired to be a detective."

"Then learn to live with it," she said matter-of-factly.

"That's what I've been trying to do. I can't help reminiscing once in a while. Are you going to tell me you never, ever, think about your husband and wish things hadn't worked out different?"

"No, I can't say that," she acknowledged, but she said no more. I suddenly felt bad, scratching her old wound. I hadn't meant anything by it, I was just defending myself. Bad tactic.

"I'm sorry, Sally, I didn't mean—"

"No, that's okay, Gil. Believe me, I'm over it long ago. And you're right, missing something—or someone—that's gone is okay, as long as you don't let it run your life."

She was talking about Rachel now, whether she realized it or not. And she was absolutely right. I'd been allowing myself to continue to feel the pain for too long. Now was as good a time as any to take corrective steps.

"Sally? Would you . . . uh, like to go out? On a date, I mean. A real one. Not like before when we did that formal prom-like routine but a real grown-up evening together?"

"What are you suggesting, Gil?"

"Nothing unseemly, I guarantee. I . . . uh, listen Sally. I like you . . . a lot. I'd like to spend some time with you, talk about you, me, the Lord. . . . The bottom line is, I'd like to find out if there's a foundation to build a closer relationship on. If that's okay."

She looked up at me, expressionless, her eyes piercing mine. Uh oh, I'd blown it. My heart started to thump, more in fear than anticipation.

Then the hint of a smile tickled the corners of her mouth.

"Yes, I'd like that, Gil. Very much."

"Great! I know this isn't much notice, but how about tonight? Tomorrow's Saturday, and—"

"Tonight would be fine."

"Okay. Good. Uh . . . dress casual, okay. Comfortable. I'll pick you up at, say, seven? That okay?"

"Fine." She smiled again and left.

As soon as she was out of sight I snatched the phone off the hook and pounded Trish's extension.

"Trish!" I shouted as soon as she'd answered. "This is Gil. I need a really big favor."

Fred Billings was manning the employee lot booth when I got there. I arrived a little before five, which I'd done intentionally to give me a chance to talk to him before Trish showed up.

"Hey, Fred," I said as I approached the booth, to let him know I was coming. He swung his chair around.

"Hey, Sonny! How's it goin'? How's the new ride?"

"Still just a big hole, Fred. It'll be awhile before it'll start to resemble something."

"These things take a lot of time now, don't they? I remember in the old days they could put 'em up in a month."

"Yeah, but they weren't as complicated as they are now. The new ride is one of those basement things; pretty elaborate, with computers and stuff."

"That'll cost 'em a pretty penny."

"Couple mil."

Fred shook his head. "There goes our profit sharing this year."

I smiled. "Maybe not. If attendance picks up because of the ride and all the other new stuff, you'll still get something. If not this year, then next."

"I hope this year, Sonny. I won't be around next year."

"Retiring?"

"Yep. Gonna pull the ol' pin."

"You've been here a long time, then."

"Twenty years. I was a cop myself, once."

"I didn't know that."

"Yep. Twelve years, back East. Got hurt, they retired me. Wife wanted to come out West, and here I am."

"You worked next to the Starcoaster in the receiving gate when they built that ride, didn't you?"

"Yep. That's how I knew it only took a few weeks to build it. They dug the foundation, poured the slab, put together the erector set and framed the building around—say, wait a second; ain't I been hearing 'bout them finding some bones or something under the 'Coaster?"

"That's right, Fred. And they've been identified. Here, take a look." I took out the photo of Stephanie Taylor and laid it on the counter in front of Fred. "Do you recognize her?"

He stared at it, leaning closer and finally taking off his glasses.

"Yeah, yeah, I sure do. That's . . . uh, what's her name?"

"Stephanie—"

"Taylor," he finished. "Yeah, she worked here for awhile. Normally I don't pay much attention to people's names, but she kinda stuck with me. You see, she reminded me of my wife when

Helga was younger. You say she's dead, huh?" I nodded solemnly. "That's too bad, Sonny. I wondered what happened to her when she disappeared. And to think, all these years she's been right over there."

My heart sped up. "Did she have a boyfriend? Or at least someone you saw her with more than the others?"

"Seems like it, Gil. Sure seems like it. But that was a long time ago, and who can remember? You know, in my mind I can picture her walking with someone, but it's not clear."

I thought I'd prod him a little. "Could it have been Jerry Opperman?"

Fred closed his eyes tightly, then shook his head. "Naw, Jerry wouldn't be seen in public with a girl that young, even if he was seeing her on the side. It wouldn't be him. Besides, he doesn't park here, he's got his own private space by his office. Truth is, I never paid much attention to who she was with, you know what I mean?"

Rats. I guess it was too good to be true. There had probably been no ulterior motive in Opperman's protests over the cessation of construction; he was entirely driven by money.

"Well, see if you can think of it," I told Fred, as I saw Trish heading my way. "If you could it'd be a big help."

"Would he be the killer?" Fred asked.

"Could be," I said. "I'd be surprised if he wasn't."

The importance of his identification came to Fred, and his face lit up.

"I'll try, Gil. I'll surely try."

"Thanks Fred."

Trish arrived and held out her hand to me. "Can you drive a stick?" she asked.

I rolled my eyes. "I could if I hadn't just fallen off the turnip truck."

"Well, let's get going then." I took the keys from her, and we climbed in her BMW 325i. She gave me a brief rundown of the unfamiliar instrument panel. I pulled out of the lot, smiling at the comfort and feel of the sports car, and accelerated up the street.

"So, what have you decided?" I asked as we neared her place.

She didn't have to ask what I was talking about. . . . She knew.

"I think I'm going to stay. It's time I got on with my life. I could rent an apartment, I suppose, but the Currans have asked me to stay with them.

"That's great! It'll be good for them, too. They really love you. But one word of caution." I downshifted and entered her driveway, braking to an easy stop.

"Yes?"

"There'll come a day when you meet someone. You're not Everett's girlfriend anymore, and they'll have to understand that. I don't think you'll have a problem with them but just be sensitive to it, okay?"

"Sure, Gil. Thanks." She leaned over and gave me a quick kiss on the cheek and a giggling smile as I blushed.

"You and Sally have fun, okay? She got out, then leaned back in and pointed her finger at me, her brow wrinkled with concern. "And drive careful!"

She winked and ran inside.

This was turning out to be quite a week.

FIFTEEN

Sally was radiant. She answered the door with an expectant smile, and, I must admit, I could hardly contain myself. I felt like a teenager. Giddy, I believe, is the word.

"So, what's this?" she asked as she came down her steps and saw the BMW poised by the curb, ready to spring into the fast lane.

"It's a BMW."

"I know that, silly. Where'd you get it? Did you finally trade in that . . . *thing* you drive?"

"That *thing* has been better to me than any other car I've ever owned. I bought it for fifteen hundred dollars and I've put eighty-five thousand miles on it. Plus it's comfortable, utilitarian—"

"And has two tires in the grave and the other two on banana peels."

"Okay," I admitted, opening the passenger door for her, "so maybe it's outlived its usefulness. Truth is, I borrowed this from Trish; I didn't want to drive you around in the van. It's not very—"

"Romantic?"

"That too. I was actually going to say it's not very reliable. We might break down somewhere—somewhere really inconvenient."

"Well . . ." her voice softened. "I'd go with you on a tractor if that's all you had."

"Really?" I grinned. "That's great, because just this afternoon I had my eye on a low mileage Massey-Ferguson. Four cylinder, shaped metal saddle, nearly new knobby tires. . . ."

We laughed, and I entered the freeway, easing the best handling sports car in the world up to sixty miles per hour. This was a nice car. For a moment I almost wished I could afford one. Then I factored in the payments, insurance, tune-ups—my van began to look pretty good.

"So . . . where are we going?"

"Well, there's a little place up in the mountains, overlooks the whole valley. Called *The Cliffs*. Ever been there?"

"No."

"Great baklava, wonderful view, big fireplace in the center of the room, interesting company. . . . I mean you, of course."

"Of course."

We drove on, our destination two hours away, talking about the park, the new rides and attractions, the possibility of the park becoming a major contender, our own aspirations and dreams. I told Sally what police work meant to me, and why I didn't feel I could start over at this late date. She related how she ended up at the park, and why she stayed so long despite the problems they'd had over the years—after all, she told me, poor management is not an unusual circumstance in business, or, for that matter, in government.

No kidding.

She reminded me what the Bible said about obeying those in authority over us, and that we don't really work for them, we work for Christ. She was right, and I have always known that, but I just get so frustrated at injustice that I almost can't keep myself from trying to correct it, even when it's like trying to swim upstream, or rollerskate in a buffalo herd, as the old song goes.

"What was that?" Sally asked.

"I don't know."

"Sounds like a warning buzzer. Did you run out of gas or something?"

"No, it shows three quar—wait! It's a phone! I forgot Trish had one." I turned on the interior light. "Now, where would I be if I were a car phone? There, by your seat."

Sally grabbed the cellular phone and inspected the keypad as it continued to ring, then pressed a button.

"Hello?" she said tentatively. "Oh . . . hi, Lieutenant." I shot Sally a perplexed glance, as if to say, *how'd he find us here?* Sally read my mind and scrunched her shoulders. "Yes, he's right here." She extended the phone toward me.

I shook my hand at it and mouthed *no*, but she insisted. With her hand over the mouthpiece she whispered, "I can't tell him you're indisposed, now can I? It's okay."

I accepted the phone with a grimace. "I'm on a date, Theo."

"Yeah, Gil, I know. Your partner, Trish Smith, told me. That's where I got the number."

"No duh. What'd you go to all that trouble for?"

"Mercer returned today, came to the station and got a release for his car. I mentioned that I wanted to interview him, to see if I could get a line on his abductors. He said to come over to his place later, that he was tired. I told him that was fine, so he wouldn't think anything was amiss—I'd yet to confront him about his true identity."

"So he still thinks we think he's Russell Albright?"

"Yep. Well, I went over a couple hours later, and when I got there I laid Russell Albright's death certificate on him without a word. He was totally expressionless as he read it. Then I showed him an old photo of him and his wife that I had her fax me."

"I wish I could've been there for that. What'd he do?"

"Went as white as a sheet. He looks up at and says, 'I don't understand, Lieutenant. What's this?' I said, 'Has it been so long you don't recognize yourself with your wife, Mr. Mercer?'"

"What then?" I asked gleefully, imagining how Mercer must have been sweating so profusely that he was almost sliding out of his clothes.

"He looks straight in my eye and says he doesn't know what I'm talking about. So I told him flat out, I'd had him positively identified, and his wife was on her way out."

"Is she?"

"No, but the ploy worked. He broke down and copped out. He asked if he was in some trouble. I told him yes, some, and asked why he did it. He said he just couldn't handle the pressure any longer, that he needed a new start and didn't think he could go through a divorce, the emotional trauma or the expense, with alimony and child support and all that. Said he figured his life insurance would take care of them."

"What about this time and this disappearance?"

"He still says he doesn't remember; it's just like he told Yuma P.D."

"Doesn't remember buying a car in Santa Vista?"

"Doesn't recall a thing after stopping at the gas station."

"Likely story."

"Yeah, so he's lying. What does that prove?" Theo queried.

"That he's hiding something, of course."

"I asked him about the bullion, point blank."

"And?"

"He said he did as he was told and handed the bullion in a box to his boss."

"Dave Whelan. That could be a lie too."

"He's either a really good liar, or he's telling the truth."

"Theo, he's been living a lie for the past fifteen years. By now he's a professional."

"Guess who picked him up at the airport when he came back from Yuma."

"I give up."

"Whelan."

"No joke. That's mighty curious."

"Kind of odd, I thought. But what do I know? They do odd things at the park sometimes."

"Sometimes?"

This wouldn't really have been all that odd, under normal circumstances. But with the theft of the bullion, it sure made Whelan look like a party to it. Then again, maybe he just wanted to do his own investigating. Or maybe he was assigned to pick him up. Whichever, it sure muddied the conspiracy waters.

"So what'd you do? Did you arrest him?"

"Mercer said he was tired from everything and not feeling too well from his exposure and the long car ride back from Yuma. He said he'd come to the station in the morning and turn himself in if I wanted."

"And you said . . . ?"

"What could I say? The false identity thing is a misdemeanor, and it's all we've got right now. Without a warrant, I couldn't arrest him out of his house. So I said I'd let him rest some, but I'd call him after dinner, I still had some things I needed to discuss tonight. He agreed. When he didn't answer the phone, I went over. He was gone."

"Flew the coop."

"I put out a teletype on him and his car. I don't think he'll get far. He didn't look good."

"Yeah? Well, last time he was *dead* and managed to stay away for fifteen years. Well, Theo, sounds like you've got it under control. I've got to go. Good luck. Hope you get your man."

I pressed the *end* button and handed Sally the phone, filling her in on Theo's half of the conversation. At this moment, I wasn't interested in pursuing it—my attention was directed toward Sally.

But Sally seemed to be intrigued.

"He's trying to disappear, isn't he?"

I shrugged. "Could be. Probably. But how can he? We're on to him this time, he hasn't had time to make a plan, to equip himself. . . . He certainly can't fake another death. He's running scared now, and people who do that make mistakes. They get themselves caught."

"Why is he running scared?"

It seemed so obvious to me I hadn't actually thought it out. "Because he's guilty, I guess."

"Of what?"

"False I.D. Maybe even the bullion theft."

"Have they found the gold?"

"No."

"Then he still has it. He didn't need to pack. He can buy new."

"You can't spend bullion, not anywhere in this country. It's illegal to possess. And speaking of possession, where is it? His apartment and car were both searched, and he didn't have it with him in Yuma when he encountered those two guys who took his car."

"If he had the gold, he'd already gotten rid of it and was on his way to pick it up."

"Where?"

"Don't ask me, I'm just a secretary."

"It was more rhetorical than anything. I was just thinking out loud."

"Well, then go over the whole thing out loud, see if something jumps out at you."

"Are you sure you want to do this? We're on a date."

"We were on a date when you told me how Christians are supposed to solve their problems. Oh, come on, no poochie lips. I wasn't being critical. But I am serious about this. We've got plenty of time, and I'm starting to get interested. Besides, I know you like to figure things out. Please," her voice quieted, becoming almost syrupy, and she leaned closer, putting a hand gently on my arm, "let's do it together."

"Unfair," I protested lamely. "Oh, all right." I exited the freeway and guided the BMW onto the road that led up the mountain.

"Well, let's see. Mercer—"

"Mercer?"

"That's Albright's real name."

"That makes it confusing."

"Okay, we'll call him Albright. Albright leaves his family in Illinois, faking his murder—"

"Why?"

"Can't handle pressure. He comes out here, gets the birth certificate of a dead baby who would have been about his age—"

"How?"

"Don't know. They didn't have those computer gizmos back then so he probably took the name off the headstone then visited the County Hall of Records. Anyway, he settles into life here, gets a job at the park, works here for eleven years or so—"

"Just eleven blank years? No girlfriends or anything?"

"Yeah, there was, now that you mention it. She called Theo when she read in the paper he was missing."

"What happened?"

"She said they went together several months, but when

things got serious between them—at least when she got serious—he broke it off abruptly. In fact, he just . . . well, disappeared. Didn't call her, didn't write. He just kissed her goodnight like everything was fine and never returned. No explanation, no nothing. Didn't even return her calls."

"But he kept his job at the park?"

"Yeah. That time he didn't flee the area. I wonder why not."

Sally suggested, "No kids, nothing to tie him down that he needed to run from. It was good enough just to stop. He hadn't crossed the line."

"Sounds like you've got him pegged," I observed.

"He runs from commitment. How far and how fast depends on how deep the commitment."

"So last week when he split . . . how do you explain that?"

"Like you said, he must be guilty."

"But why the theft in the first place? He was making good money, had retirement and profit sharing built up."

"Maybe he had another girlfriend he thought was closing in on him. It would seem his disappearance and the theft were related in some way other than he simply stole the bullion and ran with it."

It hit me like the proverbial ton of bricks, like a great spiritual truth, and I came to a skidding stop in a turnout, staring at the winking city lights spread out before us in the valley.

What came to me first was the crime corollary principle: things that happen close together in time and distance are probably related. It was basic investigative theory; Gumshoe 101.

"What's the matter?" Sally asked, concerned by my driving habits, not to mention the way I was pounding the steering wheel.

"How could I have missed it?" I complained.

"What?"

I turned in the seat to face her. "Look. We've got three separate incidents here, right? An employee disappears, what appears to be a kidnapping; we find the remains of a girl, buried ten years ago; and the theft of bullion, all three things involving the park. We connected Albright's disappearance to the theft—loosely, since we couldn't prove it—but never saw, or for that matter, seriously considered the possible link with the remains of the girl."

"How is there a link?"

"If I apply the corollary principle, it goes like this: Albright was fine as long as there was no pressure. When his girlfriend got serious, he just stopped seeing her because there was nothing happening he had to run away from. To solve that problem, he just broke off the relationship."

"Are you suggesting—"

"Stephanie Taylor, on the other hand, was pregnant. If he was her boyfriend and found out. . . . You see? He didn't need to run, he killed her instead. Maybe she refused to get an abortion. Ten years ago they weren't so easy to come by. No one knew anything about their relationship, so he was in the clear as long as she was just a missing person . . . that is, until we took out the Starcoaster and started digging. He realized she'd be found so he decided to leave, afraid they'd finally connect him to her, and when the opportunity arose to clean out the safe . . . voila, a lucky bonus. He took advantage of the opportunity by spending a little time in the train barn the night before."

"Then where's the bullion?" Sally asked. "And if he can't spend it, what good is it to him?"

"Not in the states," I said, "but in . . . Mexico? When he got messed up in Yuma, he was on his way south. That way he can also avoid prosecution for everything. He'd be set for life."

We stared at the lights of the city for a second, both of us thinking.

"I'll call Theo," I said finally. "Then we'll go on up to The Cliffs. I'm sorry, I didn't mean to spoil the evening."

"Are you kidding?" Sally said. "This is the most fun I've had in a long time. Why don't we go find him?"

"Albright?"

"You're not serious."

"Yes, I am."

"But where?"

"Why don't we start with Yuma? That's where he was headed before. Maybe by the time we get there, we'll think of something."

"You're sure. You want to go all the way to Yuma."

"Why not? After all, it's just a theory. Theo wouldn't be able to go. We're already on the way. There's no one else . . . and you're not dropping me off here while you do it alone, that's for sure."

She picked up the phone. "Call Trish. Get her permission."

I took the phone with a grin. "You beat all, Sally, you know that?"

I gave Trish the abbreviated version. She thought about it for a second, then said it sounded exciting and gave me her blessing.

"But I want the tank full when you bring it back."

"No problem," I laughed. "I'll fill it for a month. And it'll be washed and waxed." Sally gave me an approving smile, so I grinned at her and added, "Sally said she enjoyed waxing cars, be happy to do it." Sally's smile disappeared quickly, replaced by a look of wide-eyed horror, and she playfully slapped me on the arm.

"Oh, listen, Trish. Could you do something else for me? Get a hold of Lieutenant Brown—I'll give you his beeper number—and tell him about our theory. Have him show Fred Billings out in the employee parking lot booth a picture of Russell Albright. Ask him if that could be the guy he used to see with Stephanie Taylor."

Sally tugged at my sleeve and whispered something to me. "And while you're at it, Trish, talk to Mrs. Potter . . . yes, the Dragon Lady. Tell her it's for me. Ask her about Albright and Taylor. She might remember something."

"Okay, Gil," Trish said. "Boy, are you gonna owe me."

I hung up. "Watson, the game's afoot!"

"Onward and upward, Homer."

"Huh?"

Sally shrugged and smiled sheepishly.

I keyed the throaty BEEMER into life, spit some pebbles out under the rear bumper, and pointed the dual oval grille toward Yuma.

SIXTEEN

Somewhere in the middle of the southern Arizona desert, while Sally dozed in the reclined bucket seat to the lullaby of the engine drone and the music on the CD, and I gulped lukewarm convenience store coffee, it came to me.

Another tenant of criminal investigation: if it couldn't have happened that way, it probably didn't. That sounds obvious, but sometimes, when looking at a crime scene, it's easy to get caught up in trying to solve the whole puzzle at once rather than just trying to understand each piece and see how they fit together. We find a body in water with a rope around its neck and assume the person was hung then dumped in the lake, so we start looking for where he might have been hung and who hung him, when the fact is the rope was a tether, a leash, and the person actually was drowned. We were wasting our time barking up the wrong tree. The person was still murdered, but the entire scenario changes when the facts are allowed to dictate our movements, not the other way around.

For a couple hours Sally and I had tried to figure out how Albright had taken the bullion and where he had put it, when it seemed there was no way he could have. And as I stared out at the blackness all around us, I remembered the paint cans in the train barn.

He'd left the gold right where it was, let someone else unwittingly move it for him.

I eased the BMW to the side of the road, the cessation of motion waking Sally.

She yawned and stretched. "I'm sorry. I guess I'm not much of a date.

I smiled. "Nah, you're okay. In fact, you're a great date. If this gets out, everyone's going to want to drive you around the country."

She grinned and looked around, but it was too black to make anything out.

"Where are we?"

"Middle of nowhere. A flat, dark place."

"What'd we stop for? Something wrong?"

"Nope. I think I've got an idea where Albright might be headed. If I'm right, we have a chance to catch him since we got a little head start. If I'm wrong . . . well, it was a nice drive." I told her what I'd pieced together.

"Sounds good to me," she said. "Let's get going. I hope we're not too late.

"Hey, we're in a BMW!"

Her look of disdain faded my smile instantly.

"Oh yeah. Trish's BMW."

As long as there were no headlamps in my windshield or rearview mirror we were fine. At the first hint of an approaching vehicle, I coasted down to five over the posted speed. In Arizona, you get pulled over for doing the speed limit in the middle of the night: it looks like you're trying not to attract attention so you must be running dope. So to avoid suspicion you speed, just a little. When the car passed, I eased the accelerator down again just a touch and for two hours managed to avoid a red light special. It took all that time to reach our destination, but we got there without a hitch.

"Where are we going, anyway?" Sally asked as a scattering of pre-dawn lights of a small town blinked up one by one on the horizon.

"Why," I informed her.

"I'd kind of like to know where we are, that's why."

"That's the name of the town."

"What?"

"Not what, Why."

"I don't get it."

"Why, Arizona."

"You're asking me? I thought you knew what you were doing."

I laughed. "Why is the name of the town."

"Maybe I'm still groggy," Sally said, "but you're not making sense. All I want to know is where we're going."

I couldn't help myself. "Why."

"Stop the car," she demanded. "This isn't funny."

I laughed again. "There is a town in Arizona and the name of it is Why. W-H-Y. Why, Arizona. An old mining town, so named because there was no reason to build a town there. It's near the Mexican border. There, see the sign?"

"Welcome to Why," she read. "Oh. What's in Why?"

"The turn-off for New Laramie Movie Town, where the gold and Mr. Albright should be."

"Praise the Lord," she prayed.

The sun was on the rise—it had been getting light for the past half-hour—and the few clouds overhead were a brilliant pink and orange with yellow ridges as they reflected the light. The jagged rock and cactus hills of our destination that hid the sun were black, their detail invisible with the searing light behind them and in our eyes. As the first edge of the sun popped over the rim, they all but disappeared momentarily in the glare. The turquoise sky directly overhead reminded me of the jewelry one could get from local Indians at any roadside rest along the way. I decided to pick up something on the way home for Sally and me to remember this most unusual date by.

But that would have to wait. The road before us led perhaps to a conclusion, a summation of the events of the last week, or it led to nowhere. I would hesitate to call it our destiny that awaited us, since it might only be a diversion. I might be totally wrong in my assessment of everything, but I honestly didn't see how I could be. It all fit, dovetailed neatly together, so well that I wondered why I didn't come up with it before. Of course, that's the beauty of hindsight.

Sagebrush grew along the side of the road and stretched out for miles in all directions, dotted with saguaro, the spiny cholla, and organ pipe cactus. A Gila woodpecker darted overhead in the warm, early morning sun, landing inexplicably on a saguaro where it had burrowed its nest. Unseen were the tiny elf owl, who lived in abandoned woodpecker nests raising chicks the size of postage stamps. There were mule deer and musk hog here too but none I could see. They would be sleeping still and staying in the hills. Color on this otherwise forebidding landscape was provided by Mexican goldpoppies, blue lupines, megenta owlclover, and other wild flowers.

This moment of beauty and solitude was brought to you— not by the Arizona Chamber of Commerce—but by God. Even the desolate He made beautiful.

The BMW followed the road that wound through the hills before turning south and becoming a well-maintained dirt track for the last few miles. I stopped on the final ridge because of the view. An authentic western town spread out before us, a mass of brown, natural wood buildings with false fronts and covered boardwalks, hitching rails and colorful signs. The main street was broad and straight, the alleys narrow and foreboding. A shiver ran up my back. There wasn't a single shred of evidence of the twentieth century. I recognized the town and the surrounding hills with their rock formations from multitudes of movies and television shows, and that old feeling rose up in me again; that same feeling I always get when confronted by America's western heritage.

Deep down I'd always wanted to be a sheriff in the wild West.

There were no cars visible in the dirt parking lot, but I couldn't see all of it because of the buildings.

"Do you think we beat him here?" Sally asked.

"I don't know, Sal. Don't know how fast he drove, or if he stopped on the way for anything, or, for that matter, exactly when he left. I'd like to think we did, but I just don't know."

"What are you going to do?"

"I believe in the direct approach. The best way to find out if he's been here is to go on in and check."

I shifted into first and spun the tires.

As the lot came into full view, I could see it was indeed empty. We parked near the main entrance, where a rustic wood sign told us the town was open to the public on weekends and holidays only, from 10 A.M. to 10 P.M. Apparently that was to accommodate the film people. Today was Saturday, 6 A.M.

"Looks deserted," Sally said, trading her glasses for prescription sunglasses.

"They open in four hours. There's got to be someone here. Besides, they couldn't put a fence around this; it wouldn't look right in the movies. They'd have to have twenty-four-hour security."

"Where are their cars, then?"

"I bet they put them inside somewhere." I shaded my eyes and scanned the structures. "Right there," I pointed. "Livery stable. It's the only place with a big enough door, at least on this side of town." I walked over and checked for tire tracks. They confirmed my theory.

"Are you ever wrong?" Sally asked.

"I thought I was once, but I was wrong, I was actually right that time too," I said, paraphrasing Lucy Van Pelt from a *Peanuts* cartoon. "Actually, I'm just a pretty good guesser. I'm generally only wrong when I make major decisions about my own life."

"That's good to know. Seriously, Gil, we all make mistakes. Don't be so hard on yourself."

"I was joking."

"Yes, but you meant it. You usually do mean it when you joke."

"I do?"

"Yes, I think so. You may be exaggerating, or understating, but you mean it."

"Okay. So?"

"So . . . nothing. I was just saying—how did we get on this, anyway?"

"I don't know. Where were we?"

"Looking for a security guard, I think."

"Security officer." I pointed to a narrow set of tire tracks. "Electric cart. That way they can cover the perimeter quickly and quietly."

"May I help you?" The voice came from behind us, and Sally

and I both started, bumping into each other as we turned. "Town's not open for another four hours, folks."

An armed security officer sat in an electric cart, forearms resting on the steering wheel. Where he came from, neither of us could say.

"See?" I said to Sally.

He was about twenty-five, six-two and beefy, with a flattop haircut and light blue uniform, sporting a wood-gripped revolver, a Smith it looked like from here, probably .357.

"We were actually looking for you," Sally said quickly. "Go ahead, Gil. Explain it to him before he runs us out of Dodge."

"Laramie," the guard and I said simultaneously. Sally shrugged sheepishly.

"Yes sir?" The guard said patiently. But he was obviously tired, and the look on his face said I had one chance.

I introduced myself and showed him my park security badge. "We sold you guys a safe the other day—a few weeks ago, that is. It came from our western heritage museum that we tore down to make way for a new ride."

"Yeah?"

"Well, prior to shipping the safe, we had it emptied of a couple hundred thousand dollars worth of gold and silver bullion that we used to display in it behind a plexiglass front. When the bullion made it to the bank, it was found to be fake. We think an employee might have made the switch and is on his way to Mexico."

"No kidding." He perked up a little. "So why are you here if the safe was emptied?"

"Well, it was supposed to be emptied, but there's a possibility it wasn't. Since the bullion that was turned in was fake, the real stuff could still be in the safe. No one checked it before it was put on the truck for here. They assumed it had been emptied."

"Why didn't they check it when they found the fake gold?"

"They didn't discover it right away. Took it for granted it was the real stuff. Can we check the safe? If the bullion is still there, the perpetrator is probably fixing to stop here and get it."

180

"I can show you the safe. It's in the territorial bank on Main Street. But I can't let you look inside."

"Why not?"

"It's locked, and I don't have the combination . . . obviously." He grinned. "Unless you have it."

That stopped me. Why hadn't I thought to get it?

"Gil, why don't we look at it, then let Albright open it for us?"

"Good idea," I said, turning toward her, but I winced. We didn't know this guy and shouldn't give up any more information than we had to. I should have warned Sally not to divulge anything. I turned back to the guard. "Can we do that, Officer. . . ." I tilted my head to see his name tag, but he wasn't wearing one.

"Johnson," he said. "Jim Johnson."

"Officer Johnson, then. Shall we?"

"Hop on."

We climbed on the cart and rode quietly into the center of town.

New Laramie was what you'd expect. In fact, you'd probably recognize it. The Marshall's office from *Slow Draw* and *The Last Gallows*; the corner saloon from *The Gunslinger's Brother*, where that guy shot two bad guys at the same time on different sides of the building; the bank used in the famous holdup scene from *The Guns of Bad Blood*. It was all here. Although not an actual old West town, New Laramie nearly qualified, having been constructed in the twenties for the silent film, *Cowboy Creed*. Few of the original structures were left, though, due to the ravages of weather, the need for expansion, and because they weren't built to last in the first place but only as long as the picture was being shot.

The only thing I didn't know about New Laramie is that the park used to own it. I guess Mr. Golden shared my attraction for things cowboy.

Johnson stopped in front of the bank, unlocked the door, and we stepped back in time. The worn, wood floors contrasted with the L-shaped kiosk, walnut-stained and highly polished with iron grating about three feet high on top of it. Behind it stood the safe. It was open.

Johnson looked a little concerned.

"Uh oh."

Two little sounds, but they spoke volumes.

"The front door was locked," he protested.

"Our guy might have keys," I explained, going through the door to inspect the safe. "He used to work out here when we still owned New Laramie."

The safe was dark inside, even with room lights on. I felt around, but there was nothing unusual inside.

"Can I borrow your flashlight?" I asked Johnson.

He handed me a five-cell torch: the big, black, heavy, metal kind cops used to carry before the chiefs' associations got wise that they used them as attitude adjustment manipulators and made them go to plastic ones. I clicked it on and a bright, retina-burning beam flooded the safe. Johnson had apparently upgraded it to one of those new billion candlepower bulbs, the kind that need batteries capable of turning a hydroelectric dam turbine.

When my pupils constricted, I looked inside. Nothing.

As I handed the light back to Johnson, I noticed a name crudely engraved in the end cap. Anderson. I registered that bit of information in my mind without reacting.

"Is this the only safe in town?"

"This is where they said they put your safe. They took the old one from here and put it in the assay office."

"Did you see it happen?"

"No."

"Maybe they changed their mind. Can we check it?"

"Uh . . . yeah, sure. The assay office is just around the corner. We can walk." He led us outside. As he locked the door, I took Sally aside.

"What's the matter?" I asked. "Is something wrong? You're awfully quiet."

"What was that look for?"

"What look?"

"You gave me a look back there."

"Oh . . . that. I'm sorry. But you said Albright's name."

"So."

"We don't know this guy. Maybe Albright has an accomplice here, to be sure he can recover the gold."

"He would already know Albright's name."

"Yes, but he doesn't know we know. Listen, he said his name was Johnson, but his flashlight had a different name inscribed on it."

"Maybe it's not his flashlight."

"You don't know cops. Flashlights and guns are not loaned."

The guard was done with the door and walked down the boardwalk to us.

"This way folks."

Around the corner we walked and into the assay office where another safe sat against the wall, behind a high counter upon which sat a scale and some weights. This safe was closed, presumably locked.

Johnson scratched his head with a perplexed look on his face. Overly perplexed, in my estimation. He looked for all the world like someone trying to convince us he was perplexed, when in fact he wasn't.

We needed a plan.

"Has anyone else come in during the night?" I asked.

"Nope."

"You work alone?"

"No, I have a partner. He's in the office, watching the monitors and manning the phones. We trade off, though, to fight boredom."

"Is it possible to drive up here without being seen?"

"Hardly. In fact, my partner saw you drive up and called me to make contact."

"Yeah, but we weren't trying to sneak in, either. Just the same, I'll take your word for it. Is there a place we can put our car?"

"Sure. In the livery with ours. Are you really expecting this guy to show up?"

"I don't know. But if he's the one responsible for the murder, and the gold is in there, he'll have to show up. He needs that gold to finance his new life in Mexico."

"Murder?" Johnson gulped audibly as his eyes widened. B movie overacting if I ever saw it. "What murder?"

"Oh, didn't I tell you? Well, never mind now. It's a long story, and we're not in that kind of danger. If we were, this little lady wouldn't be with me." I could tell by Sally's reaction she wasn't sure if she should be appreciative or not.

"Let's get the car hidden. I want him to waltz right into our trap. If he sees our car, he might spook."

While I pulled the car into the livery, Johnson holding the stable doors open, Sally asked, "What if he doesn't show?"

"Well," I sighed, "since Johnson is sure there's no way he could already have been here and gone, that would mean my theory's wrong about the gold still being in there. It would mean he definitely has an accomplice, probably from the park, who has the gold. It means they'll probably get away, and we'll have a long drive back home."

Within minutes, we were in position. I told Johnson to meet our quarry as he did us, make him give his excuse for wanting to get into the safe, then let him do it but cover the back door of the assay office. When he came out, we'd confront him red-handed. Sally and I hid out in an alley where we could see the front door. As I scanned the territory, she bent down and fiddled with something in the dirt.

"You know, Gil," she said quietly as we waited. "You're one unusual date."

"Thanks for understanding. Or at least putting up with it if you don't understand. This is me, the way I am. When I get a hold of something, I don't like letting go. I'll make it up to you, I promise. I know a really great place in Yuma—"

"There's nothing to make up," she said with a sweet smile. "And I forgive you for the look you gave me. I wasn't being a very good policeman."

"I'm really sorry," I said. "I should have told you ahead of time and not expected you to know how to play detective."

"It's okay. I just hope I didn't mess anything up. You know,

I'm having more fun than I've ever had." She put her hand through my arm and squeezed.

"I'm glad," I said. "I just hope it works out, and we didn't come all the way out here for nothing."

She removed her sunglasses, sticking them in the pocket of her sweater, then moistened her lips as she stared down the street. I pretended not to notice, but my heart began slapping the inside of my ribcage. She shivered.

"Cold?" I asked.

"A little. Here in the shade, just standing around." I put my arm around her shoulder, and she relaxed into it, dropping her head slightly.

I was in high school again.

"Sally?"

She looked up at me, and I knew it was time. I hadn't expected to know. I thought I'd have to guess and would guess wrong, but I knew. I actually knew. I put a slight pressure on her shoulders, and she eased toward me, her eyes locked on mine. Slowly I bent my head, my brain spinning on its axis. Her head moved toward mine, almost imperceptibly. But it moved. She closed her eyes. I could feel her warm and minty breath.

Footsteps on the boardwalk across the street popped the bubble, but it was obvious Sally hadn't heard them or didn't care. I disregarded them also for the moment, pressing my lips softly into hers, but straining out of the corner of my eye to look across the street at the source of the noise.

It was him. Albright. He carried an athletic bag and stopped at the door of the assay office, unlocked it, and went in. Ah well, I had a minute or two.

I closed my eyes and gave myself to the kiss, suppressing an involuntary recollection of Rachel on the front porch in her prom dress. I was torn between wanting and not wanting to remember. I opened my eyes again, and the memory vanished.

When we broke, Sally smiled shyly.

"That was nice," she whispered.

I overcame the urge to say *you're welcome*, instead agreeing with her by nodding and giving her a wink.

"I think Albright's here," I said. "Someone went inside."

"Now what do we do?"

"We wait. When he comes out, we confront him. That should be it. The fact that he's here confirms a lot."

She gazed at me with genuine admiration, making me self-conscious. "Gil, you're awfully smart. No, I mean it."

I shrugged. "Elementary, Watson. Process of elimination. Just assemble the facts in a way so all of them make sense. Not most of them, all of them. There's usually only one scenario that fits all the facts, and that's the right one."

Five minutes passed without Albright reappearing. It shouldn't be taking this long. All he had to do was open the safe and pack the gold in his athletic bag. I was beginning to get concerned when a noise to the rear of us made us both pivot.

Albright stood there, holding a now-heavy athletic bag in his left hand. From his right dangled Johnson's revolver.

SEVENTEEN

O h my," Sally exclaimed softly. "Gil?"
I took her hand and held it tightly.

"Desperate actions of a desperate man, eh Mercer?" I said to him.

"So you know," he sneered. "Then you can understand this." He wiggled the gun.

"Why didn't you just take the gold and go?"

"Would you have let me?"

"No," I admitted.

"Well, there you go."

"How'd you know we were here?"

"The guard kindly told me."

I turned my head toward Sally. "Remind me to thank him later."

"What'd you do to him?" Sally asked.

"He's okay. He's in the alley behind the assay office, taking a little nap. You know, a bar of gold can pack quite a wallop. Now if you'll just do me the honor of telling me where all your cars are, I'll disable them and mosey on down to Mexico, and you can resume your lives, embarrassed, but none the worse for wear."

"I'd like to accommodate you, Mercer, but it wouldn't help. The police have already been called. I'm sure a sheriff's car will be pulling up any second."

"Nice try, Mr. Beckman, but I'm no fool. Oh, don't look so surprised. Everyone at the park knows who you are. Your exploits are legendary. I'm even a fan of yours. That's right. You see, no

187

one liked John Hayes. You're a cult hero. Anyway, as I was saying, I know the sheriff hasn't been called. I cut the phone lines, and I monitored police radio traffic on my scanner on the way in. You can't be too careful when you're trying to flee the country with a couple hundred-thousand dollars in gold. I've already paid once for not being too careful."

"The two guys who stole your car—the one you bought in Santa Vista?"

"You're good, Beckman. I'm impressed. But enough of this. The cars, please."

"All right. You hold all the cards. They're at the far edge of town." I pointed in the direction away from the livery stable.

"Okay, let's go. And you better be telling the truth."

I gave him my best glare and pointed my index finger at him. "One thing, Mercer. Do what you will but don't ever call me a liar. You got that?"

He smirked. "Whatever you say."

Sally was giving me a funny look, knowing I had just misled Mercer, but I only winked at her with the eye Mercer couldn't see. Later I'd explain the difference between lying and law enforcement bluffing. I turned to face him again. "Leave her here. There's no point endangering her since you'll be letting us go in peace anyway. She's not part of this." Sally inched behind me and pressed herself into my back, almost too hard.

Mercer rolled his eyes. "Quit stalling. I'm losing my patience."

I was fairly certain Mercer wasn't a cold-blooded killer. True, Stephanie Taylor had probably died at his hand, but even now, this close to Mexico and freedom, he hadn't killed the guard or us. Unless he was lying about the guard. Or perhaps Johnson was an accomplice. I still hadn't ruled that out. Shoot, I didn't know what to think at this point. I needed to stall, give myself time to think of a plan. If it wasn't for Sally, I'd have just tried to take him. But I couldn't risk her.

It was then I felt her press something into my hand, something hard, heavy and irregular, about the size of a golf ball. So she hadn't been playing in the dirt, she'd been arming herself. I was liking her better by the second. She let go of my hand, freeing me to use the stone she'd provided.

"Do what he says, Gil," Sally encouraged. "I don't think Mr. Albright will hurt us."

"Smart thinking, ma'am."

"His name's Mercer," I said with a sneer for Mercer's benefit, reminding him what a big piece of pond scum he really was.

He ignored me. "You look familiar," he said to Sally. "You work at the park too, I take it?"

Sally nodded. "I used to work dispatch."

Mercer smiled. "Ah yes. I've spoken to you many times over the radio. Now, tell your boyfriend to move it."

Sally suddenly looked past Mercer and waved, as if shooing someone away. Mercer glanced back for just a second—there was no one there—but it was long enough. I whipped my arm around and threw a fastball at Mercer's head—David and Goliath style. He ducked, firing the gun wildly—and accidentally, I thought, since there was no attempt at aiming—just as Sally and I scampered around the corner and out of the alley.

Mercer was after us immediately, but now we were moving targets and much harder to hit—I hoped. I kept myself between Sally and Mercer as we ran higgledy-piggledy down the boardwalk and onto a side street where there were places to hide. Also, I knew he was burdened with the heavy bullion, making his progress much slower. I fished the keys to the BMW out of my pocket.

"Go to the car, call 9-1-1 on the cell phone, then stay put. I'll keep him occupied." I pressed the keys into her hand. "Go!"

She fled down the street and into an alley just as Mercer peered cautiously around the corner. I ducked behind some wooden crates as he fired again, the bullet splintering the wood inches from my face. Sharp slivers imbedded themselves into my cheek.

"Okay, Lord," I whispered through the pain. "Here we go again." That was all I had time for, but I presumed He'd been watching and could figure out the rest by Himself.

"I gave you a chance," Mercer warned. "You've left me no choice."

"There's always a choice!" I shouted back, hunkering behind the crate. "You could give yourself up."

"You're a funny guy, Beckman."

"Actually I was being serious, for once. Besides, what about Stephanie? Did you give her a chance?"

"What are you talking about?"

"When you strangled her. What had she done, gotten pregnant? Was that her big crime?"

There was heavy breathing, but he didn't answer.

"You can't handle pressure very well, can you Mercer? You run from everything." At that instant, I thought about myself. I didn't do too well at it either, come to think of it. But at least I hadn't killed anyone.

"That was an accident," he said quietly, but he didn't elaborate.

I smiled. *Thanks for the confession, bonehead.*

He fired his gun again without warning, not even coming close. But this was all too uneven. He had a gun, and all I had was my wits. Good as they might have been, I think he had the advantage. Sooner or later he might accidentally shoot me. If I was going to keep getting into these situations, I would rather be armed, thank you. I filed away in my mind the need to see if I could get my old chief to give me a concealed weapon's permit.

Footsteps behind me, at the back of the alley where Sally had gone, made my heart sink. She had come back. I hunkered down and prepared myself to wave her away when the other guard stepped into view.

"I heard a shot, Jim! What hap—"

Behind me, Mercer had fired over my head. The bullet slammed into the guard's left shoulder. He reacted to the pain and the surprise and the danger by grabbing the injury and hitting the dirt. I heaved another rock toward Mercer—anything for a second or two of leeway—then crawled to the guard and dragged him around the corner, the guard pushing at the dirt with his feet to help.

"What the heck's going on?" he said through clenched teeth. I held my finger to my lips and slid the sidearm from his holster.

A Colt .45, Government Model semi-automatic pistol. I smiled. *Thank you, Lord.* "Don't move," I told the guard. "Be right back."

I hurried to the mouth of the alley and fired two quick shots into the wood near Mercer's last location, just to let him know we were now even.

"And there's plenty more where that came from!" I shouted. "Care to reconsider your refusal to give up?" There was no response, no noise whatsoever. He'd retreated, and my guess was he would try to make a break. I returned to the guard and peeled off my sweater and sports shirt, which I wadded and pressed into his bleeding wound inside his uniform shirt. I noticed his name tag. H. STREETER.

"Hold that, Streeter." I directed. "You'll be okay. We need to find a place for you until this is over, and we can get you to the hospital."

"I'm okay."

"Yeah, but you're not much good to me."

"What's this about? Who are you, anyway?"

"Later. Can you walk?"

"Yeah, no problem." He struggled to get up, and I helped him.

"Where's Jim?" he said with a wince.

"Don't know. Last I heard, he was unconscious behind the assay office, but I don't know how true that is. I'll look for him. Right now you need to get to the livery. There's a lady there named Sally by a red BMW. She'll help you and fill you in on this. The two of you stay put, but be careful, he might try to get in there to disable our cars, so we can't follow him. At least, that's what he said he was going to do. By now, he probably just wants to make a run for it and hope he beats us to the border. One more thing: I can't explain now, but your partner may be in on this. I don't know. If he shows up, keep that in mind, and use caution."

I helped him traverse the fifty yards or so to the livery. It took awhile, having to go slow to avoid stimulating his bleeding and to keep an eye out for Mercer, but we made it, and I handed him off to Sally. He kept quiet, trusting me and believing I was telling the truth, apparently satisfied that his quesions would soon be answered. Must be fresh out of the marines, I thought. If Sally was afraid, she didn't show it.

"Say a prayer," I told her.

"What do you think I've been doing?" she asked, helping Streeter inside. "You be careful, Gil," she added, noticing the gun I now gripped in my right hand. "You still owe me dinner." Then the light from outside hit me in the face and her eyes widened noticeably. "Oh, Gil, your face. . . .

"Fine time to decide I'm ugly," I said, unaware of the streaks of blood running down one side of it. I tossed her my sweater. "Keep him warm. I'm okay." I gave her one last look—a silent, brief gaze that she returned. No words passed between us but volumes were spoken in the silent exchange.

I borrowed Streeter's handcuffs, sticking them in my rear pocket, and left the livery. At long last, a fair fight. I was now the hunter, Mercer the quarry. Just him and me, and a whole deserted western town to ourselves to play in. I only wished I had had time to savor the situation.

I was, for all intents and purposes, the sheriff of Laramie, a wild west town, having it out with the bad guy, a notorious gunman. I could've giggled with delight. In all my years of police work, I'd never fired my weapon on duty, and now, working for an amusement park, in the middle of a dinner date with the boss's secretary, I'm shooting it out with a murderer and thief in a wild west town. What a job!

The first order of business was to cut off Mercer's way of escape—run off his horse, so to speak. I figured he hadn't tried to hide his car, so it was probably near the main entrance, where we had first come in.

That was just a short distance away, but there was precious little cover between here and there. Translation: none. As he might be headed to it, I decided to take the risk and lunged out into the open.

I advanced unhindered to the edge of the parking lot, the only sounds coming from my feet scraping the gravel and the rasping of my breathing. There it sat, the only car in the lot. I was surprised to see it wasn't the car he'd been driving when he originally disappeared, the one he'd gotten back from the P.D. before Theo realized he'd faked the whole kidnap/murder scenario. It looked like a rental, which explained why we were able to beat him here—it had taken him time to secure it. That also explained why he arrived undetected by the highway patrols of two states despite Theo's APB's. Mercer was certainly no dummy.

I scoured the area for him, took a breath, and raced to the car, putting it between me and town. The easiest thing to do would be to deflate a tire or two, so I unscrewed the cap on the valve stem of the nearest one, the left rear, and pushed in the core, holding it in place until the tire was flatter than a ballerina. I moved to the front tire on the same side, checking, as I duck-walked, for any sign of Mercer at the edge of town or the telltale dust from the approaching cavalry in the opposite direction. Both were negative.

Two tires were now flat, so plan B could go into effect: find Mercer and pin him down until the arrival of the posse.

I was halfway between his car and cover when he stepped out from a shadow, enough so I could see him but not enough so I could get a good sight picture. He leveled his six-shooter in my direction.

"You're starting to annoy me!" he shouted.

Without even bothering to think of a reply, I dropped to my right knee to reduce his target area, at the same time raising the .45 as I flipped off the thumb safety. As the barrel came up, I grabbed my right hand with my left to steady the weapon and squeezed twice in rapid succession, aiming by instinct alone; point-and-shoot, it's called.

These were scare shots, as it turned out, because I was too far away to be accurate. I never was much good at fifty yards, even when I had all the time in the world at the range to aim before I fired at a stationary target that wasn't capable of shooting back. Don't misunderstand, those weren't intended to be warning shots. There is no such thing in real life, only TV and the movies. My first two shots back in the alley were the exception, intentionally fired into the wall just to drive him away and give me a chance to see to Streeter. But if they'd have hit Mercer, I wouldn't have been sorry, and it would have been justifiable.

As a rule, cops only shoot to kill. Some people, Christians and non-Christians alike, have asked me how I felt about using a gun. I told them just fine. Peter carried a sword, and Jesus told him to. It's in Luke 22. Look it up. He just used it at the wrong time. Self-defense, or defending the life of another, is not only okay, it's just and right.

I had every right to shoot Mercer at this point. I tried, too, but missed. He found cover just as I pulled the trigger, but I was already on the move, and he missed by a mile, although he scored a hit on his rental car in the fender somewhere. I heard it hit, reflecting in that instant what would have happened had it been me. My cheek still burned from the close shave I'd been given earlier.

Unless he'd taken Johnson's reloads, Mercer was down to two rounds. I sprinted toward town, away from the livery stable to draw Mercer away from Sally and Streeter.

Okay, what I had to do was get Mercer into a position where I could kill him, disarm him, or just torment him for awhile. If killing was the only viable option, I'd have to go with it, although I'd avoid it if I could. I didn't want him dead—there were a lot of questions I was curious to hear the answers to—but I wouldn't cry over it, either. It doesn't make any sense to worry about someone's salvation when they are trying to kill you. If God wanted to save him, He would. He'd keep me from killing him, hopefully by having him surrender. I am not going to thwart God's plan by exercising my responsibility to protect myself and others against a murderer.

Remember, we all have choices to make. Mercer'd made his. Enough said.

I had to remain on the offensive, but I was greatly concerned that Mercer would figure out where my car was. And if he did that, he'd find Sally and the wounded security officer, a situation that was totally unacceptable. I needed a good view of the town.

Making my way cautiously to Main Street, I stuck the gun in my waistband at the small of my back and climbed to the hotel balcony. With the sun up completely, the air was beginning to warm. I jumped to the roof of the building next door, crouching behind the false front. From there, I could see most of Main Street, as well as the front of the livery stable and the hills beyond the parking lot that the only road into town wound through. It was empty. Big sigh.

In a way, I knew what Custer must've felt like, except my odds were considerably better.

Then I heard a large door creaking open, the roar of the BMW throbbing into life, and the spinning of tires as it catapulted from the rear of the livery into the parking lot and sped toward the road into the foothills, leaving a cloud of dust and pebbles in its wake. There was too much dirt floating behind it to see inside the car, but I feared Mercer had found the BMW and was making his escape. Who else would be taking off like that?

Which could only mean one thing: Sally and Streeter were in trouble.

I swung down from the roof and sprawled in the street, folding my ankle under me as I landed. The pain shot up my leg, and I probably yelled, but it didn't count since there was no one around to hear. Like a tree falling in the forest. I pushed myself up and tried to run, but fell again as I put my weight on the leg. I got up more carefully now, nursing it and putting all my weight on the good leg, and hobbled to the livery in a direct line. I still had the gun—years of habit taught me *never give up your gun*— but it was nestled securely in the back of my waistband. Mercer didn't matter to me now, only Sally. And Streeter, of course—and Trish's BMW! If I lived through this, she'd kill me!

The double doors were only secured by a wooden bolt on the inside, but the gap between them was large enough that I could stick something through and lift up the bolt. The only thing I had was the gun. I called out Sally's name but there was no answer. I stuck the gun through the crack and hoisted the bolt. The door swung open. With the .45 at my side, I stepped recklessly into the stable.

A black silhouette was framed in the light of the open doors on the far side, the doors the BMW had left through. But it wasn't Sally or Streeter, and the shadow was pointing a gun at me.

EIGHTEEN

Time decelerated, throwing me into the kind of chaos you experience when the roller coaster is suddenly snagged by the brakes and you'd swear your senses are still in motion though your body has stopped, and for the briefest of moments, you are outside yourself, aware of seconds as though each was a minute.

Without a conscious thought, my muscles tensed and flexed, and I dove, anticipating his actions, while I simultaneously brought my gun up. I saw the muzzle flash from his pistol, then a split second later heard the report, and I was unable to shoot as a scalding shaft pierced my side. Out of the corner of my eye, I sensed movement. As I flew toward the straw-covered ground, a pendulum of some sort swung toward Mercer from his blind side; a portion of the block and tackle used in the livery for wagon repair, I found out later.

When I hit the ground, the force expelled the air from my lungs with a groan. I had been unable to break my fall due to the shock of the bullet striking me and the presence of the gun in my hand. The pain was twisted and sharp in my side, yet something was oddly warm and soothing. My injured foot was tight in my shoe but all but forgotten for the moment. I bounced and rolled, there was a cry of pain, the gun was somewhere, but not in my hand, and time once again was placed on fast forward and caught up to me with a head-banging rush.

As I lay there trying to breath, to comprehend, a shadow crossed my face. I couldn't make out the details, hoping, praying, this wasn't Mercer. Remembering the weapon, I groped for it, my hand falling on it and grabbing it up with a fistful of straw. I began to raise it, to defend myself from what would surely be the final head shot that would send me home to be with the Lord, but a voice stayed my hand.

"It's me, Streeter. I got him. He's out cold."

I relaxed and allowed my gun hand to fall, but I did not let go.

He fished in my pockets and found the handcuffs I had borrowed and not needed. I could hear running steps, the handcuff's ratchets clicking, and someone moaning. No, that was me again. My head cleared, and I pushed my arms to roll to my side, regretting it immediately, but I was able to see Streeter crouching over my motionless adversary, applying the handcuffs.

Streeter had swung a pulley suspended by a rope at Mercer. It had swept silently downward then up again in its arc, and as it rose, it caught the unsuspecting gunman square in the side of the head, knocking him into next week, just as Mercer was aiming at my fallen body to fire again.

The wounded security guard who had aimed and propelled the pulley, stood and returned to my side. His uniform shirt was off and his T-shirt had been torn into strips and wrapped neatly around his wound. He knelt beside me and inspected my injury.

"Sally . . . ?" I asked

"She went to town," he explained.

"Fine time to go shopping," I moaned, trying to sit up.

"Looks like it's just a crease. Dug a little channel. I don't think it hit anything important—"

"It's all important to me," I winced.

He chuckled but stopped abruptly as his own pain twisted his face. "What I mean is, it looks like it got mostly fat—er, muscle, that is. What we call in the service an NGE. Not good enough to go home on. I think a Band-Aid will fix you up, maybe a stitch or two."

"You got some alcohol and a sewing kit?" I asked.

"Not handy," he laughed. "You'll have to let a doctor handle it, Rambo." He steadied me into a sitting position. "Sally left because the phone didn't work down here."

"Oh great. I broke Trish's phone."

"Who's Trish?"

"A friend. The BMW's her car."

"Oh. Well, the phone's okay. We're in kind of a gully here, and there was a lot of static. Sally went up to the top of the ridge to make the call to the sheriff.

Streeter helped me up to a sitting position, with some difficulty.

"How's your shoulder?" I asked, noticing he favored it slightly.

"I'm okay. It went clean through. I'm lucky, it missed the bone. Kinda ruined my shirt, though."

"Yeah, I know what you mean. I hate it when that happens." With my physiology starting to return to normal, I tried to assess my condition and determined my ankle to be the worst injury. It was already swollen and grossly bruised, but I'd done that before in high school so wasn't too concerned about it. But the bullet wound was worth far more in sympathy and hero credits. I left my shoe on and tried to stand. With shaking legs and support from Streeter—whose more serious injury was affecting him less than mine were me—I made it and ambled over to check on Mercer.

"By the way," I said, extending my hand to Streeter. "Gil Beckman. Nice to meet you."

"Hank Streeter. Welcome to New Laramie."

We stared at Mercer as the roar of several V-8s drifted down from the hills through the still desert air. Mercer groaned and stirred but didn't awaken.

"Sally told me what he did," Streeter said. I just nodded. There was nothing else to say. Streeter added, "And Jimmy never showed up. I hope he's okay."

"The cops will be here in a second," I said, seeing them bottoming out onto the flat and screaming toward the parking lot, followed by a lot of dust and a red BMW. "They can check." I kept my uneasiness about Johnson to myself. I checked Mercer's pulse, which was fine, but noted the gash on his head. I hoped he hadn't been hit too hard. I unzipped the athletic bag next to him and reached in, grabbing one of the flat, black-painted gold bars.

"Is that it?" Streeter asked.

"Yeah."

"Can I see it?"

I handed him the bar, and he hefted it in his palm. "Heavy. Why's it black?"

I explained it to him.

"You sure about that?" he asked, inspecting the bar closely as he rubbed it.

"Huh?"

"Look here."

He handed the bar back to me, showing me where he'd rubbed off some of the paint. I dropped it onto the straw and tested some of the other bars, getting the same result. They were all painted lead.

Cars slid to stops outside the doors and deputies hustled in, guns drawn. They converged on us and quickly assessed that the danger was over. I directed two of them to the rear of the assay office to look for Johnson. Sally arrived and bolted out of the BMW, almost knocking me down when she got to me.

She cried and laughed, and I showed her my red badge of courage and got the sympathy and admiration I'd hoped for. A couple deputies helped Streeter and me to a patrol car to sit while they put some better dressings on our injuries. An ambulance arrived shortly and carted Mercer away, followed by a couple of beefy deputies with scowls.

They tried to pry off my shoe, but I wouldn't let them, knowing what would happen when it was removed. I still had a date to finish.

The two deputies looking for Johnson came back empty-handed.

"There's no one there," one of them announced.

The wheels turned as my mind, despite the pain in my ankle and side, tried to process this new wrinkle. Was Johnson Mercer's accomplice? Could they have met here before and Mercer cut him in knowing he'd need help on this end? Is that why Mercer wasn't concerned about how he'd be able to get to the safe? If so, he wouldn't even need keys, but he might have needed someone here to intercept the bullion before it was found, just in case the black paint trick didn't work. It made sense. It was too risky to just hope nobody found it. It would also account for Johnson's unconvincing reactions to my story.

And had Johnson now pulled a double-cross on Mercer, whom I couldn't imagine was aware that he was trying to escape to Mexico, shooting at people, for a bag full of lead. But where was Johnson now? He couldn't have left New Laramie.

My question was answered moments later. As I was beginning to explain the whole thing to the sergeant on scene, an electric cart pulled into the stable from Main Street and Johnson stepped casually off, carrying a black vinyl bag with a horizontal white stripe that proclaimed "Security" in black letters. His duty bag. He walked right up to me and dropped it at my feet.

"I suppose you were wondering about this," he said. He unzipped the bag and hefted out one of the real bars of gold, still with black paint on it, a large portion of which had been removed.

"It had crossed my mind," I admitted. "I'm dying to hear your story."

He sat down, rubbing his head. Sally checked it, then asked a deputy for an ice pack. One was produced, and she gave it to Johnson, who held it against his head while he spoke.

"The first night after the safe arrived I was checking it out— just curious, you know—and opened it up—"

"Time out," I said. "It was unlocked?"

"No."

"I give up. Where'd you get the combination—and now that I think about it, you told me you didn't have it."

"I'll come to that, give me a chance. I was checking the outside of the safe and noticed some numbers penciled on the side, near the top edge. What the heck, I thought, I tried them. It took a few tries, but I finally figured out the directions to spin the dial and that the single digit followed by a slash before each double digit—like 3 slash 24—meant the number of spins before stopping on the number. Three turns to twenty-four, like that. Once I got the directions right, she opened."

The sergeant listening in was incredulous. "Why would the combination be written on the side of the safe? That's nuts."

200

I laughed, long and hard, holding my side.

"What's your problem?" the sergeant asked.

"I think I know," Sally offered. "The guys who worked in the museum at the park were old men, men who had been there a long time, some of them even had firsthand knowledge of some of the history and artifacts in the museum. But a couple of them didn't have much of a memory for things like addresses and phone numbers . . . and safe combinations. So they just wrote it down." She grinned and held her hands out in front of her, palms up, shoulders scrunched.

I just shook my head. "Go on," I urged Johnson, then added, "Your name is really Johnson?"

He looked perplexed. "Of course. Why?"

"Your flashlight has *Anderson* inscribed in it."

"Huh? Oh, he doesn't work here any more. He didn't take it with him, so we leave it in the cart for anyone to use. Why?"

"Never mind. Go ahead. You opened the safe. . . ."

"And I noticed the lumps inside. The other safe—the one in the bank—didn't look like that. I thought maybe it was some kind of bracing, but one of them was a little cockeyed, so I checked closer and found out I had some gold and silver bullion. It didn't look like they were supposed to be th—"

"Why didn't you call us, or report it to your supervisor?"

"I thought of that, but then I thought it'd be better to catch the crook. Besides, I didn't know who the crook was. For all I knew, it was my supervisor, or someone else here. I knew they'd be by sooner or later to claim them, so I took them out and made fakes in my kitchen using wheel weights I got from the gas station near my apartment. I figured, even if I wasn't around when they were removed, at least then I'd be able to turn in the real stuff. It's been in my locker. When you showed up this morning, I thought I'd hit the jackpot."

"That's why you didn't let on that you knew," I concluded.

"Yeah. I wanted to be sure, so I decided to wait it out. When the other guy showed, I knew you were probably telling the truth—"

"You couldn't tell just by looking at my honest face?"

He stared at me. "Not in a million years." This drew a healthy laugh from everyone.

"Everything was cool," Johnson went on, "until he came out the back door and hit me. I never saw it coming."

"You're lucky he didn't shoot you," Sally said.

Johnson, visibly relieved, answered quietly. "I know."

The sergeant wandered off for a second to oversee his deputies, leaving Johnson, Sally, and me alone. I moved over to take a look at his wound.

"So tell me, Johnson," I said slowly and quietly, "what made you change your mind?"

"About what?"

"About keeping some of the gold in exchange for information."

"I don't know what you mean."

"It's quite simple, really. That bump on your head isn't much. You said Mercer coldcocked you, caught you by surprise, knocked you out. And yet Mercer told us you told him where we were. I believe him. He had no way of knowing we were even in the state unless you told him. You couldn't have done that if you were unconscious. My guess is you waited for him to come out, had your gun on him, made a deal, maybe even for half the gold. His part was to dispatch us, after which you'd retrieve the real stuff and split it, and he'd be on his way. You gave him your gun—he wouldn't hurt you because he didn't know where the real gold was—and knocked yourself on the head, just hard enough to make it look good but not hard enough to do any damage."

Johnson stared straight ahead without comment.

"Mercer wouldn't have hung around so long if he'd had the gold. Mexico's only a half-hour away. He had to get me out of the picture first to get the gold from you. That's why you didn't call your partner for help. Streeter wasn't in on this with you. So tell me, what changed your mind?"

Johnson's head fell, and he examined the ground between his shoes. "It wouldn't work. When I saw the lady here leave in the BMW, I realized Mercer was going to lose. I knew I wouldn't get away with it. So I went and got the gold and hoped you'd believe my story. Everything else I said was true, though. About how I found the gold in the first place. I really didn't know who had planned it until Mercer showed up and said he had to get to the safe. That's when I got the idea. Not a very good plan, huh?"

"No," I said softly.

"So you gonna turn me in?"

I thought about it. "Well, I suppose I ought to be mad about you placing Sally and me in jeopardy. . . . No, I'm definitely mad about that. But I'm willing to forgive you if she is."

Sally nodded. "I think so. Maybe tomorrow when I think about it I wouldn't be so quick to . . . but, yes, I can forgive you."

Johnson was crying. Real tears of relief and guilt.

"Just one thing," I said.

"Yeah?" He looked up at me through red, wet eyes.

"Next time you get a fool idea like this, run from it."

"Th-thank you," he said, meaning it. "Are you people Christians?"

"Yes," Sally said.

"I thought so. No one else I know would be like that."

"I'm usually not," I admitted. "But I should be. You go to church?"

"No."

"Maybe you should start," Sally said.

Johnson nodded. "Yes, ma'am. I owe you that much."

"You owe Christ," I said. "He died to save you. Before I leave the area, we'll talk some more. Okay?"

"You can have dinner with us," Sally offered.

Johnson nodded as the sergeant returned.

"What's his problem?" the lawman asked.

"He's relieved we're not dead," I said. "Emotionally over-wrought from his ordeal."

"Well, he did a good job."

I agreed and said, "Sergeant, can you have your dispatcher call Lt. Theo Brown of the—"

"We already did," he said. "In fact, I believe the lady phoned him." He nodded toward Sally.

"He's on his way out," Sally said. "Taking a commuter flight."

"I'm afraid we may be keeping the gentleman for awhile," the sergeant remarked. "Assault, possession of stolen property, attempted murder, not to mention the extradition process. When we're done, you guys are welcome to him. Lieutenant Brown will want to interrogate him, I'm sure—when Mercer comes around, that is. In the meantime, after you get patched up, I'd appreciate it if you could stop by the station so we can get a complete statement."

I'd appreciate it. Sergeant talk for *you don't have any choice.*

"And here's your ride now," the sergeant announced as a second ambulance pulled up for Streeter and me. He started to help me up, but I waved him off.

"No thanks. I shouldn't be long; this is nothing. I stood up and took a step and promptly fell headlong onto the ground.

As the sergeant and one of his deputies helped Streeter and me into the ambulance, Sally spoke to the sergeant.

"Perhaps you could send someone around to the hospital. I have the feeling he'll be spending the night."

I was released the next day just before lunch, in time for Sally and me to join Theo in Gila Bend for the noon meal. We commandeered a corner booth in a small Mexican restaurant so I could put my leg up and enjoyed the warm tortilla chips and salsa while waiting for our enchiladas and chile relleno.

"You know, I've never seen an ankle quite that big," Theo mused.

"Thank you," I said. "It'll be fine in a few days. So what did Mercer have to say?"

"Nothing. He invoked."

"He refused to answer questions, or he requested an attorney? Which?"

"Both."

"Rats."

"No kidding. Without a confession I doubt we'll get a conviction for the murder of Stephanie Taylor."

"You say that as if you're not going to try."

"We've got a dead body, buried ten years, the only link being the faulty memory of an old security guard who claims he saw them together going in to work several times."

"So Fred remembered."

"For what it's worth. He saw a picture of Mercer in the newspaper. Your assistant, Trish Smith is it? called and said Fred was positive. But that only proves they knew each other. Mercer and Taylor, that is."

"Did Mrs. Potter know anything?"

Theo shook his head. "No. She knows a lot about a lot of people but nothing about Mercer and Stephanie."

"What about Mercer's statement to me that killing her was an accident?"

"Still not enough. We need solid evidence. Without it, the D.A. won't file."

"Look, Theo—you can prove she was strangled, then buried; his statement proves knowledge and since it wasn't in response to a general statement about her death, but a direct accusation, I don't know why that wouldn't do it. Add to that his previous flight from Illinois, his false identity, and the theft of the bullion and his attempt to flee to Mexico—and for that matter, interstate flight to avoid prosecution . . . any D.A. that won't file that ought to be disbarred! I don't know a D.A. who wouldn't!"

"I do."

"Who? Franklin Willis's brother?" My voice had been getting increasingly louder during my oration, and I punctuated it by slamming my hand on the table, drawing stares from all over the restaurant.

Theo sipped his ice tea. "Relax, you're going to blow an artery. I'm rattling your cage. We've got a good case."

"I knew that," I said calmly.

Sally had a question. "Why did he leave the bullion in the safe? Why didn't he just take it with him? Wasn't that risky?"

"If it was missed right away," I said, "he was afraid he'd be caught with it. And it wasn't particularly risky to leave it in there because the people in New Laramie had no reason to open it up. They probably assumed the park cleared it out before shipping it. I think he painted the bullion black just in case."

"I wish we could find out what really happened to him all

these years," Sally sighed. "Why he left his family in the first place."

"He's a jerk," I said.

"It's not that simple," she asserted.

"Sure it is. The psychologists just like to justify the expense of their schooling by phrasing it in large Greek-rooted words. What I'd like to know is what happened to him in the desert for those four or five days he was missing—and how he came out of it none the worse for the wear."

"Maybe he's just in better shape than you," Theo suggested.

"Funny."

Theo dipped a chip. "I did ask him about that, off the record. Told him it was just between him and me. He still maintains he doesn't remember."

"Bunk," I concluded. "He was all the way here before he met those guys. What about the blood in his car?"

"Lab says it's not human. Probably a convenient road kill."

"Speaking of road kill . . . ," I said as I saw the arm-laden waitress approach.

"Oh, please," Sally groaned.

Our food arrived, and we all dug in hungrily, conversation about Mercer being temporarily on hold while we attended to the really important things in life, like shredded beef and chicken and cheese and tortillas and rice and. . . .

"What a date, eh Sally?" I commented with a mouth full of refried beans and sour cream. "Just you, me, a homicide detective. . . ."

"A loaf of bread, a jug of wine, and Theo," the lieutenant said.

Sally smiled. "Definitely a contender for the *Most Unusual Spontaneous Date by an Opinionated Ex-cop* award."

"Oh, that reminds me," Theo added. "I was talking to Michelle last night—"

"During a date?" I interrupted to ask.

"None of your business—"

"That means yes," I said to Sally.

"—Anyway," continued Theo without stopping for my

rudeness," she said she spoke to that kid of yours, Joey What's-his-face."

"Duncan."

"Whatever. And she wants to see if he can make it as an artist. No guarantees, of course. Because of his age and his background, he'll be carefully watched. But he's good enough, Michelle told me to tell you, and they're willing to get him some formal training."

That pleased me. I hoped he could make it. And I thought he was beginning to come around to being receptive to the gospel. He'd be a tough nut to crack—at least until he comes to recognize and understand the nature of sin and his own guilt, and realize the need for a savior—but in Christ I had hope. I guess that's why I hadn't given up on him yet; God wouldn't let me.

My ankle was throbbing by the time we left—I needed to get it elevated and under ice again—and I hobbled to the door on crutches while Theo paid the bill, and Sally went on ahead to bring the car around. Coming in the front door as I was beginning to go out was an attractively dressed woman. I paused and smiled, holding the door while I motioned for her to proceed. She hesitated, noticing my condition, and yet apparently unwilling to accommodate my chauvinism. It was a standoff.

"I can get my own door," she said tersely, feminism fairly oozing from her tone like some primordial slime from under a rock.

"I'm sure you can," I assented with a forced smile, "but it seems I'm already holding it for you."

"I resent the attitude you men have. We're not reliant upon you, and we certainly are not going to be submissive. God didn't intend for us to stay barefoot and pregnant, She wants us free. We can take care of ourselves."

"Of that I have no doubt," I said with a sigh, my patience worn to the nub. "Do you honestly think I'm standing here in intense pain on an ankle the size of a basketball to make a political statement?" By now a small crowd had gathered behind both of us—people waiting to go in or out of Miguel's Casa de Sonora. "Lady," I continued, striving to keep my voice at normal conversational level, "the correct term for my behavior at this moment is *polite*. I'm just trying to be a gentleman. If you weren't so self-absorbed, you might realize that common courtesy transcends sex or race or age. Now get your lovely keister in here before my foot explodes!" I took a breath. "Please!"

A cheer broke out from the spectators, and my accuser's face ripened. Seeing no alternative, she tucked tail and moved forward with a huff, mumbling a quiet description of what she perceived my background to be under her breath as she swept past me.

I resisted the temptation to be sarcastic—winning, I'm sure, another star for my crown for self-control—and progressed clumsily outside, wincing with every step, unable to fully enjoy the accolades of my fellow humans. Sally pulled up just then and puzzled at the attention I was being given.

"What was that all about?" she asked as I climbed awkwardly into the passenger side of the BMW and stowed my crutches in the back seat.

"Oh, nothing. Just the Gila Bend chapter of my fan club." I settled into the leather bucket seat and put my foot up on the dash, not an easy task in a BMW 325i. "You know, God sure has been good to me—to us."

"Yes," Sally agreed softly. "He sure has." She was giving me that doe-eyed look again, the same one she'd given me in the alley. "You ready to go home?"

"Almost," I answered, as I powered up the tinted window. "Almost."